Fighting For My Heart

Moonstone Pack Series

A.L. Duncan

Copyright © 2023 Ashley Duncan All rights reserved

The characters and events portrayed in this book are fictitious. Any similarity to real persons, living or dead, is coincidental and not intended by the author.

No part of this book may be reproduced, or stored in a retrieval system, or transmitted in any form or by any means, electronic, mechanical, photocopying, recording, or otherwise, without express written permission of the publisher.

ISBN-13: 9798862933352

Cover design by: Ashley Duncan
Printed in the United States of America

For Ryan

Thank you for standing by my side and supporting even my craziest ideas. Your unwavering love has encouraged me to take risks and push the boundaries of my capabilities. Thank you for being my rock, sounding board and my forever.

Contents

Title Page
Copyright
Dedication
    1. Jasira
    2. Jasira
    3. Jasira
    4. Felix
    5. Jasira
    6. Felix
    7. Jasira
    8. Felix
    9. Jasira
    10. Felix
    11. Jasira
    12. Jasira
    13. Felix
    14. Jasira
    15. Felix
    16. Jasira
    17. Felix
    18. Jasira
    19. Felix
    20. Jasira
    21. Jasira
    22. Felix
    23. Jasira
    24. Jasira
    25. Felix
    26. Jasira
    27. Jasira
    28. Felix
    29. Jasira
    30. Jasira
Next Book
About The Author

1

JASIRA

The blustery wind howled around me, filling the night with whispers. It caressed my skin, making goose bumps rise on my arms. My black hair whipped with each gust, making it unruly. A storm was coming, and I relished it. I stood on the cliff's edge, the farthest point I was allowed to go within the pack's land.

I could finally breathe. This has always been my place of peace. Even with the impending storm, the moon stood out high in the sky, its soft glow shining on my pale skin. I basked in it, allowing the moonlight to soothe me.

I wrapped my arms around myself, yearning to know one day what it was like to be wanted. This pack was my own personal prison. Every day was hell. The only place I found peace was out here. The grass between my toes, the sound of the swaying branches, and the owl's hoot felt like freedom. I could hear the Goddess whispering, telling me not to give up.

There was no hope beyond this moment. I had given up a long time ago. I would be stuck here, wolf less, destined too never be anything. There was a time when I thought happiness was obtainable. Alpha Trenton made sure to crush that, sending his second son away to attend to pack business. Alpha Trenton hated that Hudson, and I were close. He feared that Hudson would try to make me his mate.

When I didn't shift at sixteen, like the rest of the wolves, the Alpha's fear grew. He did not want someone as broken as me to be with his son. Even if Hudson was not next in line to be Alpha. He wasn't wrong. I was broken physically and mentally. My body had become fragile from years of being beaten and malnourished. Bones perturbed where curves should have been.

My heart may ache because Hudson was gone, but I was secretly happy he left. I could never give him the love he wanted. My heart belonged to another. Even so if Hudson had asked then I would have accepted. It wouldn't have mattered that I loved a boy in a dream from my childhood, because a dream is all it was or ever would be. I would have tried to make Hudson happy, but I knew the truth. In the end, I would have tainted his beautiful soul. I would never have been enough. Hudson would have given me hope, and hope was a dangerous thing.

I closed my eyes, wishing there was more time before returning, but soon, the Alpha's men would be walking through, ensuring everyone was secure. I knew the consequences I would face if I was not where I was supposed to be. I turned my face to the sky, sending a silent prayer for strength to the moon goddess. Before I rushed back towards town, feeling like I could fight one more day.

I headed straight for the pack house to put some laundry in and cut up some fruit for breakfast. This was how I was helpful in the pack. I cooked, cleaned, and was there punching bag. Wolf or not, the pack had always treated me as if I was nothing. Trudy was one of the worst of them. She was the mate to the Beta of the pack. She made sure I received punishments regularly by her hands. Hence, the hurt ribs from earlier in the day.

I tried to avoid her, but the pack house was her home, along with several other tormentors, so it was not an easy task. If I was quiet and made myself invisible, I would be less likely to set her off.

I entered through the kitchen at the back of the house, going to the attached laundry room to get that started. The house was empty since Liam, the Alpha's son, was throwing a party. I was not invited, not that I would go. I was grateful. However, it meant I could work without walking on eggshells. I emptied the dryer into a basket, moved the laundry from the washer to the dryer, and then filled up the washer with another load. I was so focused I didn't even notice anyone was in the house. I turned to head to the kitchen and was startled by Hudson leaning in the door frame. I gasped, shaking, but quickly relaxed after seeing it was him. I wanted nothing more than to embrace him at that moment. I dug my nails into my palm, restraining myself. I didn't need to bring him into my darkness.

"Jasira," he smirked." It's been a while," he continued in his relaxed stance, clearly finding amusement in surprising me. I couldn't help the smile that made its way across my face. Maybe the Goddess was listening and knew I needed a little light to keep me going.

"Hudson, I didn't know you were back. How are you?" I asked.

"Glad to see you, that's for sure." He smiled. His green eyes searched mine. "I know I have been gone for a while, but I had to return to see you. It doesn't look like anything has changed." His beautiful face darkened.

All I could do was look at the floor. Hudson was the only one who had ever treated me with kindness other than Valentina. It had been slightly over a year since he left, and things had only worsened. Alpha Trenton saw no need to restrain himself or any other pack members with Hudson gone. I was not sure how much more I would survive, but I refused to plead or beg anyone.

Hudson approached me slowly. He reached out gently, lifting my chin to look at him. He turned my face slightly, and a slight growl escaped his lips. He inspected the faded bruise and split healing on my eyebrow. His other hand brushed my side, causing me to flinch. He grabbed the hem of my shirt, only raising it slightly to inspect my side. Horror crossed his face at my bruised, protruding ribs.

"Who did this to you, and have you not been eating?" his voice laced with anger. I turned my face away, flinching slightly, making him sigh and step back. "I'm sorry my anger is not towards you. I should have never left," his tone softened.

"It doesn't matter who did this, Hudson. This is definitely not the worst that has happened since you were gone," my voice is barely audible. I kept my gaze down, unable to look at him. A brief flash of Liam holding me downplayed in my head. I jabbed my nails into my palm, the pain bringing me back to the present. I took a deep breath to calm myself, ignoring the pain that riddled my body. I cleared my throat, holding my head up high. I refused to let Liam live in my head.

"I need to cut some fruit for breakfast while this laundry is still washing." He stepped aside, letting me pass him, but not without grabbing my wrist gently.

"I'm sorry I didn't come back sooner," he shook his head, his eyes filled with guilt. He let my wrist drop from his hand so I could continue my way into the kitchen. He followed behind me, his aura pressing against my skin, making sure I knew he was there. I kept my eyes down, trying to focus on the task at hand. I couldn't lose myself in him and letting him comfort me was the start. I reminded myself that hope was dangerous. I began pulling out the various fruits and laying them on the cutting board. I was all too aware of his eyes watching my every move.

We sat in silence. Hudson would want me to tell him what had happened while he was gone. I had locked that part away and refused to open that door. I knew him, he had a way of pulling what he wanted to know out of me. When I arrived as a child, he took me in and treated me like a part of his pack. He made the pain of losing everything I loved easier. I couldn't lie to him, so instead, I would hide.

"I will let you finish here. He spoke suddenly, drawing my attention. I don't want to cause you any problems. I will be here from now on. Things will change, I promise." He assured me warmly.

I couldn't help but meet his gaze and smile. I believed that he really wanted that, yet I knew this pack. They were cold to those who didn't fit into their box. They had made it clear long ago that I was only a burden, not part of the pack. He touched my hand gently before leaving me in silence, my dark thoughts looming on the edge, threatening to break through.

I finished the fruit just as the washer was done. Transferring the clothes over to the dryer, I yawned. I made my way out the back door, exhausted from the day. I lived in the packhouse once. It wasn't so bad then. I thought back to when everything changed.

Hope stood in the kitchen cooking for the pack as I watched her carefully. She smiled, her face held an unforgettable kindness. Hope picked me up, placing me on the counter.

"I always wanted a daughter, you know," she said warmly. I looked down at my hands, fidgeting slightly. "I know it's been hard, Jasira, but I want to make you feel at home here." She gently touched my chin, pulling my gaze up to hers. Her eyes held such love for me. A mother's love that I craved desperately.

Over the next nine months, that's what she was to me. She taught me her secret recipes, bathed, cuddled, and tucked me in. Hudson was always with us as well. He was so much like Hope. He made it easy to let him in. I missed Alpha Kai and Felix. They were home. But Hope made it okay, she made the ache from being apart from Felix tolerable. My fifth birthday came, and she made me a special cake. I celebrated Christmas with the pack, a time filled with joy.

About a month later, she became sick. No one could understand how a strong she-wolf fell so ill. The sickness progressed until we buried her two months later. I allowed myself to hope that was the problem. Fate struck again, destroying my happiness.

I shook my head, shoving the memory away. I pushed it down deep, locking it away again. I now stood in front of the shed. It was all I had, but it was my home. The door creaked as I opened it, the floor groaning in protest as I stepped in. It wasn't much, but it was enough. I had a small toilet and a sink that Alpha Trenton had installed. That was the extent of his generosity. My bed was just an old torn-up mattress on the floor, but at least it wasn't the floor. I had no other personal items, no pictures of my parents or any other family. I barely had clothes of my own. Valentina had given me some of her clothes a few times because the ones I had no longer fit.

I yawned again, reminding myself I was tired and needed to rest because morning was fast approaching. I lay down, covering up with my torn blankets. My eyes grew heavy, sleep finding me quickly. All I had was my dreams.

The air was warm, the meadow the greenest I had ever seen. Taking a deep breath through my nose, the scent of spring flowers tickled my nose. I heard giggling off to my right, my body instantly moving towards the sound.

"Felix, I hear you," I squealed, my 4-year-old self-running closer to his giggling.

I flung my body through the air and landed on top of Felix. We rolled, laughing, and wrestling with each other. Felix was two years older and larger than me, but I was faster. Making it an even fight. We tumbled down a grassy hill, squealing with delight and landing flat on our backs at the bottom. We were out of breath from laughing so hard. Felix reached his hand out, placing it in mine, and we lay there looking at the sky. He turned his face to me, his gaze never leaving mine. His ocean-blue eyes danced still with our laughter. Even at four years old, I saw my whole world in his eyes. I knew then it would only ever be him.

I was ripped from my memory by the alarm blaring in my ear. I slapped the clock to make it stop and laid my arm across my face. The ache in my chest was unbearable. Once again, I was reminded that this is what life was, that the moment's happiness would only ever be a dream.

Ugh, those 4 hours were not enough, I grunted. With no choice, I quickly dressed and headed to the kitchen within the packhouse. No one was up yet, which allowed me some peace to wake up. I promptly fried the potatoes, scrambled eggs, and started the sausage. That is when Trudy and her daughter decided to enter the kitchen.

"Is our breakfast almost done?" Trudy sneered.

"Yes, ma'am, I am about to serve it," I responded, being sure to cast my eyes downward.

"Mom, can we head into town after breakfast to do some shopping," Angelica said to her mother, not acknowledging my presence.

"Of course, dear," she smiled sweetly at her. "Hurry up, you useless girl, I have things to do today. Oh yes, I almost forgot. After breakfast, I need a brief word. Meet me in the pack office."

"Yes ma'am, of course" I nodded.

They entered the dining area where pack members closest to Alpha Trenton would be seated. I quickly finished putting breakfast on platters to serve. I placed everything on the large dining room table. Alpha Trenton fixed his plate, and then everyone immediately dug in. I waited to make sure nothing was needed. Looking around, I noticed Hudson was not seated with everyone.

"That will be all," Alpha Trenton waved me off, "I don't want to see you while I eat. I would like to enjoy my breakfast." Everyone laughed at the table. I kept my head down, quickly returning to the kitchen to the small portion of breakfast I was allotted. I grabbed my plate and hid in the laundry room, eating fast before Trudy decided I was not allowed today.

A million thoughts raced through my head about my impending birthday. I will be officially eighteen years old in two weeks. Most werewolves shifted at sixteen, but maybe I was just a late bloomer. No one believed that, not even me, but until I turned eighteen, there was a chance. I could feel my wolf, so it wasn't that I didn't have one. Even if no one believed me when I told them. It felt like she was trapped inside of me, unable to escape. I had reached for her so many times. Yet she never came even when I feared for my life. This was just another reason I was damaged goods.

When I didn't make the shift, Alpha Trenton, Liam, and Beta Stephan beat me, saying that sometimes physical trauma could bring the wolf on. That was right after Hudson left. They almost killed me. It was the first of many beatings to come but certainly the worst. This was part of being an orphan. I knew the danger of not having a place in the pack. I had lived it since I was a little girl. At least if I had my wolf, I would be strong enough to defend myself. I could have found a place, but did I really wanted to be among them. The answer was no.

This birthday meant so much more, though. Your wolf is fully connected with you, allowing you to find your true mate. Then, shortly after, you would go into your first heat. Since I had no wolf, that meant no mate. I had heard the heat was excruciating without a mate to ease the pain. Maybe I wouldn't even have a heat because I couldn't shift.

For the longest time, Alpha Trenton was hoping I would shift so he could make me some other packs problem. My nerves were getting the best of me. Waiting to speak with Trudy was doing a number on my stomach. It twisted, threatening to purge the little bit of food I just ate. I quickly cleaned the kitchen and the dining room, trying to distract myself. Once finished, I went to the pack office to see what Trudy had to say.

I knocked on her office door, waiting patiently for her to allow me to enter.

"Come in," she responded plainly. I lowered my gaze.

"Miss Trudy, you asked to speak with me." I muttered.

"Ah, it's you. Good we can get this out of the way," she huffed. "We both know you haven't been able to coax your wolf out. Not that I blame her. I wouldn't want to be connected to someone like you either," she said hatefully. I dug my nails into my palms and bit my lip to keep my mouth in check. I had learned a long time ago that it only made things worse.

"Anyway, Alpha Trent has allowed you to generously stay because casting someone out before eighteen wouldn't look good on the pack. I personally would have thrown you away as a child," she continued her face one of disgust. "You are just lucky your mother was friends with the alphas brother, so he felt obligated. That being said, you have two weeks until you turn eighteen. You will be officially removed from the pack and sold to the highest bidder on that day." She sneered harshly with a smile on her face. My jaw dropped.

"You can't do that. I am not your property." I protested. Her eyes turned cold, a cruel look on her face. She was in front of me so quickly I didn't have a chance to respond. She slammed me against the door, her hand wrapped around my neck.

"Excuse me, I thought I heard you say I couldn't do something," she snarled. "You should just be grateful. I can't kill you myself." She spat.

I tried to pull her grip loose from my throat, panic seeping in from the loss of oxygen. Blackness crept into the corner of my vision. She slammed me against the door one more time, then dropped me. I sank to the floor, holding my throat and coughing. Trudy slowly bent down, crouching next to me. I flinched, drawing a laugh from her.

"Just be grateful I am not getting to choose who you go to. If it were me, I would sell you as a sex slave," she whispered. My eyes widened, tears threatening to break free. I refused to give Trudy the satisfaction of seeing me cry. "Now get up and out of my sight," she said, standing up gracefully, straightening herself. She strutted across the room, smoothing her blouse and pencil skirt. As if nothing had happened, she sat in the chair at the desk where she had laid her things. I stood up slowly, bracing myself on the wall. I was about to exit when her crazy ass added.

"Oh yes, Jasira." Trudy looked up from her desk, "make sure to get the house groceries. We wouldn't want anyone to go hungry, would we." She said, a cruel smile forming on her lips. I fought every urge to tell her to go fuck herself.

"Yes, ma'am," I choked out, quickly exiting.

I ran through the house as quickly as I could to hide away. I briefly heard someone yell after me, but I couldn't stop. The gentle breeze caressed my face, reminding me to breathe. I sucked in a steadying breath pushing down the rising anxiety. I flung the door open to the shed, closing right away. My body was numb, trying to process what had just happened. The tears that I had held back were now flowing. I sunk down on my mattress, bringing my knees to my chest.

"Jasira? Jasira?" I felt the bed shift slightly, a hand touching my back. "Jasira? Are you okay?" It was Hudson, he had come to check on me. I glanced up, seeing the concern in his eyes. Knowing I only had so much time left with him broke my heart. He was always there for me, but he belonged here, and I did not.

"Jasira… Please talk to me. Tell me what is going on," he insisted. I wondered for a moment if I should tell him. All it would do is hurt him, but he deserved the truth.

"Trudy just told me they would sell me to the highest bidder on my eighteenth birthday." I choked out.

His face shifted from shock to anger. "What the fuck do you mean sell you?" His voice was soft but laced with anger.

"That is what she just told me." I shivered, her words fully sinking in. He got up, fists clenched. He began walking a couple of steps towards the door. "Hudson." I grabbed his wrist, and his green eyes glowed brilliantly at me. I should have never told him. He didn't deserve to be dragged down by me. I let go instantly, but he grabbed my hand before I could back away, and his eyes softened.

"This anger is not towards you, Jasira. I already told you I would never hurt you." He said softly.

"I know that I am not afraid of you" my voice a whisper. I could tell he was fighting his wolf to keep control. I looked at his hand, sighing. "You can't burst into the pack house and fight this. I already told you things have changed even more since you left. It will just make me more of a target, possibly even make you a target." I explained.

"What do you mean more has changed?" He questioned. My gaze dropped unable to look at him.

"For starters, they almost killed me about a year ago, right after you left." I said under my breath. Hudson lifted my chin again, sadness filled his eyes creeping into my soul. He suddenly pulled me into his arms. He squeezed me with his hug, but not so tight that I couldn't breathe. I let his warmth comfort me. He pulled back, holding me at arm's length.

"Hudson, I have to get myself together, then go shopping. Can we talk again later, please?" I begged. He searched my face clearly, understanding I needed time, he reluctantly nodded.

"We will be talking," he stated firmly.

Watching him walk out was heavy. I was tired of feeling so alone, even with the pain this pack had caused me. I just wanted to belong. I stood up and went to the sink to splash water on my face. The coolness slightly burned my chapped cheeks. My eyes were swollen and stinging at this point. I looked at myself in the mirror.

"I am done," I declared. I had pushed the voice inside that screamed for me to never back down for too long. It's time to bring that girl back to life. I made the decision I would escape before my birthday. I was not being sold to anyone. Even if I didn't have a pack, I would go to the city where some humans and supernatural beings lived. Since I couldn't shift, I could play off as a human.

My decision was made. Now, all I had to do was figure out the timing. I had to talk with Valentina because she needed to know she deserved that. Composing myself, I straightened up, standing tall.

I searched deep inside, finding the spark that I had locked away. I reach for it, unlocking the cage. I would fight for my life until death embraced me, whispering fear into those who would try to stop me.

2

JASIRA

*L*ost in thought, I made my way to the center of town. I spotted V at one of the shop fronts. I watched her for a moment, memorizing every part of her. A sadness settled in my chest at the thought of never seeing my best friend again. Much like Hudson, she had shown me love and kindness. Our friendship has grown more over the years.

Valentina approached me with a smile stretching across her face.

"Hey, Jasira," she said, embracing me. I held on to her for just a bit longer. I wanted to remember this. "Are you okay?" She pulled back to look at my face, seeing the sadness in my eyes.

I choked back a sob, not wanting to break in front of her. She could always read me like a book. I managed to nod, but it wasn't reassuring.

"Don't you dare lie to me, Jaz. I know you better than anyone. What the fuck happened, and who did it?" This made me chuckle slightly. Valentina was always so colorful.

"We can't talk about it here," I said under my breath. "Will you walk with me to collect my list from the market, then we can find somewhere quiet?"

"Of course," she looped her arm in mine.

We walked through the market collecting the items needed. V always had a way of making me forget. I had so many moments of happiness with her I would hold on to. We finished, and she guided me to our spot in the woods, where we would always go to escape.

"Alright, spill it," she demanded, placing her hands on her hips.

"You know I am eighteen in two weeks."

"Yes, of course I do," she pressed expectantly.

"Trudy told me today that they would sell me off to the highest bidder on my birthday." I rushed out.

"What??" she exclaimed. "They can't do that," she challenged.

"It doesn't matter," I waved her off. "I am leaving before then." Her jaw dropped momentarily, then turned into a smile.

"Now we're talking. When do we leave?" she asked. I paused, shocked by her question. "

What do you mean? We?" She stood with her hands on her hips with a, I'm not taking no for an answer attitude. This was the reason I loved her. She had a fire that sparked something inside of me.

"You heard me, I am not letting you leave here without me." I shook my head, knowing there was no changing her mind.

"You don't need to do that, V. Your parents are here along with your life." She smiled back at me, reaching for my hands. She held them tightly, comforting me like she always did.

"Jasira, you are my best friend, my sister. If you go, I go, plus I have a place where we can get help."

I couldn't help the tears that began to form.

"I am so grateful you want to do this, but it could be dangerous. The pack might try to kill me for leaving. Although I don't know why they have never wanted me here." I shrugged.

"We aren't going to be caught. I can get us out. One of the guards has a crush on me," she said with a smirk. "He will help us, I am sure of it. Besides, this will allow me to finally learn about the other part of me." The confusion on my face must have been evident because she continued. "I know that Alpha Kai helped your mother. Well, he also helped my parents. My dad comes from a long family of half werewolf and half-witches. Since he is a male, he has been able to hide the magic part of him."

"But why does it matter that he is a male?" I looked at her in surprise.

"Every female born from my great-grandmother has been unable to shift because the witch part of their blood prevents it." I was shocked.

"But you can shift V. What does that mean for you? On top of that, you're one of the strongest in the pack."

"My father has the dominant werewolf gene, and my mother is a full werewolf, not to mention born of alpha blood. Another fact we do not share with anyone." I was stunned at how all these years passed, and I had no idea.

"That being said, I am a female in my father's line, so I have all the same strengths as the females in my family. Currently, I have the power to heal minor injuries. I have been banned from using them because my parents do not want to risk me being found out. We all know Alpha Trent would banish or kill anyone different," She rolled her eyes. "Typical Alpha is scared of anyone who might have power behind them. "Anyway, back to the point, my aunts and Grandmother will help. We just need to reach a town safely and call them."

What other choice did I have? I knew no one outside of this pack. Alpha Trenton had made sure of that. Valentina's plan seemed like the best option, plus having my best friend with me was a bonus.

"I hope you're right," I conceded. "They probably would reject you as well. What good are you to them?" The nasty voice in my head whispered.

Returning to the house, I was in a fog. The world was spinning out of control, my heart hammering in my chest. I paused momentarily, shaking my head to clear it before entering the kitchen. The kitchen was empty, so I quickly began putting groceries away. I knew I had been gone for a while, but Trudy was supposed to be with her daughter.

I was loading the fridge when I heard the kitchen door slam off the wall. Shocked, I dropped the carton of juice I was holding. I was grateful it didn't burst open, but my heart rate instantly spiked.

"Well, well, look who we have here," Liam jeered as he entered the kitchen with his mate Stella. Ian, the beta's son, followed closely behind him with his mate, Breen. They approached both sides, closing me in. I stiffened, not daring to let them see how terrified I was.

"How can I help you, Liam?" I asked, trying to keep the quiver out of my voice. Liam and I had a history. A flash of Liam ripping at my shirt left me paralyzed in place. He leaned in close, so the warmth of his breath brushed my neck.

"I heard that we would be getting rid of you soon." He whispered so quietly I am not sure anyone else heard it, even with their wolf hearing. I couldn't breathe. My skin crawled, flashes of last spring terrorizing my thoughts. My gut churned as he dropped his voice to say, "Thank goodness I have my mate now, or I would have to finish what I started." He stepped back with a malicious smile on his face. He punched me in the stomach, knocking the breath I was holding out of me and making me drop to my knees.

Don't forget to pick up that juice you dropped. Liam laughed, and the others joined in. I had said I was tired of this. He turned his back to me, looking at Stella, Ian, and Breen. I decided if I was going to leave this place, why not leave fighting. I grabbed the juice, uncapping it. I could feel my body heat with anger, an energy coursing through me I hadn't felt before. As he stood there laughing, his back turned, I poured the juice slowly over his head. He turned slowly around fury, lighting his gaze. I knew I was in trouble but didn't care at this point. I had nothing to lose.

"I thought you were thirsty, Liam. I was just trying to help." I said sweetly. He immediately reached out, grabbing my throat.

"You will pay for that," his wolf on the surface. "No one disrespects the future Alpha." Liam threw me across the room into the wall. My back hit so hard it left me gasping for air. I began to stand back up, a wave of dizziness hitting me, making me stumble.

Stella and Breen were in front of me now with malice in their eyes. Stella grabbed me by my hair, yanking me to my feet. Breen threw the first punch into my side. Stella was quick to follow. I tried to grab at Breen, but Ian was there and grabbed me quickly, ensuring no hands were laid on his mate. Both girls continued with their brutal attack until I could no longer stand. I could only curl up in a ball.

"That's enough," Liam declared. "We don't want to damage the goods too badly, or no one will buy her." The girls let out a growl, displeased but clearly breathing heavily. He grabbed Stella, kissing her. "Look at how hot you are, my future Luna," he told her with admiration. She purred in response, holding his hand and pulling him out of the kitchen. Ian and Breen did the same, leaving me bloodied on the floor.

I tried to pick myself up but slipped in my blood, grunting as my body hit the floor. Why was I ever concerned about leaving this place? Death would be better than staying here. I refused to remain laying on this floor and give up. I pushed off the ground from my hands and knees, white-hot pain making my vision blur slightly for a moment, forcing me back down. Once again, I pushed myself up, I stumbled forward but was able to grab the counter to hold me up. I steadied myself momentarily, trying to allow the dizziness to subside. I took slow breaths, trying to keep it together. Without my wolf, I didn't heal like the typical shifter. The door swung open, making me stumble and almost fall to the ground. Hudson quickly rushed to my side, holding me up.

"What the fuck happened, Jasira?" His voice was laced with concern.

"Not here," I whispered, "please just help me to my room." He scooped me up in his arms before I could protest.

"Of course, let's go." He agreed. He quickly carried me to the shed. He closed the door behind us and laid me down on the bed. He went to the sink, grabbed a cloth, and wet it. He sat next to me, blotting my face gently.

"Now speak he ordered. I want to know what happened and who did this?" I sighed,

"It doesn't matter, but if you must know, it was your brother." His face twisted with anger and confusion.

"Liam did this, but why?" he questioned.

"That is not important right now," I said firmly. "I know you are Alpha's son, and you may try to stop me, but I can't not tell you. I care too much for you to leave that way. I have no choice, I am getting out of this place."

"What do you mean?" He said, a bit stunned.

"Valentina and I are leaving the pack. There is no place for me here anymore. There never was. I refuse to be sold off, wolf or not. I am done being treated this way." I raised my chin, letting my words hold strength behind them.

He nodded, "I understand, Jaz. I just wish it were different. I can help you get out and meet once you're safe."

I was shocked, "You don't have to do any of that. I am already putting you in a bad position by telling you this. I am going against the Alpha, who is also your father. The plan was to leave tomorrow night. Valentina has a guard that will help."

"You don't get it, do you. I care for you and always have. I will ensure you get out safely. Then, I will give you a way to contact me once you get to where you're going. This is not up for debate. I am going to leave now so we don't raise any suspicions. Just go about today and tomorrow like normal." I grabbed his hand.

"Thank you for this." I couldn't help the emotion that slipped into my voice.

He looked down at my hand, an emotion I didn't quite catch crossing his face. He then claimed my lips. I was stunned, hesitating for a moment before kissing him back. This was my last chance to kiss him, and I would be lying if I hadn't thought about it before. Hudson was gorgeous, kind, loving, and willing to give me everything. Not to mention the only man that had ever loved me since Felix. So, I held on to him, allowing him to deepen the kiss. It just didn't feel right, there was a voice inside of me screaming to stop. I paused, pulling away suddenly. Felix's piercing blue eyes flashed in my mind, and my heart pounded. It would only ever be him, the little voice whispered. I thought I could one day let go of Felix, that maybe Hudson could be my chosen mate.

"I'm sorry. I wasn't trying to push you," Hudson confessed, drawing me from my thoughts. I shook my head.

"No Hudson you didn't. I am just overwhelmed." He nodded quickly, embracing me, then turned to leave. He looked back at me one last time, taking me in. Hudson, being my chosen mate, was no longer a possibility.

I did as Hudson advised, finishing up the rest of the day as usual. The pack was so used to seeing me beaten they didn't ask questions. The next day went by rather quickly, I couldn't shake my racing thoughts turning the day into a fog. Valentina had met me at the cliff, and we had talked about how we would be leaving tonight. My night was full of tossing and turning. After finally falling asleep, I found peace in my dreams, where a blue-eyed boy would visit me.

The night dragged on, my thoughts racing with everything that might go wrong. V would meet me shortly after dinner when I usually went out for my walk to the cliff. It would raise no red flags, giving us time to distance ourselves and the pack. They wanted me gone anyway, so what would be the likelihood of them coming to look for us. Although if I knew anything, it was that defying or not having permission from the Alpha was a sure way to piss him off. Regardless of the fear, I knew this was what had to be done. I ignored the bubbles in my stomach. Tonight was the night I would run for freedom.

I layered my clothes even though it was late July, not knowing how much climbing or if I would get wet. I would rather be prepared to avoid adding additional injuries on top of what I have. I quietly made my way to our meeting spot. No one would suspect anything since I walked in this direction every night. Valentina was waiting for me as planned. She had a large backpack in her hand and another one on her back.

"Jaz," she whispered excitedly, rushing to my side. "Are you ready to do this? I have us a short window by the gate from the guard station. Plus, with Hudson helping, we should be in the clear."

I nodded in agreement, sliding the backpack on promptly. I should have known that Valentina would come prepared. She grabbed my hand, giving it a reassuring squeeze. Then began pulling me down the path. Valentina moved with such swiftness and grace, making sure she never released her hold on my hand.

I could see the gate, our exit out of this place. Valentina silently signaled me to crouch down. We were at the forest's edge, the trees still covering us. I looked at Valentina, asking her what was next with my eyes. She looked toward the guard and then back at me. It was indeed the one that had a crush on her. She held up her watch to see the time, then held two fingers up.

Two minutes... got it. I nodded, letting V know I understood as we waited quietly. Two minutes passed, and just as planned, the guard began to walk away. Valentina grabbed my hand again, giving me a little tug to get into position. The lights suddenly went out, this was our chance. We both darted, running as fast as we could, knowing this darkness was temporary.

I followed Valentina closely as we ran past the gate. As soon as we cleared the gate, the forest thickened, allowing us to fall back into cover. The deeper we went into the woods, the darker it grew, hiding us perfectly.

The sky opened, drenching the world. Thunder roared as if the moon goddess was daring someone to chase us. I was getting wet quickly, but at the same time, I sent a thank you for her protection. It would be hard for them to track us by scent or footprints with the rain. The thunder would drown out any potential noise we would make. The rain would wash the path of our scent. We could only hope it would stay this way for several hours.

Our feet slapped against the wet ground as we raced through the forest. Fear pumping adrenaline into our blood so we could push through the exhaustion. Valentina led the way since she was able to see with her wolf. We had been running for two hours.

"V, I need a minute." My breath came out ragged.

She stopped turning to face me, she immediately paled seeing my state. I was barely able to stand my breath coming in short pants. I felt like I was being squeezed from the outside. I was trembling with pain, unable to push on.

"What is wrong? Are you okay?" She questioned. She reached for my shirt, seeing I was holding it there. I winced even though her touch was gentle.

"What the fuck, Jaz? She gasped. Why didn't you say something sooner?"

My skin was a deep purple around my ribs. Each breath I took felt like fire. Valentina closed her eyes, touching my ribs. I tried not to pull away, but the pain was unbearable.

"Your ribs are broken, and you also have a tear in your lung. That's why you're struggling to breathe. All this running must have made the tear." Her voice was laced with anger.

"I am going to heal you the best I can." She helped me remove my shirt by sitting me down on a nearby rock. She reached out, holding my sides. For a moment, I thought I would faint, and then there was a tingling that started. The tingling became warm, moving along my side and spreading deeper within my body. Until it consumed every bit of the pain. I took a deep, shaky breath, expecting pain. When I felt none, I cautiously began to take some deep breaths. I grabbed Valentina, pulling her into an embrace.

"How did I get a friend like you? Thank you, V," I said. I was amazed with her abilities.

She smiled, handing me a dry shirt from the backpack, quickly pulling my shirt over my head. Valentina reached for my hand, pulling me up. Standing before her, she grabbed my chin, making me look into her sun kissed eyes.

"You are no longer alone, don't hide things from me, do you understand?" She asserted. "I am your best friend. The Goddess has brought us together for a reason I can feel it. Now let's get moving." I nodded, sending a silent prayer once again to the moon goddess for Valentina.

We began running again. Keeping up was much more manageable, with my body returning to normal. As wolves, our stamina was much higher than the average human. Even if I didn't have my wolf, I was still stronger. We stopped just a few times to drink water and to eat a snack to boost our energy. The sky began to brighten with color, signaling that the sun would rise soon. We had stopped running about an hour ago, enjoying the surroundings. It was amazing being able to freely speak with V.

We finally reached a small town. We scouted the area to see if we saw any of the pack. Once we were clear, we went to a small store.

"Now that we are here, we need to find a phone. We can buy one of the cheap pay-as-you-go phones at this convenience store. This way we can call my aunt, she should be able to pick us up from here." She explained.

We were in and out, still too nervous to be in public. We worked our way back to the edge of town near the forest. In the clear, Valentina dialed her aunt's number. My anxiety grew by the second as she pressed the phone to her ear.

I heard a woman answer saying "Hello?"

"Auntie, it's Valentina…."

"V, I have been expecting your call." Of course, she has. We both gave each other a look.

"We need help. Could you come pick us up? We are in a small town called Benson."

"Ahh, yes, it will take us five hours to arrive, but we will head out immediately. There is a small cottage down the road, you and Jasira can rest there. I have made the arrangements already, just give them my name. We will see you shortly," her aunt assured, ending the call.

Valentina was speechless, looking at the phone. I placed my hand on her shoulder.

"V… What happened?" I questioned.

"They were expecting our call. I mean, that shouldn't have surprised me. My Aunt Isla has visions." Valentina explained. "They are on their way, but it will be at least five hours. She has a cottage reserved for us already. We could use the rest." She paused. "The weirdest part was that they already knew your name."

"What do you mean?" Tilting my head, not understanding. "How could they know who I am, and why were they expecting you?" Valentina shrugged her shoulders, just as confused as I was. Only one way to find out, I suppose.

There would need to be a conversation. For now, we hurriedly made our way to the cottages. Sleep was a high priority right now. Once checked in we made our way to a cute cottage, relief flooded me once we were inside. Valentina told me to shower first so I could get any remaining blood off my body. I walked into the bathroom, shutting the door behind me. This would be the first shower I ever had. I was restricted to the water hose outside to clean up or the sink in the shed. Sometimes I would sneak a buck and I would fill it with warm water from the pack house.

Tears prickled my eyes as my shaky hands reached for the handles, turning them on and testing the temperature. I peeled my dirty clothes off and stepped into the shower. The hot water instantly relaxed my muscles. A small moan left my lips as the water continued to caress my body. I reached for the shampoo that the front desk had given us. Sweet cherry blossoms filled the air as I scrubbed my scalp. Not wanting to use all the hot water, I quickly applied the conditioner and cleaned my body. As I was rinsing, I looked down, and the water running off me was filthy. I scrubbed, wanting to wash not only the caked mud off my skin but the stain of the Cross River Pack. Finally feeling clean, I stepped out of the shower. I quickly finished in the bathroom, putting on the comfiest clothes I had ever worn, provided by V.

"Your turn," I smiled at Valentina. She got up to walk past, desperate to shower like I was. I stopped her for a moment, capturing her in a hug. "Thank you so much, V. For being here, for the clothes, for literally everything," I said, gripping her like she was my lifeline.

She rubbed my back, squeezed me, and then pulled back slightly to look at my face.

"You are more than my best friend, you are my sister. I love you. I'm just sorry this didn't happen sooner. Now go get some sleep, with that she gave me one more squeeze." I watched as she walked to the bathroom, a feeling of happiness creeping in that had been missing for a while. I climbed into the bed, curling up in a ball, and drifted off.

3

JASIRA

"Jasira, we need to talk," Alpha Kai said, patting his lap. My four-year-old self bounced over to him happily. I crawled into his lap, snuggling in as he wrapped his arms around me, placing a kiss on top of my head. "Jasira, my princess, I must take you somewhere safe. There is a danger coming to our pack as well as one of my sister's pack. It is not safe here for you anymore. I made a promise to your mother that I intend to keep." He explained with sadness in his voice.

"Where will I go? Who will take care of me?" I whimpered, a tear sliding down my cheek.

"My brave girl do not fear we will meet again. For now, I will take you to my brother, Alpha Trenton." He said, wiping the tear that escaped my eye. I wrapped my small arms around his neck, letting the tears flow, and then I quickly got up from his lap. Anger bubbled inside a fire I had not felt before rising. My body shook uncontrollably.

"This is not fair," I yelled. I turned and ran as fast as I could until my legs burned. I slumped to the ground, a puddle of tears. When arms embraced me, I knew who they belonged to.

"Jaz," Felix's voice was a whimper. I turned to face him. He reached out, holding my hands. "I promise I will find you, no matter what. One day, we will see each other again," He vowed.

I nodded, and we sat silently for a long time after that. Felix's arms wrapped around me, assuring me we would be together one day.

I sat up, clutching my chest from the memory. I looked around briefly, trying to figure out where I was. It had been so long since I had thought about that day. I shivered, wanting to forget. My life has never been the same since I arrived at the Cross River Pack. I looked at the clock, it was noon. Valentina's Aunts would be coming anytime. Valentina stretched, opened her eyes, and propped herself on her elbow.

"Hey girl, are you alright? You look like you saw a ghost," she questioned.

"Yes, I'm okay, just a bad memory." I shivered once more. I climbed out of the bed, trying to shake off the lingering feeling of sadness. "Your Aunts should be here soon. I'm going to freshen up." I changed the subject, not wanting to talk about it.

She nodded in agreement. Climbing out of the bed as well to start doing the same thing. About thirty minutes later, there was a knock at the door. Valentina peered out cautiously, opening the door wide when she saw her aunts were the ones there. Valentina ushered them in, closing the door quickly behind them. They both embraced Valentina, smiles on their faces.

"Jasira, this is my Aunt Deema and Aunt Isla," introducing me to both of them.

Both her aunts were beautiful and radiated power. Deema was tall, with an athletic build, chocolate skin, deep blue eyes, and short, curly black hair. I could see that Valentina shared features with Isla. She was average height, with curves for days, and her eyes were an orange sun kissed color, just like V. They both had the same coffee skin with long Auburn hair. Deema was the first to rush forward and embrace me, catching me off guard.

"I have missed you more than you know, my girl. You are so beautiful." She pulled back slightly to look at my face and into my eyes.

"Enough with all that," Isla waved at her sister, pushing her aside and embracing me. "We are sorry this didn't happen sooner, but the moon goddess has her reasons. We are here now to get you to the form you were meant to be. Besides all that we need to move now, we are too close to that wretched man. I don't want to take any chances," Isla proclaimed.

"You are right," Deema agreed, "Grab your things girls, let's get this show on the road." I was so confused with everything that happened but eager to get as far away from my pack as possible.

We piled up in the car, making our way quickly out of the town. Her Aunts were not joking when they said they wanted to put distance between us and the old pack. Deema had her foot to the floor until we had been driving for an hour. The silence was deafening, and V gave me looks like I would break any minute.

"Alright, I can't take it anymore. Deema, Isla, I need to know what you know and what the hell is going on?" I growled unintentionally.

V was shocked by the noise while Deema and Isla smiled at one another.

"That is the girl and wolf we know is in there." Isla giggled. "Listen, Jasira, we can tell you what we know of your story, but Mama Merida will be able to explain more."

"Did you know my mother and father?" I asked, hopeful.

"Yes, of course," Isla answered. "This is what I can tell you. I know you have not changed yet, that you probably think you never will." Tears welled in my eyes.

"Jasira," she continued, "I know this is hard to hear and believe, but your wolf has been suppressed by a potent magic. You will learn who you truly are, but more importantly, we must get you back to Saoirse. Once home, we can release the magic so you can become who you are meant to be." She explained. The fury inside bubbled.

"Who am I exactly supposed to be in your book? Because from where I sit, I'm a nobody. No one has ever wanted me or cared, so why have people start now?" I said haughtily. Valentina flinched as if I had struck her, making guilt rise. I reached for her "I'm sorry V, that wasn't fair."

"It's okay, you're right," she nodded. "I should have acted sooner."

"Jasira, I understand you have suffered. I truly am sorry for that, but we had to keep you hidden, not allowing anyone to suspect who you will become. You are a gift from the moon goddess herself. Her power courses through you." Deema proclaimed.

Valentina and I looked at each other, our jaws dropping. "Now, I know you want answers, but you both should rest until we get home. You will need it, believe me." Then, with a wave of her hand. Sleep took over.

I woke up groaning alongside Valentina.

"Not cool, Aunt Deema, not cool." She said, annoyed, and I nodded in agreement.

"Listen, girls, I don't have all the answers. That would have been a painfully long drive for all of us, so I did what was needed." She shrugged.

Standing in the front yard, I took in the large house. It had a homey storybook feel. We followed Deema and Isla, walking into a large entryway. An older woman with a kind face rushed in, she was ethereal in her beauty. She glowed with life and strength, like a combination of her daughters. Chocolate skin with piercing blue eyes, petite in height and curvy. She had short auburn hair with slivers of silver. She embraced Valentina first, kissing her cheeks.

"Look at how beautiful my granddaughter is," admiration in her voice. I can feel your magic, my child. We have much to discuss in the future." She moved to me, embracing me as she did Valentina. "O Jasira, you can't imagine how long I have waited for this moment." She reached up, cupping my cheek.

"You look so much like your mother." I could see the sadness in her eyes.

"Did you know my mother well?" I couldn't help but ask.

"Yes, my child, I loved your mother as if she was one of my own. I was sworn as her protector and her mother's protector by the Goddess. I couldn't protect her in the end, but that is a story for another time. We have much to prepare for the reversal ceremony. Time is not on our side right now."

"Deema and Isla, please take Valentina to get everything we need. Let Cleo know Jasira is here as well. We will need her. Jasira, I know you have a million questions, I can answer some. Come with me, and I will explain while you eat." Mama Madeira ushered me to the kitchen table. She made me a plate piled high with food. My mouth watered at the aromas as I shoveled the hot meal into my mouth. Mama Madeira smiled at me, clearly pleased by my eating.

"I know you must be so confused, my child, the truth is no less confusing. she started. Your mother and father came from two of the four remaining elemental packs that are direct descendants of the moon goddess herself."

I gasped in shock. "I had no idea any of those packs existed. I heard they were wiped out long ago in fear of their power." A shiver ran down my back, thinking about how anyone could kill someone just because of fear.

"That is what everyone believes" she said, sadness lacing her voice. "Your mother, Alpha Maeve, part of the Amber Stone Pack, and your father, Alpha Callan, part of the Amethyst Stone Pack, were both elemental wolves. They were also true mates. They joined their packs in hopes that it would make them stronger. For a long time, they lived a beautiful life together. I was a part of your mother's side of the pack until we became one. Your Grandmother was a descendant as well. I was her protector, she could use the element of water." My mouth fell open, clear that I was shocked by this revelation.

"What do you mean she could use the element of water?" I thought she was a wolf, I questioned.

"Yes, my child, she was a wolf, but this is why others feared them. The Elemental packs all had powers gifted to them by our Goddess." She explained.

I tried to process everything she was saying as she continued. My world was shifting right before me, and I was trying to keep up.

"Both of my girls were assigned to be your mother's guardians when they were old enough. They were close to your mother, being raised with her and then guarding her. She made them leave her and take you." She paused, shaking her head like it would wipe the bad memory away.

I reached out to hold Mama Madeira's hand.

"I'm sorry, I know that couldn't have been easy for them or you."

"You, my child, are the most precious gift we could ask for. She knew that" she nodded firmly. "That said, Moon Goddess Selene instructed your mother to hide you and not allow your shift until your eighteenth birthday. We were given a ritual to perform that would unleash your wolf along with your powers. The war happened quickly after that, and Alpha Kai became your guardian. He was supposed to raise you in our ways until you were old enough for us to remove the magic restraint. Until it became unsafe for you there as well. We made sure to put Valentina in place for when the time came. We knew she would bring you to us."

"You mean to say that Valentina was placed in the pack on purpose," my head spinning with everything Madeira was telling me.

Mama Madeira chuckled. "Of course, my child, she is a guardian like the women before her, except she was gifted by the moon goddess as well and has her wolf."

I was in complete shock, and disbelief.

"How can all this be true?" I asked. "More importantly, what happened to Alpha Kai?" My thoughts swirled to Felix. What had happened to him? Does this mean he was still out there?

"Yes, I figured that question was coming. Alpha Kai is alive along with his pack. They have been in hiding for a long time waiting for you. He is Alpha of the Emerald Stone pack, one of the Four." She paused, letting me take everything in. She could clearly see the pain in my eyes from speaking about Alpha Kai.

"The moon goddess showed me a vision of this moment. She told me to be patient. I know Alpha Kai has never stopped wanting to bring you back to the pack, but he respected the protector's decision. My only regret is the pain you suffered." I squeezed her hand and nodded my understanding.

"I know you are probably very overwhelmed. Let me show you to your room so you can get some rest, we will be leaving tomorrow.

"What do you mean leaving tomorrow?" I asked nervously.

"We are leaving for the Emerald Stone Pack tomorrow. Alpha Kai and his son are the ones that will need to train you." I felt lightheaded. I stood quickly to get away. This was all too much. I just needed a minute. I was shocked that I would see the boy with blue eyes. Everything was just too much, I blacked out, and the last thing I heard was Mama Madeira calling my name.

I awoke in bed, my eyes flying open to take in the surroundings. Light peeked in slightly through the curtains, revealing it was morning. How long had I been sleeping? I stumbled out of bed, finding a bathroom attached to my room. I flicked the light on it, blinding me with its brightness. I allowed my eyes to adjust before turning on the sink to splash my face. I pressed the fresh towel to my face to dry it off, then looked into the mirror. My hair was a mess, but my skin had a soft glow that it didn't usually have. This is what it must look like to have a full meal.

I looked around to find something to conquer my nest. There was a bag with my name on it. I reached for it, peering inside. It was filled with makeup, hair ties, a hairbrush, a toothbrush, and other toiletries. I worked the brush through my long black hair. I decided to jump in the shower. I conditioned my hair and washed my body. I stepped out, admiring how the waves in my hair had responded. I quickly browsed the bag, putting the lotions in the appropriate places. The makeup would have to be for another time. I had no idea what I was doing. Feeling refreshed, I went back to the bedroom.

I opened the closet to see brand new clothes with tags still on them. There was a note saying these are for you, Jasira. I couldn't believe it, I don't remember the last time I had new clothes. There was a lavender off-the-shoulder blouse I reached for. The fabric was incredibly soft. The blouse hugged my curves and was perfect. I grabbed a pair of skinny jeans to complete my outfit. They were the perfect size as well. I turned to look at myself in the full-length mirror.

The blouse made my purple eyes pop. This was the first time I had ever felt beautiful. Smiling, I slid on a pair of black flats. There was a suitcase on the bed with a note as well.

Please pack everything once you are ready for the day.

Love Mama Madeira

I grabbed the clothes from the closet, shoes, and toiletry bag. I had nothing else with me except for the backpack I came with. Carrying the suitcase, I went downstairs, where everyone was waiting for me in the kitchen.

Mama Madeira was rushing around the kitchen, finishing up breakfast for everyone. Valentina was sitting at the table with both her aunts. They all looked at me in unison when I entered the doorway.

"Morning Jaz," Valentina smiled at me, patting the seat next to her.

"How did you sleep?" Deema asked, sipping some coffee.

"You look stunning today," added Isla.

"I slept well. Thank you." I smiled, feeling my face warm from the attention. "What time is it?"

"It's ten in the morning, sweetheart" Mama Madeira chimed in. I was shocked I had slept for twelve hours, not to mention I had never slept past six.

I didn't realize how much yesterday wore on me.

"How long is the trip?" I asked. Valentina automatically reached for my hand, giving it a reassuring squeeze.

"We will be eating and then leaving, it will take us about 8 hours." Deema answered.

I nodded, and we all sat quietly after that, enjoying the feast Mama Madeira served us. I looked up several times to imprint these powerful women's faces in my mind. At this moment, I couldn't be happier. I was free, not to mention I really did have a wolf. I knew she was in there. After enjoying our meal, we placed our suitcases in a large van and set off for the hidden pack.

During the first part of the trip there, we all chatted, but as the hours dwindled to the arrival of our destination, my anxiety grew. I sat in silence, looking out the window and admiring the beauty of the forest. The fear of rejection thick in my throat, making it hard to swallow.

"Jasira, we are entering the pack lands now. We did not inform them we were coming, so I want to warn you that they may not be friendly at first." Madeira explained. My nervousness grew.

"What if they don't want us here?" I asked, sitting up straighter. When you said us, what you really meant was you. Why would they want you? The ugly voice in my head poked.

"Don't worry, child, everything will be fine once they realize who we are." Mama Madeira reassured me. Suddenly, the van brakes slammed, throwing me against the seat. Luckily, I was wearing my seat belt. I looked out the front window to see three giant wolves and two men standing in an attack formation.

"What brings you to our land?" one of the men bellowed. The others circled around us growling.

"Ladies, it's time for us to all step out of the van now," Mama Madeira instructed. I unbuckled, following their lead. I slowly opened the side door. I stepped out with Valentina following me, she stood in front of me shielding me. The realization that she was my protector, now at the forefront of my mind.

"We are here to see the Alpha Kai of the Emerald Stone Pack. He has awaited our visit. We come with Queen Jasira, daughter of Alpha Maeve and Alpha Callan." I was stunned by her announcement, and so were the two men. They looked at each other briefly, something passing between them. Mama Madeira looked back at me, snickering a bit.

"Did I forget to mention that you will be the queen that unites all the packs?" All I could do was stand there stunned until one of the men announced.

"I have informed Alpha Kai of your arrival. He is waiting for us at the pack house. Please follow us." The two men immediately shifted, taking off up the path ahead. We piled back in the van following closely, the forest felt like it was watching us. As we drove deeper into the pack lands, the feeling grew to the point of making me uncomfortable in my seat. I couldn't sit still, my stomach was in knots. The pack house came into view and suddenly the feeling eased.

A man was pacing outside. He was tall with an athletic build, he had sandy blonde hair that was tousled at the top like he had run his hands through it. His short, well-kept beard worked well with his strong jaw. I knew immediately that it was Alpha Kai, I could never forget him. He hasn't changed at all since the last time I saw him. Our kind didn't age like humans. Once we reached our late 20's, the aging process slowed dramatically.

As we pulled, he turned, our eyes meeting the most prominent feature I could remember. His eyes were green like the forest and filled with kindness. Right now, they were tainted by a deep sadness. I barely waited for the car to stop before I threw my door open, sprinting towards him. He was initially surprised, then quickly opened his arms to receive me. I ran straight for them. He quickly wrapped me up in his embrace. He smelled of sandalwood and home. I wasn't sure that he was real, for the longest time I thought my mind must have made him and Felix up.

Now, being here with him gently rubbing my back, I couldn't hold back the sob that escaped me. The dam was broken, my cries racking my body with their release. He simply held me, allowing this moment. I reined myself back in after a few more moments. Pulling back slightly to look at his face. He handed me some tissues that I am guessing one of the pack members brought during my breakdown. I took them gratefully, cleaning my face.

"Thank you," I whispered. "I can't believe I am here."

"I am as surprised as you are, sweet girl. Although you are not the little girl I once remembered now, are you." He said with a sad smile.

I shook my head, smiling back. "I am not Alpha Kai, but I have thought about this moment for so long, never believing it would actually happen." I sighed.

"Ahem," Mama Madeira cleared her throat, drawing our attention. "I don't mean to interrupt, but we should go inside. There is much to discuss with not a lot of time."

"Of course, let's go," he turned, placing his hand on my back, ushering me forward. "I made Felix wait in the grand hall for us. I didn't want to overwhelm you."

I nodded, now in a hurry to make it to the grand hall. This couldn't be real. My anxiety increased. What if he didn't remember me? What if he didn't want me here? I began to panic. We were standing in front of a giant door I assumed was to the grand hall, and I was frozen.

"Jasira? Are you okay?" Alpha Kai stopped with me, studying my face.

"I...I" my words left. Leaving me unable to say anything, Valentina was in front of me instantly. She grabbed my hands, making me look into her eyes.

"I already know what you're thinking, Jaz. You better stop it right now. These people have waited for you, they are your people. As for Felix, I know what he means to you. There is nothing for you to fear." She assured.

Heat rushed quickly to my cheeks, slightly embarrassed.

"Thank you," I breathed out. Valentina was always there when I needed her, saying precisely what I needed to hear. "Let's go," I nodded forward.

With that, the doors opened, and I walked into a giant room. The man in my dreams standing there looking more delicious than I could have ever imagined. I was in trouble. All I could do was stare, his gaze holding me captive. He had changed so much since the little boy I remember. He exuded power, demanding the room's attention. His blonde hair was to his chin and wavy, which framed the chiseled features of his face.

Valentina nudged me, breaking my trance and making me look at her. She raised an eyebrow at me. I gave her a glare as heat once again reddened my cheeks. I looked down, not daring to meet his gaze again.

"Come everyone, let's sit. I have the kitchen whipping up something for us to eat." Alpha Kai said, easing the awkwardness of the room. We all made our way to the large table in front of us. The air cracked with energy. "Felix, do you need to step out?" Alpha Kai questioned.

I didn't realize, but the energy was coming from him. It wasn't your typical Alpha struggling for control, feeling this was mixed with something. I realized that they probably had powers as well.

"I'll be fine," he insisted through gritted teeth.

Was he mad that I was here? His face was closed off, not giving any emotions away. Doubt began to trickle in again. I pushed it down, ready to listen to what Alpha Kai had to say.

"Madeira, I am happy you have traveled to us bringing our future queen. I wasn't sure when this day would come." Alpha Kai began.

Mama Madeira nodded. "I know, but it only makes sense that the goddess would bring her to us with her birthday right around the corner."

Alpha Kai rubbed his chin, clearly thinking.

"You are right, but the danger is still great." He turned to me." Did Alpha Trenton take care of you well?"

I saw Valentina flinch with his question, Madeira, Deema, and Isla lowered their gazes. I reached out my hand to them, trying to comfort them. Alpha Kai saw their response and mine.

"What is wrong, Jasira? What happened?" He questioned.

"Alpha Kai I will not go into details right now, they are not important. I was not wanted in the pack. They made that clear by treating me unkindly," I explained.

Felix growled, startling me, Alpha Kai rested his hand on his son's shoulder.

"More like abused for years," Valentina whispered. I shot a glare her way.

"It is not the time, V," I hissed back. Alpha Kai was shocked.

"First off Jasira, you can just call me Kai. I am not your Alpha, my girl. You will soon be mine. Secondly, I will be hearing more of this."

I nodded, praying to the Goddess that we could change the topic and move forward with the conversation.

"She needs to be trained, that is why we are here. She has a little over a week until her birthday." Deema announced.

"Yes, the more training she has, the better control she will have when we release her magic and wolf," Isla added.

"You're right," Kai paused momentarily. "It's settled then, Felix will train her starting tomorrow."

My head snapped to Felix, and he nodded, agreeing with his father. At that moment, the food was served. They brought out several choices of meats, pasta, fresh bread, and sauteed veggies. Everyone was clearly starving, filling their plates. We ate in silence, I kept stealing glances at Felix. I'm pretty sure he caught me a few times.

"Ladies, I will show you to your rooms," he said to Madeira, Deema, Isla, and Valentina. "Felix, would you mind showing Jasira hers." Before Felix or I could respond, Alpha Kai got up from the table, ushering the others towards the door. Felix stood first, and I followed. We stared at each other for a moment. I refused to do this, if he was unhappy with me being here, I was going to find out why.

"Are you unhappy I am here?" I asked, keeping my voice steady. I clearly shocked him. He took a step toward me.

"Is that what you think?" He asked, his brow furrowed.

"I know it has been a long time, but I was hoping you remembered me from when we were kids." I couldn't help but whisper the last part and lower my gaze.

He closed the gap between us and reached up, lifting my chin gently so that I was looking into his eyes.

"Remember you, are you serious? All these years, you are all I have thought about." He claimed.

Now, it was my turn to be shocked. Did he just say what I thought he said? I was speechless. On top of that, having him this close made it impossible to think clearly.

"Come let me show you to your living quarters." He stepped back, holding his hand out in the direction of the door. I nodded, making my way towards the hall as directed. We walked in silence, coming to a large staircase.

"You will be on the third floor with my father and me. The third floor has restricted access. The only ones allowed up there are our Beta's and most trusted circle." Felix explained. He paused once we reached the landing of the third floor. "My father is down that hall there." He gestured to the right. "Our quarters are across from each other to the left." He gently placed his hand on the lower part of my back, ushering me toward our rooms. His touch sent a shiver up my back, and I was instantly aware of how close he was as we walked.

Get yourself together, Jasira. What is wrong with you? I thought to myself. My thoughts were quickly interrupted once we reached a set of double doors.

"This is you," he said, opening the door and allowing me to step in first. The room we entered was not simply a bedroom. I entered a living room with earthy tones, modern furniture, and greenery. It was comforting, I felt close to the forest just being in this room. I couldn't help but touch everything while I stared in awe. I turned to look at Felix, who had a slight smile on his face. The first one I had seen come across those yummy full lips. He was breathtaking. I shook my head, clearing my thoughts and moving further in.

I entered the bedroom, and my eyes widened. A crystal chandelier sparkled over a regal-looking bed. The room was lavender with white accents. Luxuriously pooling window drapes were adorned with crowned light swags. There was so much to take in I was overwhelmed. Tears began to form. I swiped them away quickly. Felix placed his hand on my shoulder, turning me to face him.

"Are you okay? Do you not like the room?" He asked with concern evident on his face.

I nodded, trying to pull myself back together. I took a deep breath and closed my eyes for a moment. I opened them to Felix, still concerned.

"I could never have imagined such a room for me. This is all so much I am not sure I deserve it or am the one everyone thinks I am." My fear slipped out my lips.

He stepped closer, his body pressing against mine, grabbing my chin to look at him.

"You, Jasira, are exactly what everyone thinks you are and more," he growled. "You deserve everything here. I will make sure you will never want for anything." My breath hitched as his scent wrapped around me. There was a feeling deep in my belly that I had never felt before. I was frozen, unable to pull my eyes from his. The boy who had comforted me in my dreams was real. Standing before me looking like a damn model. His scent whirled around me making it hard to breathe. Suddenly, Felix released me, taking a step away.

"Please let me know if you need anything. I will be across the hall." He turned, making his exit.

The room felt empty, a chill crept over my body as if it were cold. I could still feel his grip on my chin as if it had been seared there. What just happened? I asked myself as I turned back, looking at my bedroom. You're stupid Jasira, that's what happened. How could you ever think someone like him would want you. There it was again the voice in my head reminding me of what I really was. Nothing.

I sighed and investigated my bedroom further, finding a walk-in closet filled with clothes and a spacious bathroom with a soaking tub.

I planned on making good use of that tub in the near future. For right now, though, I was so emotionally and physically exhausted all I could think about was curling up in that big bed. I didn't even have it in me to find pajamas. I stripped down completely, sliding into the sheets and allowing the bed to take me. I fell asleep instantly, but it was anything but peaceful.

4

FELIX

I rushed out of her room, trying to maintain control of myself. Her scent was a delicious mixture of grapes and papaya blossoms. It called to my wolf. I had not experienced this before, I never lost control.

Except maybe I had, feelings from childhood surfaced. I have always known there was something between us. I just didn't expect it to feel like this. But from the moment my father's Beta mind linked us that she was here, my emotions were all over the place.

I ran my hands through my hair, pacing my living room. Why was she having such an effect on me? But she always had, hadn't she?

When we were kids, she would enter a room and be the only one I could see. I thought she was beautiful as a little girl, but now goddess help me. She was sexy as hell. Especially when she smiled, her plush lips mixed with those dimples had me reeling. It had killed me to not take her in my arms and feel her soft body against mine when she walked in.

The feeling only grew stronger until we were in her room together and all I could think about was running my hands down my curvy body. I had to get away, but I hadn't missed the flash of hurt in her eyes as I walked out.

To top all that off, my uncle hadn't taken care of her like he had promised. My anger rose, my wolf pushing his way to the surface. I didn't know what she went through, but I would find out. I would kill anyone who had touched her.

I tried to drag myself out of the dark road I was going down. I needed to keep my powers and wolf in check. But it wasn't happening, not when I knew she was right across the hall from me.

The door opened drawing my attention. Declan and Gage walked in, their faces morphing into concern.

"What's up Felix?" Declan asked.

"Nothing I am fine," I snapped.

"Clearly, that is not the truth" Gage quipped.

I sighed, debating on how much to tell them. They were my best friends, and I never hid anything from them. I stopped pacing and plopped down on the couch.

"Pour me a drink would ya." I gestured toward the bar.

Gage was closest, he grabbed three glasses filling them. Declan sat across from me, watching me closely. Gage handed my drink to me and sat next to Declan.

"Do you remember how I have been looking for someone" I asked even though I knew the answer.

"Yes. How could we forget? You have been searching since we met you." Declan claimed.

"She is here and right across the hall." I explained.

"That's great. Isn't it?" Gage pressed. Gage was always the one to push me or ask the hard questions.

"Yes, the fact that she is here is great. But I am barely holding on to control of my wolf. We see her as pack" I wasn't ready to admit the actual reason. "She came from a bad situation. She was abused by the pack my father sent her to." My body shook with anger just thinking about it.

"Sounds like they need to be taught a lesson." Gage said cracking his neck.

"That may be true, but it is not happening right now. Felix, you clearly care for this girl. You need to make your wolf see that he doesn't want to scare her off," Declan stated.

"There is something else you guys should know. She is Alpha Maeve and Alpha Callan's daughter."

They both stared at me, their mouths open in shock. Declan was the first to get it back together.

"You mean thee Alpha Maeve and Alpha Callan." Declan shook his head trying to process everything.

"The one from the stories we all heard about as kids. The child that is blessed by the Moon Goddess." Gage added.

"Yes, that's the one. Her name is Jasira, and she will be our Queen," I proclaimed.

Gage and Declan had a ton of questions. I answered them the best I could, because in the end there was still a level of mystery around Jasira. We had been told her parents stories as children. They were heroes to the Elemental wolves. Madeira's mother had a vision of Jasira before Madeira was even old enough to be a protector. She had passed down the prophecy to Madeira, letting her know that one day a wolf would be born of two powerful Alpha's. That wolf would be the Queen of all the packs and unite us. The prophecy was more in depth than that, but we all got the picture.

I yawned, exhausted from the day. Talking to them had given me some relief. My wolf was calmer now. We said our goodnights, all of us needing sleep. Even after our talk they were still in shock when they left, but excited to meet her.

I decided to take a shower to relax a bit. The hot water cascading over my body felt amazing. All I could do was think about her. I had to control myself, Declan was right. But damn it was going to be hard. My wolf wanted her, but he didn't want her to be uncomfortable with us either. Or worse scared of us. Until I knew what she had been through I would need to tone my aura down.

I stepped out of the shower, frustrated in more ways than one. I lay across the bed, trying to will myself not to think of Jasira. Until I heard her scream, I ran to her, fear engulfing me.

5

JASIRA

is hands pushed me down on the floor, pinning me in place. I tried to kick, twisting away.

"Please, Liam, let me go," I cried. "Please don't do this." He slapped me hard across the face.

"Shut up, I am your future Alpha," Liam growled. "You should be grateful that I would even want to touch you."

He held both of my hands in his one. He was so strong there was nothing I could do, and he knew it. He reached with his other hand, ripping my shirt along with my makeshift bra and exposing me. Panic ran through me. I bucked harder, trying to get him off me. He laughed at my efforts, and he knew I was weak. He let me go momentarily to undo his pants, allowing me the briefest opening. I pulled my legs out from between him and twisted, rolling to my hands and knees, kicking out at his stomach. I scrambled away as I heard him grunt an angry growl tearing from his lips. He grabbed my ankle, and I screamed.

I sat up straight in the bed, panic coursing through me in the dark room. The door burst open, and Felix rushed towards me. I couldn't breathe, my throat tightened, my heartbeat wildly, and my stomach turned. Felix reached out to make sure I was ok. I flinched away, the dream still fresh.

"Jasira, listen to my voice. I need you to take a deep breath. You are safe, I won't let anyone hurt you." He slowly reached out again to touch me, careful not to startle me. The moment his hand touched my arm, I felt warmth spreading up my arm.

"I'm sorry," I sobbed, pulling my knees to my chest, "I didn't mean to disturb you." I apologized in fear of being punished, the past still fresh.

He pulled me into his arms, and my body tensed in an automatic response, but once pressed against him, a wave of calmness came over me.

"You have nothing to be sorry for." His voice was soothing. "What happened? Please talk to me."

"I am afraid," I said, looking up at him.

"I won't let anything happen to you," he repeated. I shook my head.

"I am not afraid of them. I fear that once I let you in, you will toss me aside like everyone else. I just got you back," I whispered.

"You don't ever have to worry about that, Jaz. I will always be here." He said, giving me a slight squeeze. I was suddenly very aware that I was completely naked, with only a sheet covering me. I panicked, standing up too fast, losing my footing along with the sheet that had been hiding my nakedness. I felt myself falling to the ground when strong arms wrapped around me, catching me. Now, I was pressed against his chest. The room instantly became too hot. Damn, his chest was so firm. He growled slightly. He made sure I was balanced before letting me go and stepping back. I will wait in the living room. He quickly turned, leaving me standing there. I sprang into action the minute the door shut. I grabbed a T-shirt and yoga shorts from the closet. Why was I so hot and bothered by this man? I had bigger things to deal with right now. I thought to myself.

I walked into the living room. Felix was sitting on the couch waiting, not so patiently. I could tell he was tense.

"Will you sit and explain?" he asked. I nodded, sitting across from him.

"I want to tell you everything, but now doesn't seem like the time." I hesitated.

"You don't have to tell me everything right now. How about we just start with why you were screaming." He pressed gently.

"Alright, I can do that. Valentina knows pretty much everything the pack did to me. She even knows about the time they left me for dead". A growl escaped his lips. "She does not know about this, so if we could keep it between us, I am just not ready to share it with her." I realized then how safe I felt with him. Knowing I could share this weight with him, he could help me bear it.

"I promise, however, you will tell me about that other incident as well." He said his voice was tight.

"I was alone cleaning the living quarters of the pack members. The Alpha had taken his trusted advisors who lived in the pack house to some big meeting. Liam stayed behind to be Alpha while Trenton was away, so he was out doing who knew what. While they were gone, I was assigned to deep clean all the rooms. I was finished with everyone except for Liam's room. I didn't hear him come in. He came up behind me, wrapping his arms around me. I pushed away from him." I spluttered.

"I asked him what he was doing, and his response was putting me to good use," I whispered. "When I refused him, he attacked me, throwing me to the floor and pinning me down." A flash of him throwing me to the ground made me turn away from Felix. I couldn't look at him.

"I fought him. I tried so hard to get away that I briefly broke free when he was unzipping his pants." I choked out, trying to fight back my tears. I dug my nails into my palm focusing on that pain instead of the memory. Felix took a sharp breath. I pushed forward, knowing I wouldn't be able to tell him if I stopped now.

"I got out from under him, but he was too fast. He grabbed my ankle, pulling me back. He choked me, slamming my head against the floor a couple of times. He then began to pull my pants off." I cried, no longer able to hold back, the memory had forced its way in. "Liam must have heard something that made him pause. He climbed off, pulling up his pants quickly. He left me there, but not before he kicked me several times and then threatened if I ever told anyone that he would kill me."

I felt Felix next to me again, holding my hands and soothing me. I looked up at him and went back to my living room. "I found out later that Trudy had come home early. He found his true mate at the Super Moon Ball a few days later. Lucky for me, he didn't have any interest after that," I scoffed.

I searched Felix's face for a hint of rejection. His hands balled into fists, shaking slightly. He was so hard to read, my anxiety grew. What would he think of me, now that he knew how weak I was?

"I am going to kill that mother fucker," he cursed.

I was surprised by his proclamation. What did he mean by that? Did he really care for me that much? A million questions raced through my head. But none of them were answered. Felix's muscles rippled with anger. I could tell he was fighting for control of his wolf. His aura poured out, all alpha. Most would have fled or cowered away, but this was Felix, and I wasn't scared. I placed my hand on his knee, without even thinking. The contact causing a spark between us, I went to pull my hand away in shock. But Felix placed his hand on mine, pinning it there. Our gazes locked, his blue eyes, an undertow sweeping me out into oblivion. I took a deep shaky breath. Felix pulled his hand from mine, looking away. The moment was gone, maybe I had imagined it all. I yawned then, and realized how tired I was.

"Why don't you go back to bed, Jasira. We have training tomorrow morning you will need your rest," he breathed.

"I know we just reunited, but could you stay with me?" I asked shyly. I needed to feel the calmness he could provide. I still wasn't sure why, but he had this effect on me as a kid as well.

"Of course," He nodded. We made our way to the bedroom, He grabbed a few pillows off the bed to begin making a spot on the floor.

"Umm, Felix?" I said, feeling brave. Maybe I hadn't imagined that moment, maybe there was something between us.

"Yes," he stopped what he was doing to look at me.

"This bed is huge. If you're comfortable with sleeping up here with me, you can." I kept my voice strong so he wouldn't think I was questioning my decision. He paused for a moment.

"Are you sure? "He asked. I nodded my assurance. He grabbed his pillows back up, placed them on the bed, and climbed in, ensuring he gave me my space.

"Good night, Felix," I whispered.

"Goodnight, Jaz," he replied. With that, I closed my eyes, feeling safe because of a blue-eyed man.

I woke up feeling better than I had in a while. A weight lifted off my chest. I looked to where Felix was sleeping, but he was nowhere in sight. I sighed, getting out of bed. A small bit of me was disappointed that he wasn't here. Girl, you need to stop, I whispered to myself. I showered, getting myself ready for the day. I dressed in comfortable shorts with a tank top. It was August, which meant that it was sweltering outside. My stomach grumbled, reminding me I better get a move on if I wanted to eat before training. I was tempted to knock on Felix's door but resisted. I remembered my way down to the dining area and headed in that direction. Valentina, Madeira, and her aunts were eating at the table.

"Good morning, everyone," I smiled happily.

"Hey, Jaz," Valentina exclaimed. "You're just in time. Breakfast just got here."

6

FELIX

I woke up earlier than I usually do. Jasira was still sleeping peacefully, so I decided to sneak out to avoid disturbing her. Her scent lingered on me, and my wolf was pleased. I took the shower I had planned on taking last night. My mind was racing with everything she told me. I was so grateful when she asked me to stay with her. I couldn't have left her if she wanted me to. The pain in her face chewed at my insides. I decided to mind link my father.

"Dad, are you up?" I asked.

"Yes, everything ok?" He replied.

"No, not at all. Let's meet in the office in five minutes." I said.

"Okay" he responded, I closed the connection. I jumped out of the shower and quickly dressed. Then, I made my way to meet my father. When I opened the door, he sat at the large table where we had council meetings. He immediately noticed the anger and pain on my face.

"What is wrong, son?" He asked, waving to the seat across from him. I began pacing, not able to sit now.

"Last night, Jasira screamed out in her sleep. She was having a nightmare about her old pack." My father stiffened slightly, then acted normal like I wouldn't notice. "What do you know?" I growled at him. He sighed, realizing I wouldn't let this go.

"I spoke with Madeira and Valentina about what they knew about her life. After the comments at dinner, I had to know," his face twisted in pain.

"Felix, you need to keep your emotions in check. I know you care for her, but tearing the house down will not help her." He said calmly.

"I know that" I gritted my teeth. "Just tell me," I sat down, showing him, I was in control.

"She was abused regularly, and they did horrible things to her. Especially the beta's wife, Trudy. When she didn't shift at seventeen, they nearly beat her to death. Valentina didn't know the details, but she was the one who healed her. Jasira wasn't healing fast enough and wouldn't have survived." My father explained.

A roar ripped from my throat. This was my fault, I should have found her sooner. The guilt was eating me alive.

"There is something else Felix." I looked at my father, needing to hear it all. "She left because they were going to sell her to the highest bidder." He finished.

My blood boiled, my wolf was begging to rip them apart. "Don't worry, we will kill every last one of them." I told my wolf, soothing him.

"This is our fault. We should have never left her." I shook my head. The guilt and anger had me spiraling.

"I am going to kill them all," I said to my father.

"We can't risk it. Felix, she needs to grow her powers and train." He answered.

"Liam tried to rape her," I shouted, throwing the chair in front of me across the room.

My father was in complete shock, but that quickly turned to anger.

"What the fuck did you just say?" he snarled.

"That's what she was having the nightmare about. The only reason Liam stopped was because he was interrupted. V doesn't know. No one does." I said, taking some calming breaths.

"They're fucking dead, all of them." He growled out. I nodded in agreement.

"The kitchen just mind linked me, and everyone is waiting for us." My father announced. "Let's go eat breakfast with Jasira. We have already missed too many with her," He continued. He was right. We had so many moments missed. Time we would never be able to get back. I may not be able to change the past, but I was damn sure going to be there for her future.

"Yes, let's go," I affirmed. I patted him on the back as he rounded the table. "I am making it my personal mission to train her so that she can remove Liam's manhood from his body." I smiled at the thought. Walking by my side, a darkness filled his eyes that I hadn't seen before.

"I expect nothing less, son.

7

JASIRA

The dining room doors opened, and Alpha Kai entered with Felix. Alpha Kai came to my side, kissing the top of my head.

"Good morning, dear did you sleep well?"

"Yes, thank you, Alpha," I responded with a smile.

"It's Kai to you, young lady. I hope you found your room to your liking," He chuckled.

"You have no idea how grateful I am to you for your kindness. The room is perfect." I replied.

Felix took a seat right next to me. I looked at him with a smile, I could drown in the depths of his eyes. My heart rate increased a little. I looked away, reaching for the syrup as a distraction.

"Did you sleep well?" I asked Felix, trying to play it cool when I looked back at him. The corner of his mouth turned up into a sly smile.

"I slept great, thank you." I couldn't help the happy dance that I did inside.

"We usually have some of the pack here for breakfast, all our closest friends. However, I arranged for it just to be us today. Tomorrow, they will join us." Alpha Kai said, interrupting my thoughts. "You will meet several of them today during training. We can't wait to introduce you. We will go to the training grounds right after breakfast." He continued.

Mama Madeira clapped her hands excitedly.

"That is great news, Alpha Kai! While Felix trains Jasira, I will be training Valentina." She told him. "That way, she can train alongside you when you shift." Madeira said to me. I had to admit I was excited to train. I was never allowed in my old pack, which left me defenseless if we were ever attacked. Or when I was attacked, a shiver ran through me briefly. Felix touched my hand slightly, letting me know he was there. I relaxed and finished my breakfast, eager to fight.

After breakfast, Felix walked me to the training grounds. A nervous energy fluttered in my belly. As we entered a sizeable gym-like room, I couldn't help but look around at everyone. At least fifty pack members were warming up, waiting on Felix, I presume. A man jogged up to us with a smile.

"This must be Jasira," he said warmly. He had a kind face, and I was instantly comfortable with him.

"Jasira, this is my Beta Declan," Felix introduced.

"It's so nice to meet you, Beta Declan," I said with a smile.

"Have you set everyone in groups yet, Declan," Felix asked.

"Yes, everyone is warmed up and ready for you." Beta Declan nodded.

"Why don't we put you in Gina's group?" Felix said. We walked over to one of the groups. "Gina, I want you to meet someone," Felix said. The auburn-haired woman turned around. She was drop dead gorgeous. She was petite, but her body was muscular. Her face reminded me of a model. She smiled at Felix and then looked at me. She was clearly accessing me, almost as if to see if I was a threat.

"This is Jasira. She is the daughter of an alpha from a neighboring pack. We will be training her. I was hoping you would help with that." Felix stated. I wondered why he didn't tell her the whole truth and decided I would ask him later about it.

"Of course, anything for you, Felix," she replied sweetly. I instantly disliked her and how she batted her eyelashes at Felix. Am I jealous? I thought to myself. I shook the unfamiliar feeling off and focused.

"Just show her the basics," Felix said, then turned to me. He placed his hands on my shoulders, ensuring he had all my attention. "If you need me, just come find me. Don't push yourself too hard. I will come back shortly and check in. I will also train you a bit," Felix said in a hushed voice. My heart warmed for this man.

"Okay," I replied, nodding my understanding. He turned to go make rounds to the other group's training.

"Let's see what you have," Gina said, breaking me out of my daze. She got into a fighting position, and I did my best to copy her. I had never fought or trained before, so I wasn't sure if I was doing it right. I certainly wasn't going to tell Gina that, though. I steeled myself to take some hits. She was fast, speeding towards me before I knew what was happening or how to react. She had me on my back, the air leaving my lungs on impact. With a grunt, I got back up. I looked up and swore I could see an evil gleam in her eyes.

"So, tell me," Gina said. "How do you know Felix? You seem close, yet I have never heard of you."

She began circling me, getting ready to strike again.

"Why would you have heard about me?" I was puzzled. She lashed out again, but I was expecting her this time. I barely moved out of her way.

"Oh, you don't know I will be Felix's Luna soon." She poked. This threw me completely off, and she took advantage of it. I twisted slightly, trying to break the fall. It mostly worked, but I felt my ankle bend in a painful way. I held in the cry that I wanted to let out. Who does this bitch think she is? I am pissed now.

I stood back up my ankle protesting, but I didn't give a shit.

"Hmm, you said future Luna. Felix didn't seem to mention that when he was in my bed last night," I spat. I knew it was a low blow, but I was done with being pushed around. It was time for her to learn her place. Her face turned red with fury, and I swear I saw a flicker of flames in her eyes. But my own fire was ignited in my soul. She came at me for the third time, but I was ready. Her mistake was she did the exact same stance each time she charged me. Without realizing it, she gave her move away.

She charged, but I pivoted, grabbing her arm as she went by me, bringing her back to face me. I pulled my fist back and swung, hitting her in her pretty face. She stumbled back, reaching out to grab me, stopping her fall and balancing herself. She reached for my arm, holding it with a firm grip. I then felt an unexplainable pain in my arm. It felt as if my arm was on fire. I screamed, the burning growing more substantial, along with the smell of burnt skin. She removed her hand, stepping back with a cackle. All I could see was the scorched mark of a handprint. My arm was bubbling, the pain increasing by the second.

My ankle chose that moment to give out, making me stumble forward, pulling my arm to my body to protect it from hitting anything. I tensed, expecting pain again as the floor neared. Strong arms wrapped around me, balancing me.

"What happened?" Felix demanded. I noticed Gina was back playing Miss Innocent again with an I don't know look on her face. Felix paid her no attention as he accessed my arm. "Gina, did you do this?" he growled out.

"I... um...I didn't mean to. She made me do it." Gina squealed. Felix immediately scooped me up, holding me close to his chest.

"I need to get you to the infirmary and call for Valentina." He commanded someone. He ran, trying his best not to jostle my arm. Great, now he will think I am weak. Plus, what was the deal with Gina being his Luna? I need to put some space between us. The thought had my heart aching.

We reached the infirmary, and he laid me on the bed as the Doctor came in.

"What's going on, Felix? Who is this?" The Doctor asked.

"This is Jasira. She is the child of Alpha Maeve." The Doctor gasped as she looked at me, then immediately saw my arm.

"What happened here?" She asked me.

"Just a friendly disagreement," I said sarcastically, hissing at the pain as she inspected it further. Felix growled. The Doctor looked at him.

"Felix give us some privacy, maybe find her protector" she ordered.

It was interesting seeing a future Alpha ordered by anyone. But Rebecca was clearly older, probably knowing Felix as a pup, so they paid no mind.

"I will be outside the door waiting for V to get here," he said unhappily. I nodded, trying to focus on not being sick from the pain.

"I am Doctor Rebecca, it is so nice to meet you Jasira," she spoke while she turned to look for supplies. "Tell me what happened here?" Doctor Rebecca asked. I hesitated for a moment." Listen, I need to know if this is magical or if it's caused by nature." She insisted.

"It was Gina. She burnt me with her hands," I sighed.

The Doctor shook her head. Sitting in front of me, cleaning my wound. That girl is nothing but trouble.

"I have told Felix to watch out for that one." This was my chance to find out what the deal was between the two of them. She seemed to know what was going on.

"She seems to think she is the future Luna to the pack, and Felix is hers." I started trying to seem nonchalant.

"She is delusional," the Doctor grunted.

I was going to try to get more information from her, like why she would think that, but before I could ask, Valentina burst into the room. She had a look of pure anger on her face but quickly shifted to concern when she got a look at my arm.

"Who did this to you?" Valentina rushed to me, taking my arm from the Doctor.

"It's not a big deal, V," I responded.

"It is, in fact, a big deal. You are to be the future Queen. No one should lay a hand on you." She said, "I am going to heal you, but this will hurt. I must reverse the magic, then heal the wound." She continued.

"Felix!" she shouted. Felix entered the room immediately.

"I will need you to hold her," she nodded in my direction. Before I could say anything, Felix put his hands on my shoulders, holding me in place. The feeling of being held down had panic bubbling to the surface. Memories began flooding back, and my chest tightened. Felix must have sensed my anxiety. He lowered his face in front of mine. Filling my vision with only him.

"Jasira, I will never hurt you, I promise." His voice a soothing balm to my anxious thoughts. His smell swirled around me, and I breathed it in, letting it fill my body with comfort. Felix nodded at Valentina, and then she began.

The pain wasn't bad at first, just a gentle tugging. The tugging became stronger until it turned into an unbearable ripping feeling. I felt as though someone was pulling my skin from my arm. I screamed, unable to hold it in. My vision began to tunnel into blackness as the intensity of the pain grew. I thrashed, trying to escape the burning, the feeling consuming me.

Finally, the pain began to ease. Felix's smell engulfed me, comforting me. I looked up at him, and his face was a mixture of concern and anger. I didn't even realize I had been crying, but he gently wiped away the tears. I was so tired my eyes were fighting to stay open.

"It's okay, Jaz, just rest. I am sorry that hurt so much," Valentina whispered. I tried to fight the overwhelming sleepy sensation, but it was useless. Blackness came whether I wanted it to or not.

8

FELIX

"What the fuck happened?" Valentina asked harshly. "I left her with you because I thought she would be safe. How could you allow this?" She was shouting now.

My guilt swirled to life reminding me that I had failed her yet again.

"I would like to know the same thing, V. When I left, she was in a group training with my people," I growled.

"May I interrupt for a moment? I may have some insight." Doctor Rebecca said, coming in to check on Jasira.

"Please do speak freely," I insisted.

"Jasira told me that Gina was the one to do this to her," Doctor Rebecca stated. My mouth fell open in shock. Why would Gina do this? I thought to myself she was someone I trusted. As if reading my thoughts, the Doctor continued. "Jasira mentioned that Gina was stalking a claim on you, saying she was to be the future Luna of the pack."

"Are you kidding me? You put Jaz with one of your love interests." Valentina accused. "You should know she wolves don't share their territory very well." I growled at the thought of Gina being a love interest.

"Gina is not a love interest or my mate. She is a trusted friend, or so I thought," I said sharply.

"Then why would she think you are hers and she is to be the future Luna?" Valentina pressed her hands on her hips.

"That would be the council's fault. Everyone knows an Alpha needs a Luna. I have no mate yet, so they discussed Gina since she was a strong warrior and has always loved me. They gave me three years to find my mate. If not, then I was to mark her and make her my chosen mate."

I could tell Valentina wasn't happy, but she understood the duties of an Alpha. "My pack had to be my priority. I have a fated mate, I just needed time to find her. I just agreed to their nonsense to hold them off. It doesn't matter now, though." I explained.

"Why is that? Because it kind of looks like it does matter, since Gina is out here claiming you. Valentina huffed.

"It doesn't matter because I have found her. Even if she doesn't know it yet" I whispered looking at Jasira. "I am guessing Gina saw that connection as well."

"So, how do we deal with Gina?" Valentina asked with a new understanding.

"I will take care of her, friend or not. She just made a huge mistake." I answered. Valentina seemed satisfied with that response. We both sat quietly lost in our thoughts waiting for the only person that mattered to wake up.

9

JASIRA

A wave of emotions hit me as I awoke. There were voices in the room I recognized talking in hushed tones. I lay there momentarily, eyes closed, processing what had happened. What was I going to say to Felix? He would want to know what had happened. Plus, the whole Gina being his Luna made a different emotion rise inside me. One that made me feel as if I would burn the world down. I took a deep breath, opening my eyes. This immediately drew the attention of Felix and Valentina. They were both at my side in an instant.

"How are you now?" Valentina asked, holding my hand.

"I am fine, V," I smiled, trying to reassure her. The pain was gone completely, thanks to her healing. She let go of the breath she was holding in relief.

"Thank the goddess," she whispered. Giving my hand a slight squeeze.

"How long was I out for?" I said, trying to sit up to get out of bed. I was done lying down and being the victim.

"Woah, take it easy. You should rest." Felix insisted. I glared at him, my anger about his relationship with Gina still at the forefront.

"I am done laying here. I would like to train, learn more about my history, and discuss the next steps. I am done being pushed around." I spat. "Don't you have a pack to worry about right now, along with a future Luna?" I said sarcastically.

He visibly flinched at my words, and I realized what I had said. Guilt immediately followed, he had been nothing but kind to me. My emotions were running crazy.

"I am sorry, Felix, that wasn't fair. It is not my place to be upset about such a thing." I whispered.

Valentina cleared her throat.

"I am just going to give you some space. Jaz, I will see you at dinner." She walked out the door, pulling it to leave Felix and me to work out whatever this was.

"Felix," I started, but he held up his hand.

"Please don't apologize," he uttered. "I am the one who should be sorry. I shouldn't have put you in that position. I should have told you about Gina," he professed.

A knot in my stomach formed, the thought of him having feelings for Gina broke something inside.

"So, tell me then. What is your relationship with her?" I mumbled, barely able to speak the words.

"There is no relationship with her," he growled. "The whole thing about her being my future Luna was a council decision. If, after three years, I had not met my mate, then I would claim her. This would bring stability to the pack and ensure the Alpha line continued. Believe me when I say I had no desire to do such a thing." His voice filled with anger as he spoke. "Gina doesn't matter to me. She is simply a friend." He explained.

Relief filled me. I released a breath I didn't realize I was holding. Why was this man affecting me so much? I began to get out of bed, but Felix insisted on helping me. I suddenly was standing in front of him, our bodies pressed together. I looked up into his eyes, realizing how close he was. I could feel his warm breath on me. He hesitated, but his eyes dropped to my lips briefly. That was all I needed. I leaned forward, kissing his soft lips briefly. I had never done such a thing before, but I couldn't help it. The need to kiss him was so strong. The sexiest growl I have ever heard escaped his lips. I pulled back, about to apologize, but he kissed me back before I could say anything. I jolted slightly in surprise, then closed my eyes, relishing his soft lips pressed against mine. I can still feel his lips on mine as he reluctantly pulls away. He held my face as he rested his forehead on mine.

At that moment, Doctor Rebecca walked in. Felix and I both stepped away from each other like we had been caught. I couldn't contain the heat that crept up on my face as she smiled at both of us.

"I just wanted to check in. If you're feeling better, you are clear to go," Dr. Rebecca informed.

"Thank you, doctor." I said. She then turned and left.

"I must go check in with the pack. I will see you at dinner. Beta Declan's mate, Liana, will be waiting right outside, and she will stay with you." He said, reluctant to leave. I rolled my eyes.

"I will be fine Felix, just go."

After Felix left, I couldn't help the giggle that escaped me. I touched my lips. The warmth from our kiss still lingered. I had to pull myself together before I could go to the waiting room. I quickly spotted Liana, she was hard to miss. She rushed up to me excitedly with a vibrant smile across her kind face.

"You must be Jasira. I am so happy to meet you," she said with sincerity in her voice.

I couldn't help the smile that blossomed on my face. Liana had such amazing energy.

"Yes, that's me, you must be Liana," I replied. She nodded, hooking her arm in mine, and pulling me along with her. I chuckled at her.

"Would you mind if we went back to my room so I could shower? It's been a bit of a day?" I asked.

"That sounds like a plan to me. Let's totally get you dolled up for dinner." She eagerly guided me to my room, her bubbly mood infectious. By the time we reached the room, I was in stitches.

Alright, you go get in the shower, beautiful. I will look through this extensive closet of yours. I was actually excited to have a laid-back, girly moment. Liana's aura was pure and bright. I showered quickly, intrigued to see what Liana had planned for me.

When I entered the bedroom, she had two dresses laid out for display on the bed.

"I just couldn't decide," she said, delighted by her choices. I smiled at her and picked up the first dress.

"Should I try both of them on?" I asked.

"Most definitely," she replied. I grabbed both dresses excitedly. I entered the bathroom, quickly sliding on the first dress. I stared at my reflection in the full-size mirror. I couldn't believe this was the same girl that wore torn, stained clothes a week ago.

The emerald green dress was stunning. The lace made the dress soft and elegant. I stepped out, showing Liana.

"Oh my gosh, Jasira, you look incredible." She jumped up and down excitedly. I blushed at her compliment.

"Thank you," I said politely.

"Alright, let's see the next one" she waved me along. I re-entered the bathroom quickly, making the swap. I took a moment to check how the dress looked. I felt sexy in this one. It was meant to grab attention. The deep burgundy material was silky soft, fitting every curve of my body. The dress went to my knees as well, but there was a slit that went mid-thigh. It was halter style with a plunging back. I gathered my courage, ready to show Liana. As I stepped out, she gasped.

"Hot damn girl, that is definitely the one. We will make sure that all eyes are on you at dinner," she said.

"You think it looks good?" I questioned. Spinning around to give her a better look.

"Umm...Absolutely, it looks better than good." She insisted. At that moment, Valentina walked into the bedroom.

"Holy shit Jaz" she exclaimed, making me laugh.

"V, I'm so happy you're here." I introduced the two to each other, excited to have Valentina join us in getting ready. Valentina and Liana decided this was a good time to do my hair and makeup. I had never felt so pampered. V grabbed us some wine, filling our glasses as Liana worked on putting soft curls in my hair.

"Who is going to be at this dinner anyways?" I asked, sipping my wine.

"We have a usual group that dines with us, so it is likely everyone who is close to the Alpha. It's like you're coming out for dinner." Liana answered. This made me nervous. What if they don't like me, I thought. "Typically, it would be the Beta Michael, his mate Shayna, Colton Alpha Kai's Delta, Alpha Felix, Declan, Jax, Gage, Gina, and me." She listed everyone for me. Gina would be there. Great, I now had to deal with that. I thought to myself. I was glad to be wearing this dress. I felt sexy and powerful, so tonight, I would show Gina exactly who Felix belonged to.

I sat looking at myself in the mirror of the vanity. I couldn't believe how incredible I looked. The light makeup Liana had done was perfect. Liana smiled brightly at me from behind,

"You look stunning, Jasira."

"Thank you," I said, unable to contain the giggle that slipped from my lips.

"Alright, my Queen, let's get you to dinner," Valentina announced, squeezing my shoulder. I chuckled, rolling my eyes. I would never get used to being called a Queen. At this point, I am pretty sure these people have it all wrong.

We went down to the dining area, not wanting to keep everyone waiting. Felix paced back and forth at the entrance of the dining room. He froze in place, looking up at us. His eyes found mine, I knew I should look away but couldn't. A low growl escaped Felix's lips, sending a shiver up my spine. Valentina gently touched my back.

"We will see you there." Valentina smirked, drawing my attention, and snapping me out of whatever had just happened with Felix. I nodded to her, both of them leaving us alone. Felix approached me, grabbing my hands.

"You look beautiful, Jasira. That dress is incredible," he proclaimed.

I could feel the heat of my cheeks rising, causing me to blush. I couldn't help the smile that turned up my lips. This man made me feel things, things I didn't ever think I would get the chance to experience. I couldn't let myself grow attached. I knew I needed to protect my heart.

Felix cleared his throat. He had been watching me, waiting for me to process my thoughts. His expression was guarded.

"Everyone is waiting for us. We should go in," he said, pulling me towards the door.

"Wait," I insisted, grabbing his arm. He paused, his expression now concerned.

"Is there something wrong?" he asked as he looked me over.

"No, I am okay, but" I shook my head, my cheeks growing pink, but not for the same reason as before.

"But" he raised a brow, waiting for me to continue.

"I know Gina is in there". A low growl escaped him at my statement. I placed my hand on his chest, not realizing what I was doing. His beast calmed as I continued. I would like for you to let what happened earlier go. I want to deal with it in my own way. I said confidently.

"Do you know what you are asking of me, Jasira?" His voice was dangerously low.

"I realize this is against your Alpha instincts but hear me out."

"Alright, let me have it," He sighed. I put on a serious face, but inside, I was smiling. "If I am to be Queen one day, I must show them I deserve to be. I need to prove my strength because you won't always be there to defend me." His eyes glowed again, his wolf clearly on the edge, his body tense.

"I will always be there, Jasira. No one will hurt you as long as I breathe," he snarled. I stepped toward him, pushing my body against his. His alpha aura radiated off him, making me want to cower, but I refused. I wrapped my arms around him instead. He growled, but it was one of satisfaction this time.

"I didn't mean it like that. I'm sorry." I felt his body relaxing.

"Fine, but I can't promise you if she tries to hurt you again that, I will restrain myself," he grumbled. I could see his unhappiness with letting it go as I turned my head up to look at him.

"Thank you," I said, realizing I was still in his arms. I began to step back. He pulled me into him, so I was pressed against him. I sucked in a breath as a zap of heat made my core ache. His lips crashed down on mine, surprising me. I quickly met his mouth with eagerness, parting my lips slightly. Alpha Kai suddenly cleared his throat. We both pulled away abruptly. My hands pressed to my lips as I turned away, unable to look at either of them.

"I was just checking to make sure everything was alright out here," he said clearly, trying to keep a straight face.

"Um, yes," Felix cleared his throat. "Everything is great, Dad. We were just headed in." Felix replied, his voice still slightly husky.

"I see that," Alpha Kai chuckled. "I will see you both in a moment then." He turned back toward the dining hall, leaving us. I couldn't hold the laugh any longer. It bubbled out of me, startling Felix.

"I'm sorry," I said in between laughs.

"You have no reason to be," he chuckled.

"Do you remember when we were kids, and he would give us that same look when we were being mischievous?" I laughed out loud.

"Yes, he really did," Felix said, laughing with me. We both sighed, reigning the laughter in. I couldn't help but smile at him as he led me into the dining room.

He reached for my hand, holding it tightly, sending warm tingles running up my arm, comforting me. He stopped in front of everyone, not letting my hand go. He cleared his throat, drawing everyone's attention.

"I wanted to make sure I introduced you all to Jasira before I let everyone in the pack know." He started. "Everyone who sits here is a trusted member of this pack. So, it is essential you know who Jasira is. She is the daughter of Alpha Maeve and Alpha Callan." An audible gasp came from several pack members. "Jasira is the Queen we have all been waiting for.' He smiled with admiration as he looked over at me briefly. "Now let's eat dinner together," he announced, pulling out a chair for me and promptly sitting beside me. I looked around the table, excited to sit with a pack and feel welcomed. Food came out right away and served on platters. It all smelled terrific, and my mouth began to water. We all waited patiently for Alpha Kai to begin.

He looked at me with a smile on his face.

"I would like it if you started the meal, Jasira" he claimed. My mouth fell open, I was in shock. The Alpha of the pack always puts the first item on their plate. No one else but Gina was shocked by this revelation. The pack nodded their respect to me.

"I am honored, Alpha Kai," I said, trying to keep my voice from wavering. I grabbed a buttery roll from the basket before me and placed it on my plate. Then, everyone joined in filling their plates with the assorted foods. My appetite had grown this past week, so I piled my plate, excited to dig in. The pack chatted with one another, and I couldn't help but look around, admiring everyone. Mama Madeira and Alpha Kai chatted like old friends catching up. Valentina was engrossed in a conversation between her two aunts. Warmth filled my chest.

Could I really be a part of all this? I looked at Felix. He was turned, talking to Declan. That's when I looked at Gina, who was staring daggers at me. I didn't understand the hatred. I had done nothing to her, she wasn't Felix's mate. I reached for Felix's hand for comfort before I could stop myself. He turned to me, his attention now solely focused on me.

"Are you okay?" he asked sweetly.

"Yes, I am great," I replied, beginning to pull my hand from his. He tightened his grip, clearly not ready to let it go. I looked towards Gina briefly. I swear her eyes had flames in them. Giving my attention back to Felix, I squeezed his hand and smiled at him.

"I am tired. I think I will go rest," I said, beginning to stand. Felix stood up as well.

"I will come with you," he insisted.

"You don't have to, I know my way," I reassured him, but I could tell by the look on his face he was not taking no for an answer.

We both said our goodnights to everyone, leaving them to continue chatting.

Both of us were silent as we made our way up the stairs. It was driving me crazy by the time we got to my room. Felix opened the door for me and then shut it behind as he entered.

"Is everything alright?" I turned to ask him. He was only inches away from me, and I had to resist the urge to close the gap between us. His scent wrapped around me like a warm blanket on a cold night, begging me to get closer.

"No, everything is not alright," he said, his voice low. His response surprised me, but before I could ask what was wrong, he continued. "I can't seem to stay away from you, Jasira. I have never felt like I would lose control, but I am barely hanging on when I am around you." His words sent shivers down my spine.

"Maybe I don't want you to control yourself," I whispered. Looking up at him, his eyes glowed the brightest blue, clearly showing his wolf was at the surface. Felix stepped forward and our bodies pressed against each other. His hand reached up, caressing my cheek. I leaned my face into his caress, closing my eyes.

"You don't know what you're saying. I can't do this. I'm sorry," he said, pulling away slightly.

A heaviness pressed on my chest. I sighed, knowing Felix was right. What if he found his mate, or if I found my mate when I shifted. I didn't want to lose my friendship with him. I was probably just imagining our feelings. I bet he just felt guilty. Pitying me for everything I went through. I turned away from him, tears fighting to escape. I didn't want anyone's sympathy, but I would be lying if I didn't admit that the thought of him finding a mate killed me inside.

"I am exhausted. I think I will just go to bed," I announced. With that, I walked to the bedroom, closed the door, and left Felix standing there.

10

FELIX

I ran my hands through my hair and let out a huge sigh. I could tell Jasira was hurt, but what else could I do. I turned to walk out of the room. I made my way across the hall, pouring a glass of whiskey and throwing it back. She would shift in just a few more days. I knew she was my mate, I could feel it. I couldn't risk hurting her. I was too afraid that my wolf would lose control and mark her. I didn't know if a human could survive that or what it would do to her shift. There were too many risks. Earlier that night my father had walked in on us kissing, and I had been grateful for the interruption. I had an overwhelming urge to take her right there. I needed to control myself, but it was getting more complicated daily. Her sweet smell of grapes with a hint of papaya blossoms was enough to drive me crazy.

I poured another glass, drinking it immediately. I was pacing the living room when Declan came in.

"What is going on with you?" he questioned.

"She is driving me crazy man, my wolf is clawing to get out. Did you see that dress on her tonight?" I anxiously replied.

"I most definitely saw that dress on her tonight. Who didn't?" Declan said, chuckling. I growled in response, making him hold up his hands, feigning innocence in return. "I was joking, calm down. "My mate does good work, though," he poked, earning him another growl. He rolled his eyes at me. "Have you considered that she might be your mate?" He asked.

"She is my mate." I snapped. I had not yet told him or anyone else for that matter. My father probably suspected, because I had spoken with him about my connection with her as a kid. Declan's face was one of shock and hurt.

How long have you known? Does she know? He pressed.

"I have always suspected, but now, as her wolf strengthens, I am positive." I confided. "But no, she doesn't know." I sighed. He nodded his understanding. Honestly, if she hadn't had her wolf locked away, she would have shifted when she was a pup. Elemental wolves usually shift around five or six so we could feel the connection with our mates sooner.

"When we were kids, I felt as though she was mine. Even then, I just didn't understand the bond. As a teenager, I recognized the feelings I had as a child and suspected we were mates." I confessed. Declan startled me when he spoke again.

"What are we doing about Gina?" he asked. I grunted at his question.

"We are doing nothing. Jasira wants to handle it herself," I explained unhappily. Declan stood shocked for a moment. "I want you or Liana with her when I am not to keep her safe. I will train her in private sessions starting tomorrow until she gets her wolf. You will be taking over the pack training until then." I stated.

He nodded, agreeing with my plan. We chatted more about the pack training before he left to find Liana. I drank a few more glasses of whiskey to help me sleep. I lay in bed, exhausted from the stress of the day. I closed my eyes, willing myself to sleep. After tossing and turning for a while, sleep finally found me.

11

JASIRA

"Jasira...Jasira," I heard a voice in the distance, pulling me out of my slumber. I blinked several times, clearing my vision.

"Liana, is that you?" I asked as she promptly pounced on my bed. Yep, definitely, Liana. I stretched a yawn, escaping me.

"What is going on?" I asked. I could tell it was morning, but it was still very early.

"I am here to take you to your first training session," she answered cheerfully.

I swung my legs over the bed and went to the bathroom. I couldn't believe someone could be that happy this early in the morning. I brushed my teeth, splashed my face, and quickly threw my hair in a messy bun. I grabbed a sports bra with some leggings and then went to the door where Liana was waiting.

She looked me up and down.

"Are you trying to become the big bad wolfs snack?" She grinned, wagging her eyebrows at me. I shook my head, chuckling at her. I didn't know what she was talking about.

As always, though, her pleasant mood rubbed off on me. We were joking around as we walked towards the packhouse gym. The room was empty when we arrived, leaving me wondering who would be training me. I knew Felix said he would do it, but after last night. I wondered if he had changed his mind. My heart sank at the thought of him pushing me away.

"Felix will be here shortly, he just had to get training started with the rest of the pack. So, we will just warm up together." Liana announced, pulling me from my thoughts.

We started by doing a few laps to warm up our bodies but quickly transitioned into defensive positions. Liana was a good teacher. She was patient and made sure to check in after each step. When we began working on the offensive side, I quickly realized that she was also an excellent fighter.

"You're doing great," she encouraged as Felix walked in about an hour later. I smiled at her, trying not to look Felix's way. I could feel a soft pull to him, my body trying to betray me.

"Thank you, Liana. I appreciate you stepping in." Felix commended her.

"Your welcome Felix," she said as she gathered her things patting me on the shoulder. I was very aware now that I was alone with Felix. The pull became stronger, forcing me to take a step toward him. What was wrong with me? I made the mistake of looking at him, his eyes ablaze with hunger. I broke our gaze, reaching down for my water and gulping it down. I suddenly was very hot. He approached me with a smile on his face, and his body relaxed.

"I'm sorry I was late. I know I promised to train you." I kneeled, playing with my shoes, keeping my eyes on the ground.

"No need to apologize, protecting your pack is more important," I replied. He was in front of me in an instant. He grabbed my chin, pulling my gaze to him.

"Nothing is more important than you," He growled. My mouth fell open. I had no idea what to say. He just said he couldn't do this last night, and now he lays that on me. I am so confused. We both stand up. He is facing away from me, his hands in his hair. I see him taking deep breaths before he turns back to me. He has an unreadable expression on his face. Which makes me even more confused.

"Let's see what you got. How about we start there?" Felix pressed. Is he about to pretend that none of that just happened? Okay, then, two can play that game.

"Sounds good," I said, schooling my face to look nonchalant. We spared for the next hour, him showing me how to throw and land a punch. It actually was empowering, even though I am still unsure about his mood, I leave feeling better. We head straight to the dining hall to eat and then to the giant library. He walks me there in silence, which is becoming increasingly infuriating.

When we reached the library, I saw Valentina and Mama Madeira. I rush to them both, embracing them. Before I can look back, Felix has disappeared. A growl escaped my lips before I even realized it.

"Ah, trouble with your Alpha," Mama Madira chuckles. My frown deepens.

"No, because he is not my Alpha," I huffed my chin up. I catch the look between the two, making me want to scream. Valentina reaches over, placing her hand on mine.

"Calm," she demands. I felt a warming sensation, and then a wave of calmness filled me. I nodded, grateful maybe now I can focus on learning magic.

The history of the elemental wolves and magic is fascinating. Time passes quickly as I soak in everything, they share with me. Before I knew it, they announced that we should go have a late lunch. I am not hungry, so I tell them I want to walk a bit. Valentina is hesitant but finally gives in. I quickly found a back door in the library that leads outside. There is a small path that leads to the outskirts of the forest. I take it, being sure to stay on the trail so I don't get lost. I can't help but close my eyes as a gentle wind blows. The smell of the forest soothes me. I open my eyes, continuing my walk, which leads me to a small creek. I slid my shoes and socks off, dipping my feet in the water. The wind blows again, but a different scent is mixed with it this time. A smell I would know anywhere.

Felix is headed in my direction. If his face is anything to go by, he is unhappy with me. I steel myself for Felix's anger, which I can now feel radiating off him as he moves closer.

"What are you doing out here?" he snaps.

"I didn't know that I needed permission being a queen in all" I sassed back. His eyes glowed, and he shook with fury.

"You are supposed to have someone with you to keep you safe," his voice a deadly whisper.

"I haven't had someone to keep me safe all this time, and I am still here. I think I will be just fine," I threw in his face. My anger was a growing pressure in my chest, threatening to explode. "Plus, you're the one who said you couldn't do this." I pointed my finger back and forth between the two of us. "So why do you care?" I choked. His face softened.

"What do you think I meant by that, Jasira?" He asked firmly. I could feel the breakdown coming on. I refused to let him see me cry. I turned my back on him.

"If you didn't want me, you should have just said that." I stuttered out. Tears slid down my cheek, but I quickly wiped them. He grabbed my shoulders, forcing me to face him.

"Look at me, Jasira," I refused. "I said look at me." He used his alpha tone. My eyes wandered back to his. "I want you to hear me when I say this. I want you more than anything. I just am afraid I will hurt you." He said gently.

"Hurt me when you find your mate," I accused. He looked at me like I had three heads.

"No, hurt you like mark you before your first shift," He shouted. Shock rippled through me, I was not expecting him to say that.

"Oh" is all I could manage. He shook his head, and sighed.

"I want you to feel the mate bond. I want you to be sure." He said softly. I couldn't help the tears that poured out. He wanted me. It was like a weight lifted off my chest. I hadn't been imagining the feelings between us. He pulled me into his embrace, soothing me. We stood there for a long time talking about our memories until my stomach rumbled. I wasn't ready to leave, yet everything seemed okay in the world with him by my side. Felix, however, would not ignore my hunger even if I was willing to.

"You need to feed your body. Your wolf is getting stronger every day. Plus, you need the nourishment," he flinched slightly, thinking about my previous pack. I touched his arm reassuringly.

I could see that no matter how much I protested, there would be no winning this fight. "Fine," I huffed, rolling my eyes.

"Did you just roll your eyes at me?" Felix hissed.

"Maybe I did. What are you going to do about it." I threw back at him. Felix's wolf flashed in his eyes a hunger I hadn't seen before, making me press my legs together from the instant heat I felt between them. I stepped back, suddenly feeling like prey.

"Where do you think you're going?" he said, scooping me up and throwing me over his shoulder. I shrieked with surprise.

"Put me down, Felix. I am not a child."

"Tsk Tsk, someone needs to be taught some" manners he chuckled. I wiggled around, trying to break free from his hold, but his arms were a steel vise holding me. My efforts only made him chuckle more. He swatted my bottom, surprising me.

"Did you just spank me?" I squealed, my cheeks reddening.

"I sure did. That was just a warning. If you're naughty in the future, I will do more than just give you a little spanking." His voice low with heat. I really tried to look offended but couldn't help but think that I might just have to be naughty to see what else he had in mind.

I was so lost in my thoughts that I hadn't noticed we were back at the pack house when he set me down. I turned my nose up as I straightened my clothes. He raised an eyebrow and gave me a smile that had my insides doing funny things.

"I can see right through you, Jaz," he whispered in my ear. "You want to be mad, but you know you liked it." I flushed slightly, hating that he was right. I quickly turned my head, capturing his lips. He was stunned but immediately let out a soft groan. I kissed him fiercely, nipping at him, then suddenly pulled away, halting the kiss. I turned, walking straight to the dining hall, leaving him surprised and racing after me. Two can play that game, I thought to myself with a smile.

Dinner was great, as usual, but exhaustion hit me right after, so I excused myself and headed straight to my room. I curled up under my comforter, feeling safe for once. Before I even realized it, I had drifted off to sleep.

My exhaustion grew worse each day that passed. I could feel my wolf's presence more and more each day. She was eager to be released, and the closer my birthday came, the more she affected me. I felt on edge constantly, my emotions going crazy. I couldn't believe tomorrow was my birthday. The week passed quickly, with the daily routine mainly consisting of training. Liana greeted me as usual this morning, bouncing excitedly, waiting for me.

Instead of going straight to training today, I was headed to see Doctor Rebecca. She wanted to have a check-up before the ritual tonight. I agreed, but only because Felix wouldn't let it go. Pushy Alpha's, I thought to myself, but I couldn't help but smile at the thought of him. I have been spending a lot of time with Felix. I would be lying if I said I didn't enjoy it.

"Thinking about a certain Alpha," Liana nudged me playfully, wiggling her eyebrows. I rolled my eyes.

"Of course not," I said, trying to sound affronted. However, I couldn't keep the smile away, and she wasn't buying it.

"You can say what you want, but I know the truth," she teased. Luckily, we reached the Doctor so I could change the subject.

"I still don't get why she wants to see me." I shrugged. Liana gave me a knowing look but allowed the topic to change.

"You are about to experience something no one has before. She wants to make sure that tonight can go as smoothly as possible. She reassured me. "Now go, I will be right here." She added. I sighed, making my way back to the room. The nurse took my vitals as I waited for the Doctor.

"Good morning, Jasira," she greeted, entering the room.

"Good morning" I replied with a smile. Although I didn't like going to the Doctors, I was fond of Rebecca and trusted her.

"Your vitals look good for a wolf, but how are you feeling?" she questioned.

"I am fine. My wolf has been making her presence more known, though." She nodded her understanding, telling me that was perfectly normal. I fidgeted a little, knowing I had a question to ask, but I was slightly embarrassed.

"What is it, Jasira?" She pressed, clearly seeing my anxiety.

"I... It's just," I sighed, knowing I needed to come out with it. "When I shift if Felix is my mate," I paused.

"Yes," she encouraged me.

"Well, if we, you know, have sex, but I am not ready to have a pup," I said quietly, looking down. "I mean, I want to have a pup, but what if I am not good enough to be a mother. What if Felix doesn't want one with me?" I stumbled over my words. My anxiety now making everything pour out all at once.

"Woah woah woah," she said, stopping me. "Jasira, you don't have to make any of those decisions right now. In fact, your shift is going to be stressful enough, so it hardly seems like the time to worry about all this. You will not get pregnant unless you are in heat. However, we have birth control for she-wolves here. So, you don't have to worry about anything." I sighed, grateful for her understanding. She explained that I had to take the pill every day until I felt ready to conceive. I got up to walk out feeling relieved.

I met Liana in the waiting room, she jumped up from her chair the moment she saw me. So, what did the Doctor say she asked as we walked to the packhouse training gym. She said I am perfectly healthy.

"See, that wasn't so bad," she teased. I stopped right outside the gym.

"Can I ask you something, Liana?" I said nervously.

"Yes, of course anything, Jasira." Her voice grew serious for once as she listened intently.

"I assume you have gone through heat before with Declan. Did you automatically want to have a baby? I mean, I want a baby. But I am unsure if I want one anytime soon or if I would be a good mother." I whispered the last part. Liana reached out, touching my shoulder, seeing my distress.

"To answer your question, yes, I have been through heat. I am not ready yet to have a baby, so I take a birth control pill from the Doctor. I didn't know why I wasn't ready until I met you." She started, making me look up at her in surprise.

"What do you mean because of me?" I asked.

"I need time to serve my queen to help her bring peace before I have a whole bunch of pups." She answered. I couldn't help but pull her into a hug.

"Thank you," I whispered.

I stood in the packhouse training gym. It was much smaller compared to the one that the pack trained in. Felix stood across from me, looking like a god, his skin glistening from our morning strength training. I felt stronger after this week of training, but still, without a wolf, I was no match for Felix. He was doing his best to teach me how to defend myself. I praise the Goddess he was so patient.

"I know you don't have your wolf or magic yet, but that is changing." You have been doing so well. He said encouragingly. "You are strong, I can see it," he continued.

"I'm glad you think so, but my ass says differently since I have landed it on five times already," I snapped.

"Come on, Jasira, reach deep in there. Your instincts are there," He chuckled.

Alright, he wanted me to reach deep down fine then. I closed my eyes, took a deep breath, and looked inside myself for my wolf. I tilted my head a bit, this was weird. I could feel something in there that hadn't been before. I felt power. Just slightly seeping out behind a locked door I didn't have access to. I reached for it, drawing what I could be closer to the surface. When I opened my eyes, I let my body do what it wanted. I moved forward slowly, maintaining the defense position Felix had taught me. He was fast and agile, shifting on his feet. Every time he had punched before, it was too quick. I couldn't get out of the way. He would throw me off balance and then take me down.

Not this time, he threw the first punch, and my body felt a burst of energy. I twisted my body to the left, making him miss me at the same time, raising my left hand out towards his face, hitting him with a strength I hadn't had before. This knocked him off balance, and though he didn't fall, he stumbled. I stood there frozen, not knowing what had just happened.

The look of shock was evident on his face.

"I... I am sorry, Felix. I don't know what just happened," the words spilling out of my mouth apologetically.

"There is no reason to apologize, I asked for it," He laughed, and I couldn't help but laugh with him.

"I am exhausted," I said, picking up the towel to wipe my face.

"I would imagine so you just let out some magic you are not supposed to have yet," he smiled. "Tonight is the night we will do the ritual, it doesn't surprise me that things are changing." He assured me, then grabbed his water to drink.

I was grateful we finished training for the day, my eyelids felt so heavy. We ate lunch before Felix had to attend to some pack matters. Declan joined me in walking back to my room.

"I heard training went well," he remarked. I nodded in agreement. "How are you feeling about tonight?" he questioned.

If I was honest with myself, I was scared shitless. What if my wolf didn't come out? Would they throw me away like the others had? Not to mention, once I shifted, what if Felix wasn't my mate. My stomach turned at the thought.

"I'm nervous, and my mind is spinning," I replied honestly. We reached my door, and another wave of exhaustion hit me. I said my goodbyes to Declan and made my way inside. It was late afternoon, and dinner wasn't for several hours, so I decided to shower and nap.

I didn't want to be exhausted for tonight. The shift on a regular basis was draining. It was always painful the first time, so I didn't expect anything easier for me. I quickly showered, washing the sweat off my body from our training session. I still had the towel wrapped around me as I lay on the bed. Before I could think about changing, I fell asleep.

I stood in the middle of a meadow surrounded by forest. It was dark, but the moon shone brightly, illuminating my surroundings. The wind whirled by me, drawing my attention to the edge of the woods. The feeling of someone lingering in the darkness raised the hair on the back of my neck.

"who's there?" I called out. Ready to fight if need be. A beautiful woman stepped out of the shadows. Her skin glowed brightly as if the moon only shone for her.

"There is no need to fear my child," she said in a voice like a song. "I am Selene, goddess of the moon." My jaw fell open in shock. I tried to form words but couldn't. I have to be dreaming, I thought. She chuckled, "you are not dreaming, Jasira."

"How did you know what I was thinking?" I stuttered out. She smiled brightly at me.

"I do not know what you are thinking, however your expression is clearly one of shock. I simply made a deduction of your thoughts." Her body moved quickly, gliding towards me. She reached for my hands, and I cast my eyes down, showing her respect. "My child, do not look down, for I want to look into my daughter's eyes." I looked up, meeting her gaze. Her eyes were a bright purple like mine.

"Are you saying you are my mother?" I am so confused. She reached up and caressed my cheek.

"I know this is confusing. I am sorry that you have so many questions. There is only a short time I must tell you what I need to." She explained. "Your mother was one of the strongest alpha females, her bloodline was a direct descendent of my children. As you know all the elemental packs are, this is why they have powers. When your mother was battling alongside your father, she almost died. She lost the ability to bear children." I gasped.

"But then how did I?" I questioned. She smiled.

"I came to your mother one night and asked her to carry my child. She agreed, but I made her swear not to tell anyone. You are my daughter. You are a demigod." I shook my head in disbelief,

"How could this be? Why did you let all those bad things happen to me?" I asked angrily. She flinched slightly from my question, her eyes filled with sadness.

"I am sorry, Jasira, that was not the path I wanted but the path you had to take." Before I could respond, she pressed on.

"We are almost out of time, my love. I will see you again, but please let me finish." I nodded even though I didn't know how I would see her again. "Tonight, at midnight, the magic holding you will be released. You are stronger than anyone knows. Please only tell those you trust most what you have learned. There is a war coming, a division in the packs. They want to destroy all the elemental wolves. It won't stop there. You must stop them." She said urgently.

I noticed the meadow begin to fade away, her voice becoming more distant.

"Mother," I shouted, "who is doing this?"

"Trust your instincts," she whispered as she faded away.

I sat up straight in my bed, breathing heavily and clutching my chest. Holy shit, Batman, my mother is the Goddess Selene.

I raced out of bed and barged into Felix's living room. Felix and Declan were talking but promptly stopped, and I slammed the door shut behind me.

"Jasira are you okay?" they both asked, concern evident on their faces.

"We need to talk now." I said, looking at Felix, "Declan, please excuse us." I demanded. Declan was slightly stunned but nodded, making his way out of the room. Felix crossed the room in a few strides, searching my face.

"What is going on?" he said, holding my hands.

"I have to tell you something. I have been told only to share with the people I trust most," I said out of breath. His smile made my heartbeat increase even more. Focus, Jaz, you need to tell him what you just learned.

"I am listening," he assured me.

"You have to swear this stays between us," I insisted, knowing he would never share it. He nodded. I took a breath, "I am the Goddess Selene's daughter." I whispered out, barely audible. He was a wolf, so he could hear me being so close.

"What??" he asked, shocked. I promptly told him about my dream, knowing it wasn't just an ordinary one. It was too real. He was now pacing, running his fingers through his hair. He always did this when he was upset or thinking.

I smiled being in his presence was so calming, I couldn't believe how close I felt to him again after all these years. He stopped turning to me, catching me smiling at him. His face softened as he looked at me.

"You are special, this news shouldn't surprise me." He said, making me blush. "The Goddess is right though, we need to be careful. No one can know, especially since you don't have your powers right now." I nodded, agreeing with him.

"That will change in about six hours," I said anxiously.

"Why don't we go to dinner now? You need to put some food in you. The shift will be draining as it is," Felix insisted.

As we walked to the dining hall, my stomach was in knots. I just couldn't help replaying the dream over and over in my head. The only thing helping me keep it together currently was the calm that Felix provided. The only people from the pack who knew about the ceremony tonight were Alpha Kai, Declan, and, of course, Felix. We had kept it secret from everyone else. The Deltas of the pack were instructed to stay on high alert so there would be no interruptions. As we entered the dining hall, my stomach growled, letting me know it agreed with the splay of food. Felix chuckled, nudging me.

"I even heard that, it's good you're hungry" he said. I giggled back. He always knew how to brighten my mood. I sat next to Valentina, leaning my head on her shoulder.

"Are you nervous for tonight?" she asked. I nodded, unable to say anything. I could feel her send me calming magic.

This past week, we worked together to build our magical connection. I now recognized Valentina's magic. It's very similar to how each shifter has a distinct scent. I thanked her for the pick me up and dived into my plate.

We ate in silence, everyone anxious about what was to come. The people at this table were my family. I could trust them all with my life. I knew whatever tonight brought, they would be by my side. As I finished dinner, I memorized them all at that moment just in case this was the last time I saw them.

Everyone cleared the dining room leaving Felix and I alone. I had been lost in my thoughts at dinner, silently watching everyone. But I wanted to go for a walk with Felix now, just in case this was the last one we shared. It had become an everyday occurrence, one that I enjoyed. He took my hand guiding me outside to our usual path. These last few days were the best of my life. Felix had shown me what it felt like to be in a pack. Stirring emotions inside me that I promised myself I would keep locked away.

We walked until we arrived at the creek. The heat of the day had passed, and a gentle breeze caressed my skin. The night sky was aglow with a canopy of glittering stars. I looked at Felix catching him staring at me.

"Thinking about anything good, or do you just have a staring problem?" I winked at him. His laugh filled the night, my heart skipping a beat in awe of him.

"Both, I suppose," He replied with a smile. "We should get going. The ceremony starts soon." My anxiety hit me like a wave, stealing my breath slightly. He reached out, pulling me into a hug. "Don't worry," he whispered into my hair.

I pulled back slightly, looking into his eyes. I knew that this might be the only chance I got. I grabbed his face, my lips crashing down on his, a hunger inside of me rushed forward. He met my urgency, letting his tongue slide into my mouth. He tasted incredible. I never wanted our kiss to end. He pulled back suddenly, a war waging on his face.

"I am sorry," I whispered, "I had to just in case that was the last one I get to have with you." Hurt flashed in his eyes, he reached up caressing my cheek.

"I promise you Jasira, this is just the beginning."

12

JASIRA

I had kissed him like my life depended on it. I just couldn't bear the thought of not making it out of the ritual and not kissing him again. Or worse, not being his mate after my wolf was set free. We walked back in silence to the house. Both of our nerves were on edge now. Valentina was in the foyer waiting patiently for us.

"I am glad you guys are back," she said. "I have some people I want you to meet." We followed her to the meeting room, where a group of people were waiting.

As I entered, I heard a gasp. I was seriously confused about who they were and why one looked familiar. Alpha Kai was chatting with a woman and a man on one side of the room while the other stared at me.

"Uncle Theo, Aunt Chloe?" Felix asked.

"Yes, Felix, it's us, Chloe," she said as she rushed to hug him. Chloe then turned to me. "You must be Jasira," she said, resting her hands on my shoulders. I nodded, still in shock.

"Jasira, this is your mother's sister, Alpha Amelia." Alpha Kai introduced as he came to my side. I was suddenly frozen in place. The room spun a bit. Felix immediately steadied me.

"I thought I had no family left," I whispered. Alpha Amelia approached me.

"No, Jasira. I have just been hiding, waiting for the day that I will be needed." She pulled me into her embrace, and I felt a tear slide down my cheek. All I ever wanted was a family. I knew I would die fighting for it now that I had it.

Alpha Amelia stepped back, giving me room to process my thoughts.

"I am happy you are all here. However, the big question is why?" I asked.

"I can explain that one," Valentina said, stepping forward. "Each elemental pack was gifted a stone from the goddess. They are used in ceremonies to strengthen the pack and give protection. The stones are entrusted to the Alphas. Alpha Theo, Alpha Kai, and Alpha Amelia are essential to the ceremony we will perform tonight. They have brought their stones here for you because all packs will be one under you." Valentina stated. Alpha Kai made his way to me taking my hand in his, I am guessing he sensed my anxiety.

"I know this is overwhelming, but we are all here to support you." He soothed.

"We must go to the woods now to perform the ceremony. Mama Madeira is waiting, and so are my aunts." Valentina insisted.

We all walked outside, the wind had picked up since we returned from our walk. The wind became more robust as we walked, pushing us forward. The forest felt alive, as if it knew something was happening, making shivers run up my back. The walk to where we would perform the ceremony was about 15 minutes. This was the first time I had been in this direction. When we stepped out of the woods, I gasped suddenly at the open meadow before me, my body frozen in place.

"Jasira, What's wrong? Are you okay?" Felix was immediately in front of me, trying to see why I had stopped.

"Felix, this is it," I said in a whisper.

"What do you mean by that?" Alpha Kai asked, standing behind Felix, concerned as well. Everyone was now looking at me, waiting for my response. Mama Madeira and the aunts had approached as well, seeing my pause.

"There is something I need to tell you all," I announced. "Are you sure?" Felix asked me.

"Yes, I trust everyone here." Nodding, he stepped aside so that I could address everyone. "I am not Alpha Maeve's biological daughter," I started. Immediately, I was interrupted.

"How can you say that I was there for your birth?" Alpha Amelia protested. Mama Madeira shook her head.

"Child don't be silly. Of course, you are her daughter," Madeira declared. I held my hand up to silence them.

"Please let me finish." I asserted. Everyone went silent, even the forest and the wind grew quiet. "Alpha Maeve was injured in a fight. She survived but lost the ability to bear children. The moon goddess came to her and asked if she would bear her child in secret. She agreed, swearing to tell no one. My mother is Selene, the moon goddess, and I am a Demi-God." They were all shocked by my revelation. "I know this because Selene visited me in this very meadow earlier this evening." I proclaimed. Felix stepped forward.

"We must protect Jasira with our lives. She is more important than any of us realize, and there is more that the goddess told her, but we do not have the time to waste." He spoke to them, reigning everyone in.

"Felix is right. We must begin the ceremony. Come, let's move to the meadow's center." Mama Madeira ushered.

I was grateful to Felix for breaking everyone out of their daze. I mouthed a silent thank you to him and received one of his brilliant smiles in return. The Alphas seem to know their places, walking to each of their candles. Alpha Kai stood to the North, representing Earth, next to the green candle; Alpha Theo stood to the East, representing Air, with a yellow candle; Alpha Amelia stood to the South, representing Fire, with a red candle; and finally, Felix stood to the West representing water with a blue candle. Everything moved in slow motion. Mama Madeira, Isla, and Deema were getting everything in place, creating a circle. Valentina walked me to the center, and she hugged me tightly.

"I am here no matter what," she said as she held me. "I promise my life to protect yours. I love you, Jasira," she whispered.

"I love you too, V," I said, choked up. She walked away, taking her place next to her grandmother and Aunts, all of them holding hands. It's time Isla said the four of them closed their eyes.

"Moon Goddess Selene, we call on you tonight to release the magic restraining, Jasira Selinofoto. Earth, we call upon you to ground us," Madeira's voice rang out. Alpha Kai aimed his hands at the ground. Vines suddenly sprung up, reaching for his hands. He turned his hands upwards, and the vines followed. They wrapped around his fingers, glowing slightly. Isla turned to Alpha Theo.

"Air, we call upon you to balance us," Isla called out. Alpha Theo moved his hands gracefully, and the wind began to circle around him. The wind chased around his body, creating a slight glow as it progressed.

"Fire, we call upon you to protect us," Deema called out. Alpha Amelia held her hands together, slowly separating them, creating a ball of Fire.

"Water, we call upon you to provide us with wisdom," Valentina called out. Felix held his arms out wide, slowly pulling his hands into his body. Tiny tendrils of water gathered, creating a significant movement of water as he swirled his hands in a circle.

The four women began to chant something under their breath. As their chanting hastened, the Earth started to shake. I stumbled slightly but kept my balance. Vines reached out, grabbing my feet, and holding me in place. Their chanting grew, and with it, the wind picked up. The wind became strong, howling at me. My hair whipped crazily around me. They were now chanting even louder. I still could not understand the words because they were clearly written in a different language. The Air grew hot, and a circle of flames lit around me. The flames licked and bit at my skin. I couldn't help but cry out, looking to Felix for comfort. I could tell he wanted to rush to me but wouldn't break the circle for fear of what would happen. The four of them were not yelling. The wind had become so loud I could barely hear them. The sky opened suddenly, releasing a downpour of water. It immediately cooled my skin, easing the heat of the flames. It was all too much. The world began to spin, and darkness clouded my vision. The last thing I saw was Felix's face as I collapsed.

My eyes flickered open, and the dark meadow came into view. Except there was no chanting, there was no one. Silence filled the space. I sat up quickly, looking around. *What the hell is going on?* I thought. A wave of dizziness hit me from sitting up so fast. I closed my eyes momentarily, letting the spell pass. *This is the meadow from my dreams again,* I looked around in search of the Moon Goddess. As if knowing I was looking for her, she came forth, her ethereal body gliding towards me. She smiled a bright smile as she helped me up off the ground.

"My child, happy birthday," she said warmly.

"Thank you, Goddess, but why am I here again?" I questioned. She chuckled.

"You do not need to address me formally. You may call me Selene or Mom, whichever you are comfortable with. You are here because the ceremony worked. Your magic has been released. I was able to pull you to this realm briefly before you wake up and complete your shift". She remarked. I could only imagine how concerned Felix must be.

"What are they doing while I am here? Why can't I see them?" I questioned.

"All good questions. The protectors are closing the circle, so when you awake, you will be able to shift and run. As for why you can't see them, well, that comes with learning your magic over time. This is a different plane, a thin veil lies between. Once you become strong enough, you can walk among others without them knowing. It is how gods and goddesses watch over you." She explained. That was a lot to take in, I had no words to respond to what she had just told me. "Now, before you go," she continued "I wanted to give you something." She pulled out a beautiful necklace that glowed softly,

"This is a Moonstone," she said, gently turning me to clip it around my neck. I touched it, feeling a slight pulse coming from the diamond-shaped stone.

"It is beautiful mom," I said in awe. She spun me back around, holding my shoulders. "If you ever need to come to me, you can use the moonstone." She said, smiling.

"Now, you must go back. Shifting will be painful, so I apologize in advance." With that, I was sucked back to where everyone waited for me.

"Jasira, wake up, please" I heard a muffled voice. The sounds of what was happening around me came back in a rush of waves. Instantly, my body felt like it was on Fire. A scream ripped out of my throat as my eyes flung open. Felix was there by my side, his breathing shaky. He tried to provide me with comfort, but nothing helped. I felt my wolf rippling along my skin, forcing her way to the surface. I rolled to my stomach forcefully, trying to get on my hands and knees. My bones began to break throughout my body. My nails became sharp claws as I grew fur. My head felt like it was going to explode with pressure. All I could do was scream, the pain becoming unbearable with each passing moment. As the final transformation took place, I panted, a blast of energy radiating off me, knocking Felix and everyone else down.

I stood there in the center of my destruction on all fours. The pain had finally stopped, and I looked around. Everything came to life. I could see perfectly even though it was dark. I could hear the smallest of sounds. I took a deep sniff of the world. What is that fantastic scent? I wondered.

"Mate!" A voice inside my head screamed, startling me. Well, I need to get used to that. My wolf urged me forward, demanding I find the scent. It wasn't hard to find, for it was the man only a few steps away, picking himself off the ground.

Felix rose, facing me with a growl escaping his lips. He shifted effortlessly to his wolf form. My wolf jumped back and forth eagerly, ready to play with her mate. A large pale blonde wolf stood in front of me. Felix walked forward, nudging me.

"Mine," He purred through our mind link. I was so happy to hear his voice inside of my head.

"I am yours, Felix," I said back, my heart exploding with happiness. "But you will have to catch me first." I giggled while taking off. Surprise registered through our mind link, then a primal growl.

"I will catch you, my little Queen, but I don't think you are ready for when I do." His voice was full of heat when he spoke. A shiver ran down my spine, anticipating what the rest of the night would bring.

13

FELIX

Jasira stood in the middle of the circle, a storm forming around us with all the elements. I could feel the power radiating off her. Her cries of pain piercing the night. All I could think about was running to her, but I couldn't. I had to wait until the circle was closed, I wouldn't risk harming her more. When she collapsed, my heart stopped. My wolf clawed at me trying to escape. But Madeira had already begun closing the circle the moment Jasira hit the ground. I gritted my teeth forcing my wolf to back down. I didn't take my eyes off Maderia, watching and waiting. As soon as it was safe, I rushed towards Jasira. I threw my body to the ground, gathering her in my arms.

The storm was gone, and the forest was silent. As if it was holding its breath to see what would happen next. Minutes passed my Jasira began coming to. I was not prepared for the scream that tore from her lips. My wolf's howls rang in my head. My heart breaking with each additional cry. The shift was taking over, the ceremony had worked. We all waited in anticipation, as there was nothing else we could do.

She was almost entirely shifted when a massive blast of power filled the air. I flew through the air, landing on my back. It knocked the wind out of me and everyone else. I quickly sat up, ignoring the pain. I gasped at the sight of her.

"Are you seeing this?" I mind linked my father. He groaned slightly, sitting himself up as well.

"Oh, my goddess, she is incredible," he exclaimed. She, indeed, was a sight. Her fur was pure black with streaks of purple glowing through it. Her purple eyes glowed intensely now, she had to be the most beautiful creature I had ever seen. She walked towards me, sniffing the air, and on instinct, I followed suit.

I had been so distracted with her shift I hadn't realized what she was smelling. She smelled good enough to eat, Jasira was my mate. My wolf yipped happily inside of me, fighting to get free. He needed to be with his mate. She stood before me in all her glory, I couldn't resist the urge to shift any longer. My wolf wanted to take her right there and mark her. That wasn't going to happen, though. I wanted our first time to be special. Plus, her wolf had been locked away for so long that she needed to run free.

I steeled my resolve, disappointing my wolf slightly. Mine is all I could growl out through the mind link to her. She nudged back, agreeing. She suddenly took off running, but not before adding,

"You will have to catch me first." I stood there stunned, she wanted to play that game did she. My restraint lessened slightly with her teasing. My wolf, now more eager than ever to take her. I chased after her, knowing when I caught her, I would make her scream my name.

14

JASIRA

Having my wolf was the most incredible feeling. I finally had that missing piece I had been waiting for. Not to mention that Felix was my mate. I was on cloud nine right now. I ran through the forest excitedly, knowing that Felix was not far behind. I looked forward to him catching me after seeing the heat in his stare. That didn't mean I had to make it easy, though. I ran until I reached a creek, not knowing the entire pack lands had put me at a disadvantage. Felix was hot on my tail, and I knew there was nowhere else to run. I quickly called on my wolf to let me shift back. I stood there naked, waiting for Felix. He stopped several feet away from me, quickly shifting back.

His gaze locked onto mine, lighting a fire inside of my soul. His eyes trailed down my body, taking in every inch, leaving my body burning with need. The forest was silent, waiting for one of us to make a move.

"You are playing a dangerous game," he growled. His eyes glowed, his wolf still close to the surface. I am trying to show restraint, but it is not easy when my wolf is screaming for me to mark you. His voice strained.

"Maybe that's the problem Felix, who said I wanted you to resist" my voice a breathy whisper. The warm feeling in my belly grew with each step he took closer. I could feel the slickness between my legs, my arousal thick in the Air.

We closed the distance between us, the need for our bodies to touch becoming unbearable. My breasts touched Felix's naked chest, making me shiver. I reached up, running my fingers along his chest. He grabbed my chin, tilting my face up to look at him.

"You are incredible," he said lovingly. I bit my lip, blushing at the compliment. He growled, his lips crashing down on mine. I returned his urgency, my lips parting slightly, allowing his tongue to slip inside. His hands slid down my body slowly, tingling following his touch. He grasped both ass cheeks, lifting me in the air and wrapping my legs around him. He moved from my lips, kissing down my neck until he reached the spot where he would mark me. He nipped, sucked, and licked, causing a moan to escape me.

"I want to take you, but not here" he whispered in my ear. I could feel his hot breath on my neck as he breathed me in.

"Well then, it looks like we need to return to the pack house. Do you want to shift and run there?" I asked.

"There is no way you are getting down, I am barely holding my wolf back as it is. I will carry you." His voice deep with need.

He switched my body around to a better position to carry me. I laid my head on his chest as he ran. Exhaustion settling in from the earlier shift. We reached the packhouse in minutes, not stopping until we were in my room. He gently laid me on the bed, his body on top of mine. The heat from our touching made me ache in a way I hadn't experienced before.

He gently kissed my neck, his hands exploring my body once again. My lips parted with the feeling of him touching me, making my core throb. He worked his way down to my nipples, my breath catching as he took the hard nub into his mouth. He sucks, then licks, making me moan softly. He moves to the next one, repeating his delicious assault. I ran my fingers through his hair, arching my back, needing more. He complies, moving down my stomach, trailing kisses on his way. He spreads my legs, leaving me open and exposed. I blush, butterflies filling my stomach.

"You are so beautiful, Jasira, and I can't wait to taste you," he says, his voice filled with heat. I watch, frozen in anticipation.

He lowers his head to my aching, wet sex. His tongue gently slides between my folds, caressing my pulsing clit. My grip tightened on his head, a loud moan escaping me.

"Please don't stop Felix," I growl out, waves of pleasure filling my body. He chuckled briefly, then began a circular motion with his tongue. I was panting my body, desperate for a release. He continued licking and sucking as I climbed higher and higher. My body bucked as I exploded, my muscles contracting as I screamed his name. He continued to lick a moment longer, sending tingles up my body and making me wither beneath him. I pulled his hair slightly, prompting him to climb back up my body. There was a fire burning inside of me that only he could extinguish.

"I need you now," I groan as I claim his mouth, tasting myself on his lips. He reached down with his two fingers circling my entrance, letting my slickness coat them. He slid one finger inside of me, making me gasp. I grab the pillows, moaning into them. "Please, Felix," I beg, wanting more. He slid a second finger into me, expertly working them in and out. I moan louder, I need him inside of me.

"Felix, I need you," I pant out. His eyes glowed his wolf on the surface. He slowly removed his fingers. He situated himself between my legs, rubbing his hard length up and down my slick folds. I whimper at his teasing. He coated himself in my juices, sliding the tip in at first. He slid in slowly letting me adjust to his size. I let out a gasp in shock at the sudden stretching.

"Are you okay?" he asked, his voice husky. It burned slightly, but he held still, letting me adjust. The sensation faded away quickly, leaving behind an ache for him.

"Yes, I'm okay. Please, Felix, I need you," I plead. He began moving slowly, his length gliding in and out.

"You are fucking perfect," he hisses, capturing my mouth.

"Yes, Felix, I need more," I beg. He picked up his pace giving me his entire length into me. I can feel the fire building low in my belly again, but this time, I'm afraid it will break me. He drove into me harder and faster, my body needing every inch of him. He began kissing down my neck, stopping at the place where his mark would go. I felt his teeth grow into fangs as he sucked and nipped.

He moved swiftly, biting down, claiming me. It hurts for only a moment before the fire that was building becomes a volcano about to erupt. My legs wrap around him, pulling him to me. I grabbed his hair, exposing his neck on instinct. I bit down marking him, his taste on my tongue making me combust. I scream out his name, my muscles tensing around his length sending him over the edge. My name leaving his lips as he spills his seed inside of me. Both of us breathed heavily, he licked my neck, stopping the bleeding. I do the same.

He gently removed himself, laying next to me. He pulled me to him, my head resting on his chest. I can feel the mate bond spring to live between us. He is mine, and I am his. I wanted to stay in this moment forever, but my eyes were heavy. I tried to fight sleep, but it claims me anyway.

15

FELIX

Jasira snuggled into my chest, falling asleep quickly. I was beyond happy that she was my mate. I breathed her in her scent instantly, making me hard. I couldn't wait to have more of her, but for now I would settle with cuddling up to her and letting sleep take me.

I woke before her untangling her from my body. I gently slid her over and she whined in her sleep making me chuckle. She clearly didn't like the distance I placed between us. To be honest I didn't either, but I had a big day to plan for her. I mind linked everyone to meet me in the office. I quickly but quietly got dressed sneaking out.

As I entered the conference room everyone was smiling. My father was the first to come over to me. He patted me on the back.

"Congratulations son," he said warmly.

"How is our birthday girl?" Valentina winked. I couldn't help but roll my eyes and laugh.

"She is still asleep, I am pretty sure she will stay that way for a while," I answered. I could feel her exhaustion through our bond. I wasn't surprised after everything she had been through.

Liana clapped her hands excitedly.

"Well then there is no time to waste she we have a birthday celebration to plan." Liana clapped her hands excitedly. I smiled ready to give Jasira everything she had missed all these years.

"I will distract Jasira until it is time for her to get ready. Liana and V, you are going to take over then," I said. They nodded their agreement. We broke down all the details for the party before we all left for our assigned duties.

I went to the kitchen to grab a tray to bring her breakfast in bed. I quickly made my way back to the bedroom. I was almost to the bedroom when her beautiful voice rang through the mind link.

"Felix...Felix where are you?" Her voice was full of concern.

"I am almost back to you, beautiful" I replied. I picked up my pace rushing to our bedroom. Walking in the room she was sitting up with concern on her face. She only had the sheet covering her body, looking delicious. I placed the tray next to her, unable to restrain myself from capturing her mouth. Her lips were soft against mine, she parted them slightly allowing me access to slip my tongue inside. She tasted delicious, my erection straining against my pants. I pulled back both of us panting slightly.

"I brought you breakfast, how about you eat so I can have mine?" I said winking. She giggled in response, making my heart sing.

16

JASIRA

Waking up I looked around quickly realizing I was alone. I panicked, was last night all a dream I thought. My heart hammered, my chest squeezed but the mate bond pulsed reminding me it was there. I took a shuddering breath.

"Felix...Felix where are you?" I tried to sound normal but knew I had failed. I could feel his concern, he quickly let me know he was on his way. I breathed easier, propping myself up in the bed. He entered the room moments later, his eyes roaming over my body.

I felt a shiver run over my body with hunger in his eyes. He approached me, his lips crashing on mine. I needed him again, all of him desperately, but he broke the kiss leaving me aching and panting.

"I brought you breakfast, how about you eat so I can have mine" his voice deep and breathy. I couldn't help but giggle and squeeze my thighs together at the same time. The thought of his mouth on my body again had my core heating already. The smell of the food had my mouth watering as he placed it in front of me. I didn't realize how hungry I was. I began digging in immediately a small moan escaping as the first bite hit my mouth. Felix chuckled as he watched me stuff my face.

"The first shift always makes you feel like you're starving. It gets better though I promise," He assured. I quickly made work of the breakfast in front of me, rising from the bed. "Where are you going," he challenged, grabbing my hand pulling me back to him.

"I need to get ready for the day, you know pee, shower, dress for training." I blushed.

"I think not my queen, I have a whole day planned for us." He countered, rising from the bed. "Now I am going to run us a bath, you just wait here" he demanded scooping me up then tossing me back on the bed.

"Yes sir" I laughed. His eyes darkening slightly.

"Be careful little wolf or you won't make it to the bath" a wicked smile on his face. I watched as he walked into the bathroom, closing the door. I can't believe that this man is my mate, thanks mom I said praising the goddess. He opened the door only moments later completely naked. I gasped at the sight of him, my body was screaming in excitement instantly.

"Come here Jasira" he commanded. My legs felt like jelly as I climbed off the bed. I could smell a fruity aroma as I walked towards the door. I took a deep breath, it smelled amazing. My breath left me as I entered the room. Tears pricked my eyes threatening to spill over as I looked around seeing flowers and candles everywhere. It looked like something out of a romance movie.

"Felix this is incredible" I whispered, turning to him.

"Anything for you Jaz" he cooed, grabbing my hand leading me towards the tub. The bath was a milky color, vibrant flowers floating on top of the water. I had only seen something like this in a magazine. I used to sneak a peek at them when Trudy wasn't paying attention.

The thought of Trudy darkened my mood for a moment, a tingling sensation starting in my fingers. It quickly turned to anger, my old pack almost stole all this from me. I tried to close my eyes, but my emotions began to spiral, flashes of all I went through played across my mind. I felt so hot, like I would burst into flames.

"Jasira. Jasira, come back to me. I need you to calm down." A soothing voice pulling me back.

I opened my eyes, flames rose from my hands and arms. I instantly panicked, what was happening Felix I looked to him. Oh, my goddess, had I hurt him. As if he read my thoughts, he shushed me.

"I am fine" water danced along his skin creating a protective bubble against the heat. He approached me unafraid of the fire. He wrapped his arms around me, his water cooling my flames.

My body relaxed completely. I let him hold me as I took deep breaths clearing my mind. "Are you ok?" concern lacing his voice.

"I am now," I answered my face pressed to his chest. I breathed his scent in letting it calm my soul. He stepped into the tub pulling me in front of him. The water felt amazing as it lapped against my skin. I closed my eyes, relaxing against him, willing the water to wash away the memories for now.

"Do you want to talk about what happened there?" He asked his fingers trailing up and down my body. An ache between my legs started, making me press my thighs together.

"No not really" I responded slightly out of breath. He worked his way up to my breast running his touch feather light. My nipples became painfully hard.

"Please" I begged. Felix chuckled, sliding his hand down my belly, I held my breath anxiously waiting for him to touch my throbbing bud.

His fingers slid between my folds instantly finding my spot. He moved in a steady circular motion making the ache turn to pressure that continued to build higher and higher. He was relentless, speeding up as he went. I cried out as I peaked, soaring over the edge. As I trembled with my legs shaking, he grabbed the soap washing me. He kissed my neck trailing down to my mark, his teeth gracing it. I moaned, wanting him.

"Felix" I whined. I could feel his hardness pressed against me. I turned my body completely around mounting him. A surprise look crossing his face. I needed him now, the feeling bordering on unbearable. I situated myself slowly lowering down on him. He hissed through his teeth, grabbing my hips. I moaned as I pressed down, taking his full length. I began rocking back and forth allowing my instincts to take over. His grip on me tightened as he began to slam into me. Our bodies worked in sync as my body shook with need. An earth-shattering wave of pleasure ripped through me. My walls clenching around Felix, both of us finding our release. I collapsed down on to him my body spent.

I nuzzled into him as he began washing me off once again. He then stood up from the bath, my legs wrapped around his waist as he carried me to the vanity. He sat me on the counter drying me carefully. I couldn't help but smile at his sweetness, no one had ever shown me this much care.

"Thank you" I said, running my hands through his hair.

"There is no need to thank me you are my mate" he replied with a shrug.

"I wish I could share with you what these small things you do mean to me." I explained. Use your bond, show him your pain my wolf encouraged.

"Felix" I said, prompting him to look. He waited patiently for me to continue. "I think I need to show you my past. You asked me what happened earlier." He nodded but didn't interrupt. "I had dark memories flashed through my mind making me so angry. I have never felt that kind of rage, it triggered the fire. I am not sure what kind of powers I have yet, but my wolf thinks this will help."

"Alright Jaz, but how will you show me?" he asked, tilting his head. That was a great question. How was I going to do this? I thought to myself.

"Take his hands, reach for the mate bond then let your powers guide you" my wolf assured.

We both got dressed then made our way to the living room. We sat on the couch, and I grabbed his hands.

"Are you ready?" I asked. Felix nodded. I closed my eyes, finding the mate bond with ease. I could feel a warm sensation filling me, Felix was a small orb of blue light I could touch. I reached for it, a purple surge of light wrapped around the blue one connecting. \

"Now remember" my wolf whispered, then I fell down a dark path landing in a meadow Felix promptly followed.

"Jasira, where are we?" Felix asked, getting up from the ground. Before I could respond a young boy and girl tumbled through the grass playing, laughing.

"That's us" I whispered, Felix's face was shocked.

"This is one of your memories" he said stunned.

"One of our memories actually. I remember this day it was one I often thought of when I needed solace from the pack."

The sky darkened and rain began to fall, twisting the memory into something else. Alpha Kai stood on the porch with Alpha Trenton at the Cross River Pack house. I held Felix's hand, tears streaming down both our faces.

"Thank you brother, for watching over her". Alpha Kai said. A woman came out of the house carrying lemonade of course Alpha Kai.

"It is our pleasure," she smiled at me.

"That was Hope, Alpha Trenton's mate. She died a year after I arrived. I had almost forgotten about how kind and loving she was. Alpha Trenton was different then, something died inside him when he lost her." I said to Felix not able to look away from the memory.

We moved to the next memory, it was three months after Hope had passed. Beta Stephan had met Trudy, and she quickly became the head woman of the pack. She came into my bedroom, her expression cruel and twisted.

"It's time for you to move to your new space half breed" she spat with disgust. She grabbed me by my arm, painfully dragging me down the door and outside. Tears streamed down my cheeks. I was too young at this point to realize crying made everything worse. She walked to the edge of the woods where there was a small red shed. Opening the door, she tossed me in.

"This is where you will live now, I expect you to clean the pack house everyday" she snapped. Slamming the door and walking away. I curled my knees to my chest, falling asleep trying to keep warm. Felix was growling, making my attention snap to him. I placed my hand on his arm.

"This is just the beginning" I shook my head knowing what was coming. As each abusive memory passed, I could feel the tension in the air growing from Felix. The next memory that came was of Hudson and I the day he was leaving. We clung to each other saying our goodbyes, he had turned sixteen about three months earlier.

"When I come back you will have your wolf then we can run together." I smiled through the pain of losing one of the only friends I had. Felix looked at me.

"Who was that?" he asked, his jealousy thick in the air.

"Just a friend, Felix" I said, rolling my eyes. Before he could ask anything else another memory surfaced. A dark memory I didn't care to relive. This was going to be hard to watch.

"You might as well be human" Trudy spat as I sat tied to a chair. "Alpha Trenton wants to see if pain will bring your wolf on, she rolled her eyes. I said I would babysit you until they all got here." I shook in the chair, fear consumed every fiber of my being with the hateful look in her eyes. She had several hits on me before Alpha Trenton, Beta Stephan and Liam arrived.

"You can go Trudy, "Alpha Trenton commanded. She left unhappily missing the show. "I can't believe my brother left such a worthless half breed for me to support. The only thing you are good at is cleaning. Luckily you can do that. I made a promise to make sure you lived but that's it." He punched me in the stomach, then grabbed me by the throat. He didn't stop choking me until my vision blurred, darkness creeping in. When he let go, I gasped for air coughing as I struggled to fill my lungs.

"I have things to attend to Stephan give it your best shot, Liam you can help. Stephan is crafty, he will show you the ropes." With that Alpha Trenton left. Stephan faced me with a wicked smile on his face. His eyes showed his demons this man was sick. He pulled out a worn leather case laying it out on a small table. Silver glistened in the light, I squeezed my eyes shut not wanting to see what was coming. My screams filled the air as he cut into my body.

Shifting us to the next memory, Felix watched on as Liam tried to rape me. All I could do was stare at Felix, he was shaking at this point barely in control. Several more memories played through showing Trudy's growing cruelty towards me. Until we reached what happened just a couple weeks ago. Hudson coming home, Trudy telling me their plan to sell me, Breen and Stella beating me in the kitchen.

After the last memory showed we were sitting back in the living room staring at each other. Felix shook uncontrollably, his eyes glowing, his wolf begging to be set free. He roared in anger, his claws extending, fur began to grow. Declan busted into the room hearing his Alpha's call. His eyes glowed as well.

"What is wrong Felix?" He growled. I stood up instinctively.

"Calm down" my voice commanded.

Declan calmed instantly shocked, Felix eyes met mine, his wolf battling against the command. Felix, please come back to me, I said gentler. His eyes softened, he took me in his arms breathing me in deeply.

"I am sorry I lost myself for a moment" he whispered to me.

"I understand you have no reason to be sorry" I soothed.

"Umm hello, did you just alpha command me" Declan cut in.

"I am sorry for that Declan." I chuckled.

"No need to be sorry my Queen, I am just stunned. What was that all about anyways?" he questioned.

"We can discuss it later. Today is about Jasira" Felix said, smiling down at me. If I was being honest my wolf was right, I felt stronger now that Felix knew everything. I was in control of my emotions now and did not have to bear the pain alone.

Valentina and Liana came in with worried looks on their faces.

"Is everything ok?" Liana said, caressing Declan's face.

"Yes, my love" he comforted her.

"Ladies, I am happy you are here. Declan and I have some pack business to attend to." Felix announced. Confusion showed on my face as I looked at Felix.

"Don't worry, I will see you shortly" he captured my lips briefly leaving me slightly breathless. With that they both left, leaving me with the girls.

Both the girls approached me excitedly taking turns hugging me.

"Congratulations" they squealed. I couldn't help but laugh at their excitement. "What are you two up to?" I eyed them suspiciously.

"Well, we are here to get you ready," Liana sang jumping up and down. Her energy filled me with happiness.

"Ready for what?" I chuckled.

"That is for us to know and for you to do whatever we say," 'Valentina asserted. I held my hands up in surrender letting them take me back to the bedroom to have their way with me.

They worked their magic as I explained to them all that had happened since last night. Including the walk down memory lane with Felix.

"I have never heard of anyone being able to do that" Liana said in awe.

"I suspect that you have all the elements inside of you, along with the spirit or life element." Valentina informed.

"I didn't even think of it, but that makes sense especially since the moon goddess is your mother," Liana gasped.

"I am not sure what that means but I am sure we will find out" I shrugged. I looked in the mirror barely recognizing the girl from my memories now. I felt so different from her. I smiled at both of my girls. "Thank you both for this. I feel amazing. Now what will I be wearing to whatever we are doing" curiosity eating at me.

"Ah yes the dress, hold on I will be right back." Liana rushed out of the room coming back with a dress bag. They unzipped the bag, revealing a black dress covered in rhinestones. It was beautiful, I was eager to try it on. I stripped the robe off. I had changed into slipping the dress over my curves. The straps were made with rhinestones as well, the dress hugging every part of my body stopping right below my knees.

"It's perfect," I whispered.

"Yes it is," V said resting her head on my shoulder. "Now let us throw on our dresses and get moving." They made quick work of getting changed then hurried me out the door.

"Do I get to know where we are going?" I asked.

"Just come on nosey" Valentina ushered. We made our way to the second floor, I hadn't had the chance to explore all the packhouse because I had been so busy training. We stopped in front of a large set of doors.

"You wait here" Laina commanded and without another word they both took off.

"What the hell guys?" I shouted after them. "Am I just supposed to stand here until I get some type of smoke signal?" A smoke signal I got, Felix stepped out of a room further down the hall, his eyes instantly roaming my body. My heart raced, my body heating under his gaze. He looked good enough to eat in his black suit with a black shirt. He made his way to me in a few strides.

"You look magnificent Jasira" he growled. I blushed. "May I?" He held out his arm to me, I took it still confused. The double doors opened in front of us, he pulled me in, giving me a view of a large staircase with the whole pack waiting at the bottom.

"Surprise", they all shouted confetti raining from the ceiling.

"Oh, my goddess. What is this, Felix?" I said shocked.

"It's your birthday party Jasira. Happy birthday, my queen" he whispered into my ear a devilish grin rising on his face.

Tears spilled down my cheeks in happiness. I could not remember the last birthday I had, let alone anyone doing something just for me.

"This is too much," I said looking at him.

"It will never be too much for you Jasira, you deserve the world." He proclaimed.

He claimed my hand leading me down the stairs where everyone awaited. Nervousness made my tummy flip, what would all these people think of me? Doubt crept into my thoughts like poison. My heart began racing and my chest constricted, I became lightheaded suddenly. Felix must have sensed something from the mate bond because he was immediately pulling me to him wrapping his arms around my waist.

"What is wrong?" he asked through the mind link holding my gaze.

"I'm sorry I just need a minute this is all overwhelming." I responded honestly. Valentina came to my side.

"How about me and the birthday girl step out on the balcony for some fresh air" she insisted.

Felix paused clearly, not liking the idea of being away from me but nodded in agreement anyway. Valentina guided me to a large set of double doors that led to a large balcony. The air was warm, but a nice cooling breeze tickled my skin. I breathed in the surrounding forest allowing it to calm me. There was a staircase that led off into a lush garden. I couldn't help but admire their beauty, wanting to get closer. I turned to Valentina who stood there in silence.

"Thank you for bringing me out here." I am grateful for my friend.

"Of course, Jaz, I will always put what you need first," she declared. I knew what she was telling me, that no matter what Felix or anyone else wanted she would stand by me. I smiled, grabbing her hand to pull her back to the party.

We walked back into the party, Felix gaze immediately, finding mine. He was talking to a group of pack members, so I approached to join the conversation. Felix held out a hand drawing me to his side.

"I am happy your back" he kissed my neck. I blushed not use to the show of affection in front of others. "This is Jenna and Rosa, Jenna is our packs midwife. Rosa is her mate he introduced. Jenna was just talking to me about the recent pups born into the pack." He continued.

"It's lovely to meet you both" I affirmed.

"Why don't we go dance? Jenna, Rosa we will chat later." Felix said, whisking me away.

Felix pulled me to the dance floor even though I protested about not knowing how to dance. He however knew what he was doing, taking my hands, and placing them where they should go. He took the lead allowing me a chance to relax into his steps. We danced for a while, Valentina, Declan, and Liana joined us along with several others. As upbeat music played the dancing became wilder, making laughter flow from everyone. Eventually the music changed, becoming slow and romantic. I couldn't help the shivers up my spine as he pulled me closer, his strong arms holding me tightly. I looked up at him getting caught in his eyes, I could drown in them forever.

"This has been amazing, thank you" I admitted.

"I knew you would like it," he chuckled, leaning in, placing a soft kiss on my lips. He searched my gaze for a moment.

"I love you Jasira, I always have" he expressed. My heart felt as if it would burst with happiness. "I love you too, Felix" I professed with a shaky breath. His face lit up the song coming to a finish.

"I need to go check on something. Will you be ok for a few moments?" he questioned.

"Yes, I will be fine," I responded.

I watched him walk away. He really did look delicious in that suit, I thought to myself. Why I had a moment I figured this would be a great time to use the bathroom. Jenna was close by, so I asked her where it was. She directed me to a door, saying it led to the dressing rooms and both sets of bathrooms. I waved her a thank you rushing towards the door before Felix came back. The hall was quiet as I walked towards the restroom. I slipped off my heels allowing my feet to rest. Dancing in heels was not easy, my feet were not used to it and ached. I walked into the bathroom with several stalls lining the wall. No one else was in here so I was able to pop into the first stall quickly doing my business. As I was finishing, I heard the door swing open, but no one came to the stall area. Probably using the mirror Jasira, stop being such a worrier. I thought to myself. I couldn't shake the growing anxiety as I flushed exiting my stall. As I rounded the corner to wash my hands it was clear why my senses were on high alert.

Gina stood looking into the mirror, an innocent look upon her face. She tried to act surprised that it was me that came around the corner, but I could see through her fakeness. I ignored her washing my hands, if you don't pay her attention, it will be fine, I thought to myself. I began to turn to walk out but she stepped in front of me.

"Excuse me Gina," I politely said, trying to keep everything calm. A cruel smile marred her features.

"Did you think I would just let you brush me off?" she hissed. I took a step back putting some space between us, I was not trying to fight her especially not knowing what my powers could do.

"Gina, I am not here to fight you, let me pass. Felix will be waiting for me." Her eyes lit up with anger, she took a step towards me.

"You think you can come to my pack and steal my place as luna? I am the strongest female in this pack I deserve to be luna not you" she snapped. She was delusional, clearly, she needed to be put in her place. Maybe then she would leave me alone.

"It's not going to happen Gina, so move on. Felix is my mate." I snarled. She grabbed for me like she had done before but I was ready stepping out of her reach. "Listen Gina, you don't want to do this." I sneered.

"You have no idea how badly I do want to do this," she growled fire dancing from her fingers. As she raised her hands to aim at me, I felt an electrical sensation come over me, everywhere tingled. Her hands extended shooting fire directly at me but never touched me.

My skin glowed with a purple aura around it. Water formed a protective bubble around me stopping her. Her face was one of shock, taking in what had just happened. I waived the water away,

"Gina let's just not do this" I said hoping she would get the hint. Bullies never do though, in fact I think I enraged her more.

"You're a water elemental wolf" she laughed "you think a little water will stop me." She stepped forward again, letting her arms engulf in flames. She cackled like a crazy person as she moved forward with her attack.

Energy still pulsed through me growing by the minute. I was angry now, all my life I have been pushed around. I am not letting it happen to me anymore. I am a Queen, I thought to myself. As the rage built wind began to pick up making my hair blow, my body engulfed in flames and the ground shook. I could see the fear in her eyes as she backed away seeing the shift in me happen.

"What that is not possible" she said, stuttering as she backed up.

I was done playing her games, she wanted some of this she was going to get it. The mirrors shattered as the building shook. I could see her sweat from the heat coming off my body even though her element was fire. I reached out my hand commanding the wind to wrap around her throat.

"I warned you" I said in my Alpha voice. She shook in fear.

"I…I am sorry" she wheezed out around my grip. The door flung open at that moment Felix, Declan and Valentina entered the bathroom.

17

FELIX

The whole room shook as if an earthquake was happening. I reached out through the mate bond to find it blocked by rage. I rushed out the door looking everywhere for Jasira, something had set her off. I ran to Valentina who was looking around frantically.

"Where is Jasira?" I asked worry filling my voice.

"I am not sure she was with you, I just felt the quake and began to look for her." Rage filled me.

"Where was my mate?" I roared. Jenna and Rosa ran to me.

"What is happening" they said trying to keep their balance as the building trembles increased.

"Have you seen Jasira?" I growled hoping someone had seen her. Jenna nodded.

"I told her where the bathroom was a little bit ago."

I took off, Valentina trailing behind. In all the commotion Declan had found me as well now following as I slipped down the hall to the restroom. As I swung open the door, breathing heavy rage coursing through my body, I had to step back at the sight of Jasira. She was incredible, power radiated off her making her skin glow. She was beautiful, even in her rage. I heard the gasp of Valentina and Declan as they trailed in behind me.

"Stop" she shouted in her Alpha voice. I stopped pushing against the command, Valentina and Declan stood frozen shock on their faces.

"Jasira, my love what is going on?" I tried to soothe her. Her eyes looked at me at the sound of my voice. I looked at Gina growling at the thought of her trying to hurt my mate.

"Gina has challenged me for Luna," she laughed darkly. "What she doesn't realize is that I am not a Luna. I am an alpha, and a queen." She roared.

"There is no competition Jasira, you are the things you say. More importantly you are my mate." I continued trying to calm her. "This is not what you want. You are kind, fair and loving. I have seen you as the alpha you are, and it is not this" I insisted. Her grip loosened on Gina as she looked at her.

"You are right" she agreed, her voice back to normal. She dropped Gina to the ground. The building no longer shook, and the wind calmed. She approached me still glowing, commanding the room's attention.

"When I awake, I will deal with her," Jasira demanded.

With that she collapsed into my arms releasing everyone from her alpha hold. I walked back to the grand hall where everyone was chatting amongst themselves. My father spotted me then Jasira. He rushed to us, concern evident on his face, he reached for her face making my wolf growl.

"Calm my son, I will not hurt your mate. I am simply worried" he defended.

"I think she is fine, just depleted. I want to get the doctor to look at her." I said impatiently. As if hearing me, Doctor Rebecca was by my side.

"Let's just take her to the clinic, so I can have a closer look," She advised. I nodded my agreement allowing her to lead the way.

18

JASIRA

My eyes fluttered open. I looked around the room, realizing I was in the clinic.

"Ah, my child, you're back with us." Madeira sat next to my bedside, her kind face staring at me. "You gave Felix quite the scare," she patted my hand. "I heard you lost control a little back there" she continued. I looked down, not wanting to see her disappointment. "Look at me, Jasira," she coaxed. I met her eyes, mine slightly glossy. "I am not upset with you, dear. I am proud that you kicked that girl's ass." She chuckled, "It is understandable that you lost control. You have all this power, yet no training. Your emotions are high because you just shifted, and the supermoon is only a week away." She chided. I had totally forgotten about the supermoon, which is also when the annual Festival is. "What's on your mind, child?" Madeira inquired.

"I was just thinking about the Festival, I have never been allowed to attend. The pack would go, but I was forced to stay to clean." She listened, humming her acknowledgment. I sat up, confident in my next decision, looking at Mama Madeira. "All the elemental wolves will be attending the Super Moon Festival as the Moon Stone Pack." I proclaimed confidently. A grin spread wide across Madeira's face,

"Now that's what I am talking about," she encouraged.

"What are we talking about?" Felix asked as he entered the room, coming to my side. "You scared me, beautiful," he whispered, kissing my forehead.

"I'm fine," I insisted. "I do have something to talk to you about, though." I swung my legs off the bed, standing up. This was going to happen, and I knew my mate would not like it.

"I will leave you two to it," Madeira said, heading towards the door.

"Actually, Madeira, I would like you, Deema, Isla, and Valentina to meet us in the grand hall in one hour. Would you kindly assist Declan with gathering the pack?" I held my chin high, trying to radiate confidence. Her warm smile gave me all the reassurance I needed. "Of course, my Queen." She nodded, leaving us. I mind-linked Declan my instructions as well.

"What is going on, Jasira?" Felix questioned, confusion evident on his face.

"It's time I start acting like the Queen I am. My question for you is, are you ready to stand by my side?" I challenged', waiting for his reaction. His eyebrow cocked a sexy smirk on his face.

"I will follow you anywhere, in fact I love this commanding Queen." He reached out, grabbing my waist and pulling me against his body. I could feel him hardening against me, he tilted his head down kissing my mark. I giggled in response, the ache between my legs making me aware of how close our bodies were. He released me, taking my hands in his. "What can I do to assist you, my Queen?" He asked, warmth in his tone.

I explained to him that I needed to see Gina. She was in the holding cells waiting for me to wake up. To say Felix wasn't happy with my request was an understatement, but I insisted. Before I could go to see her there, I needed to speak with my mother. Felix was unhappy with me going alone, so I compromised and took Valentina. V waited for me in the foyer of the pack house. She grabbed me, pulling me into her embrace the minute she saw me.

"I am fine," I assured her. I shifted my wolf, coming much easier this time, the pain tolerable. Valentina followed as I led us to the meadow. I still couldn't believe how amazing it felt to let my wolf free. Clearly, my wolf approved, she wanted to play with Valentina, but time would not allow it right now. I shifted back once we reached the meadow, breathing in the fresh grass and feeling the gentle breeze caress me. Valentina came up behind me, shifting as well.

"What are we doing here?" she inquired.

"I needed to speak with my mother," Valentina looked at me like I had two heads, making me chuckle. "Trust me, I know it sounds crazy, but she told me I could contact her. Do you trust me?" I asked, grabbing Valentina's hands.

"With my life," she responded. With that, I closed my eyes, holding my necklace in one of my hands. I still held tightly to Valentina, hoping that I could bring her with me. I reached deep, feeling the energy built inside me. It grew frantic, pressing to escape. I thought of Selene, picturing our meetings together. The power erupted from me, the world shifting around us until we stood before my mother.

Valentina gasped, stumbling back, almost falling, but a man caught her. She quickly stepped away from him, sniffing the air. Her eyes went wide.

"This is not happening," she exclaimed. I looked at the man, seeing confusion, marring his godlike features. Selene clapped excitedly, and a brilliant smile lit up her face.

"Well, here I was thinking I would have to send you to Earth on an errand. Well done, my daughter." she gleefully announced. The man looked at Selene, still confused, searching for an answer.

"My Goddess, what does this mean?" he questioned. She pointed at both of them.

"You two are mates, silly," Selene giggled. I shook my head, trying to catch up. "Alright, I guess since we are in a time crunch, I can explain." she continued. "I wanted to honor you, Valentina, for being Jasira's protector. So, I made Evander your mate, he has been loyal and deserves to experience love. But enough about that, you two can get to know each other later." She waived, leaving no room for questions or arguments.

I sent Valentina an apologetic look. Goddess knows best, I thought to myself. As much as I would have loved to chat, I came here for a reason. and was in a hurry.

"Mother, I first want to thank you for my mate," I said, expressing my gratitude.

"Well, of course, my darling, it was only fitting that I pair you with a legacy."

"A what?" Once again, I was confused.

"Ah, yes, that will be a conversation for another time. Felix's mother was a demi-goddess herself," she answered, pressing me to continue. My mind reeled with a million questions. I knew I needed to stay on track because, apparently, my mother couldn't.

"That is definitely a conversation we will be having," I murmured.

I explained to her my plans step by step. She looked pleased as I laid everything out. "The more important question here is, can I feel someone's true intentions and feelings, and whether they are being truthful? "I inquired. My wolf had told me that this may be a possibility that would help with my future decision. Which is what prompted the visit to my mother. I, of course, had other questions, but I had to start with this next step first.

"I am so happy you came to me for help. I always wished my daughter, and I would have a connection," she smiled. "The answer is yes, you can do that. You simply need to connect with the same energy that brought you here. You have the four elements, Jasira, and the Aether element. Some know it as the soul or spirit element. It is everything that surrounds us. You will discover all the things you are capable of. I will be here when you need guidance", she finished. I nodded my understanding, grateful for her explanation.

"I do have one other question for you, mother." I pressed, knowing time was of the essence.

"What is it, you may ask me anything?" She encouraged.

"Why do some of the other packs want to eliminate the elemental wolves?" I asked, figuring if I was going to help bring everyone together. I should know why this all started.

"Ah, that is a good one, my girl," she replied with a pondering look. "You see, there is a story behind this that dates far beyond the oldest wolves' years. I know you're in a hurry, but the short of it is. They are not the same as you, which, among all species, creates distrust and fear. Yet we all come from Chaos, so we are the same." She proclaimed in a goddess like way. I was a bit confused, which I think she realized.

"Listen, Jasira, you will understand, but for now, know this. Those wolves come from a line that has fought the elementals for generations. The original four lines of wolves are blessed. This is why they shift naturally at a young age. The other wolves come from a curse, this is why their magic is held captive." She further explained. "You must go now, speak with Madeira. She is wise." She gave no other warning but a wave of her hand, sending us back to the meadow.

Valentina looked at me, wonder and uncertainty in her face.

"Was that a dream?" she said, rubbing her head. I laughed.

"No, it was real." I pointed towards Evander, who stood quietly. "Looks like we have a new addition, he is quite dreamy" I joked wagging my eyebrows at her. She gave me an I will kill you look, making me laugh further. "Come on, let's get this party started," I said, still laughing. I called my wolf to me. This time, the transition was instant. It was time to go speak to Gina.

I arrived at the entrance of the holding cells. Felix was pacing, his hands running through his hair as I approached. He turned, rushing towards me, scooping me up in a hug and claiming my lips.

"Miss me?" I whispered, my voice slightly husky.

"You have no idea," he said, a smile replacing his worry. He looked over my shoulder, seeing Evander, "Who is that?" He eyed suspiciously.

"My mate," Valentina murmured, rolling her eyes. I giggled, patting her on the shoulder. Felix gave me a look asking to explain later, I nodded refocusing on the task. He led us through the holding cell area, where Gina sat on a cot. She looked up as we entered the room, fear evident in her gaze, before looking at the ground. I turned to Felix.

"Could you open the cell, please?" He gave me a crazy look but did as I asked. He tried to follow as I entered the cell, but I held my hand up, stopping him. "I will be fine," I insisted. "I needed her to listen to find out what I needed to know." As I approached her, I could feel the fear coming off her in waves, yet she straightened her back and held her chin high. That was why I was here. I released some energy toward her, allowing her to feel I meant no harm. As my power caressed her skin, she looked up at me, gasping slightly in surprise.

"I am not here to hurt you," I assured. "I just want to have an honest conversation," I stated.

"I'm listening," Gina said, trying to sound unfazed. I sat down beside her, taking her hands into mine. A shocked expression passed momentarily on her face, then changed to suspicion. Felix growled from outside the cell, and I waved him off. I reached deep for the energy I had felt before, and it came to me quicker this time. I focused on calming it, then released it gently through my hands to hers, forming a connection. I felt her try to pull away for a moment, but then she relaxed.

"Can you hear me?" I asked through the link, needing to be sure that it had worked. It was similar to the mate bond. I could sense her emotions, feel her truths, or lies.

"Yes, what the hell is this?" she asked, trying to sound haughty, but I could feel her nervousness. I ignored her.

"I feel like we got off on the wrong page. See what I think is you are in pain. You have gone unnoticed despite being the best fighter in this pack. You grew up alongside Felix, hoping to be a part of his leadership. He never showed interest in you, which hurt because you were willing to step up even if he wasn't your mate. The council talked about you becoming Luna, and you had hope again. Then I came in and destroyed that for you." I spoke to her through our mind link.

"All I ever wanted was to be important, to be seen as the fighter I was." She snapped, and her hurt seeped in even though she tried to sound angry.

"I come to you as an alpha and a Queen. I recognize your fighting ability, your strength. I can see your heart, Gina." She wept through our mind-link, realizing she couldn't hide. The anger from being passed over grew inside her, poisoning the loyal heart I saw. I wiped the anger away, absorbing it before I knew I was healing her inside. I released the connection, pulling her into my arms as she wept like a small child. I shushed and soothed her. I looked briefly at Felix, seeing the confusion and wonder on his face. Valentina looked at me with warmth and pride. I pulled back from Gina. Her sobs had stopped, and she wiped her face.

"Now I have a question for you," I said, drawing her attention. She sat up straight again, her chin held high.

"Yes, my Queen," she responded with strength in her voice. I smiled.

"I can't imagine anyone better suited to protect me and the pack. Would you be my Delta?" So many emotions crossed her face.

"I...I. It would be my deepest honor," she finally got out.

"Good, then let's go." I grabbed her hand, standing her up. Felix opened the door, shaking his head. As I walked past him, he gave my ass a little slap making me chuckle.

"You never cease to amaze me, my Queen." He announced with pride. Let's just see what he thinks of what I do next, I thought.

I stood at the top of the stairs, looking down at everyone in the grand hall. I hadn't had the chance to meet many of the pack members. That didn't matter. Now, they would know me, and I would take time to get to know everyone. Felix stood by my side, waiting to see what I would do next. He touched my back, his support clear through our mate bond. Warm shivers made their way through my body. I smiled at him, sending my gratitude in return.

I stepped forward, ready to begin. I reached for the wind to send my voice among the crowd so all may hear.

"My name is Jasira, and my mother is the Goddess Selene." Gasps could be heard among the crowd, followed by whispers. "I will be taking my rightful role as Queen over all elemental wolves, with Felix, my mate, as your king." The crowd had different responses. Some were uneasy, some confused, some angry. "I know this is a lot," I continued, "but I promise I will prove myself to you all." All the alphas stood to the side at the bottom of the stairs. I acknowledge them by bringing them forward. "These faces here are ones you trust, they believe and follow me." The Alphas nodded in agreement. "They will be the voices of the people because we will become one pack." This brought on louder chatter, and fear was evident.

"Quiet while your Queen speaks" boomed Alpha Kai's voice. The room grew silent, and he smiled up at me. "We have hidden in fear for too long, separated ourselves from families. No longer will we do this. We will all be one under the Moonstone Pack."

"You all know Felix's Beta and Delta. I would like to introduce mine. Liana," I turned to her. "Would you be my Beta?" She had been a trusted friend since the moment I arrived. Her face lit up with a smile, her head nodding yes in excitement. I grasped her hand, giving it a squeeze before letting it go. "Gina will be the Delta of the pack," this leads to several gasps. I ignored them, pushing forward. "The moon goddess has blessed me with a protector," I usher Valentina forward. "She is my most trusted friend and sister."

"This is a lot to take in, but there is more. Everyone has heard of the Supermoon Annual Festival." I could feel the crowd's anxious attention. I could feel Felix tense next to me, his unease coming through our bond. "You have had to stay away, hiding in fear. This has prevented many of you from finding your true mate. I can't imagine a life without mine." I continued smiling at Felix. He returned my smile, bringing my hand to his mouth so he could kiss it. "You shouldn't have to either," I proclaimed, returning to the pack. "The festival is in ten days. We will be taking those of age looking to find their mate. We will talk again before we leave." With that I concluded my first announcement to our now conjoined pack. I walked out with Felix by my side as we headed to have our first new council meeting.

He pulled me into him, wrapping me up in his arms. His smell, his warmth, swept all my thoughts away. All I could do was breathe him in. I hadn't realized how tense I was until I was in his arms.

"From now on we talk before you do something like that," he growled. "You may be Queen, but you are mine. I will do whatever is necessary to keep you safe." I looked up, meeting his eyes, his wolf clearly on the surface. I could feel his alpha aura rolling off him in waves. I would be lying if I said that it didn't turn me on. My core turned into molten lava, my arousal in the air. I watched as he took a deep breath, his eyes turning dark with desire. He slammed me up against the wall, displaying his dominance. His lips crashed into mine, taking what he wanted. I could feel his tongue tasting my lips, my mouth opening in response. He suddenly pulled away, leaving us both panting. I whimpered in response to the loss of his lips.

"I am so proud of you, but I am also scared for you," He murmured into my hair, trying to reel himself in. "I am struggling. My instincts say protect what's mine, shelter you, make you stand behind me, so I am hit first. But I also know everyone has controlled you your whole life." He whispered his confession to me. I sighed.

"I understand, but I will be safe if we are together. We are stronger that way," I reasoned. He nodded. "Plus, I know you want my old pack to be punished as much as I do." He growled a low, deadly noise.

I sighed again, pulling back to look up at him. I reached up, caressing his cheek. Everyone was waiting for us, but my mate needed this moment. I grabbed his hands, taking a step back. My body instantly felt colder.

"Felix, it is now our duty to protect our people, but I won't put myself in unnecessary danger," I promised. He blew out his breath.

"Alright," he replied gruffly.

We started walking back, not wanting to postpone the meeting any longer. I, for one, just wanted to get this done so I could climb in bed with my mate. The warmth spread across my chest as my stomach danced at the thought. I daydreamed as we walked, thinking about the first time with Felix. As we entered, everyone lowered their eyes, bowing their respects. I felt so honored with all these powerful wolves willing to support me. Felix touched my back, gently guiding me to the head of the table. It was usually the Alpha's seat, but he nodded in approval, sitting to my right. Everyone else sat down, joining us.

"We are here because we need to discuss the Alpha ceremony and mating ritual for you, too. We must do this before we are to go to the festival," Alpha Kai announced. I hadn't really thought about this. A wave of uncertainty plagued me. What else had I not thought of? I criticize myself. "You are so over your head. You will never pull off being a Luna, let alone a queen." The ugly voice inside me sneered. Felix reached out, took my hand, and returned me to the table.

I took a shuddering breath, willing my doubts away. Though they were still there, they were not as loud and allowed me to think.

"Since that is a priority, let's make it happen. I am sure I can entrust my beta to help handle things". I paused, thinking for a moment. "Aunt Amelia and Aunt Chloe, would you assist Liana as well in getting things together?" They both nodded happily. The meeting took longer than I hoped. We discussed the changes to come along with going to the Super Moon Festival. That was clearly a hot topic since everyone was divided on the idea. It just felt right. This was where we needed to announce that we were a pack. We could see all our enemies' faces right there if there was pushback. No one would be able to hide. Hopefully, we could discover who was going to be a problem this way. Plus, we needed to allow everyone to find their mate. I had talked with Felix when I first found out that he didn't have a mate. He had explained to me that many young elemental wolves did not. Apparently, between the division of the elemental packs for their safety, not many had gotten the chance to find a mate within their packs. Even if Elemental wolves shifted when they were just children, their chances of finding their mate did not happen until their late teens.

We finished up by laying out my needs with training. I would train with Felix privately. This was because anyone who tried to offer received life-threatening growls from the Alpha. I relaxed a bit as we walked back to our rooms. The thought of sleep was so enticing I was exhausted from the day. We paused in the hall looking at each other clearly, us having separate rooms wasn't going to work out. Felix wanted me to choose where I was most comfortable, so I decided on his room. I loved that every part of it smelt like him the minute you walked in. It made me feel at home and safe. He chuckled at me happily with whatever I chose. He told me he would have the staff bring everything over tomorrow.

I walked into Felix's room, or should I say our room now. My body drained, and I flopped on the bed. Felix climbed on top of me, tickling my side and making me giggle until I couldn't breathe. He leaned down, placing a soft kiss on my lips. Felix tried to pull back, but I wrapped my hands around his neck, pulling him in and deepening the kiss. That was all the encouragement he needed. He quickly lifted me off the bed, my legs wrapping around his muscular waist. He held me as he crawled to the top of the bed, laying me down, his hands exploring my body. I was no longer tired, my body buzzing with excitement. The earlier warmth in my belly started while my core dampened at his touch.

He growled as my body responded to him. Nipping his way down until he reached my most sensitive spot. He teased me with gentle kisses and bites. Then followed with feather-light licks between my soaked folds.

"Please, Felix, please," I said, my fingers wrapped in his hair, trying to make him give me more. He chuckled.

"Tsk tsk, such an impatient little queen we have here." He stopped momentarily, making me whine, but quickly slid his fingers in between my slit, wetting them before he thrust them inside. His mouth then captured my clit, suckling and licking it. I cried out as my climax rocked through me.

He then grabbed my hips rolling me over, he pulled my ass towards him plunging into me showing no mercy. I could feel the sweet ache of his fullness inside of me, trying to stretch to fit him. There was no pause this time, he was going to show my wolf who the Alpha was. His deep thrusts started slowly but grew faster with each one.

My wolf howled in pleasure, responding to our mate dominating us. I was on fire, burning alive from the inside. With every second, I grew closer to exploding. I was so close to release he reached around, his fingers grazing my swollen bud, and began rubbing it. I saw stars again crying out, but his name left my lips this time.

My body shook as the waves of pleasure spread through my body. He found his release with me. My insides spasmed from the intensity of the orgasm. We collapsed, both panting, our bodies slick. He held me to his chest, kissing me on the head as he caressed my hair. His soft breathing and earthy scent were a lullaby to my soul. Snuggling in deeper, I found sleep instantly.

I woke up alone, my mate nowhere in sight. My wolf was in a panic. I dressed quickly to search for him. I felt a desperation I hadn't felt before, anxiety eating at me. I busted into the dining room doors.

"Where is he?" I shouted, feeling more wolf than human. The energy I experienced during a shift was caressing my skin. Everyone turned in surprise, and Alpha Kai slowly came toward me with his hands up, showing he was not a threat. I growled as he got closer, making him stop.

"Jasira, it's just me, calm down," Felix said gently.

"I said, Where is he?" My voice was a deadly snarl.

"Felix went on patrol near our borders. There was activity there early this morning. He should be back soon." He soothed. I began to pace.

"What is wrong with me?" I started crying, my emotions everywhere.

"I am sorry," I whined at Kai.

"It's okay" he reassured, finally feeling safe enough to approach me. "Why don't we go to your room so you will have his scent around you until he returns?" I whimpered but nodded my agreement, following him back upstairs. Once, I was safely tucked into the bed. Kai grabbed a few of Felix's shirts to bring to me, I quickly snatched them out of his hands growling at him. He retreated slowly away from the bed, my wolf watching his every step.

Valentina peeked her head in the door moments later. I was now up frantically walking around the room, but hearing the door open, I turned, ready to attack, letting out a growl to warn the intruder. She approached me with caution but still came in, determined to soothe me, while Kai called Felix. I came out of my haze for a moment, recognizing Valentina. I rushed to her, crying on her shoulder as she rubbed my back.

I doubled over while I was standing there, startled by the sudden burning sensation that filled my stomach. Valentina guided me to bed while trying to figure out what was happening. The pain eased slightly for a moment, allowing me to hear what Kai was saying even though he was in the living room.

"Felix you better come back, something is wrong with Jasira." He paused, allowing Felix to respond. "She is not hurt physically, but something is going on." another pause. "I am calling the doctor, but she needs you now." He hung up the phone and then called the doctor before returning to my room.

I tossed my body around the bed, trying to get comfortable, but was unable to. I felt like I was overheating. I began stripping my clothes off not caring who was around, the doctor chose that time to enter. I hunkered down on the bed, growling at her. How dare another she-wolf come into my den. I wasn't thinking rationally anymore, my wolf was in control I was just along for the ride. I snapped my teeth at her, warning her not to come any closer. Kai stepped in front of the woman, holding his hands out.

"It's okay, Jasira. We will leave until Felix comes back." I whined at my mate's name, digging my nose into his shirt, taking a deep breath. The fog of my wolf lifted slightly.

"I can't control her, I am sorry," I croaked as they backed out the door, leaving me to wallow in my bed.

19

FELIX

My phone rang, instantly making my heart race. My father wouldn't be calling unless something was wrong. He knew I was tracking and would not want to distract me.

"Felix, you better come back. Something is wrong with Jasira," he said, his voice riddled with worry.

"What do you mean?" I pressed. All he could tell me, though, was that she wasn't injured. I shifted immediately, knowing that I would be faster this way. I wasted no time getting to my mate. It had been 45 minutes since the call. My body was riddled with anxiety when I got closer to her emotions coming through our mate bond. I could feel her desperation as I entered the room. My father stood guard at our bedroom door, Rebecca and Valentina were also there.

"Dr. Rebecca could not look at her. She wouldn't let anyone in," he claimed.

He stepped aside, allowing me to open the door. A growl escaped my little mate, who was clearly not herself. Her fangs were extended along with her claws, but her growling stopped the moment she recognized me.

"Felix," she whimpered, my heart breaking at the sound of her distress.

"Yes, I am here," I purred, approaching her slowly. She visibly relaxed the closer I became. I took her in my arms, allowing her to breathe me in. She nipped at my body, leaving love bites in several places. Her arousal was thick in the air, making my wolf go crazy. I purred, calming her until she was more Jasira than her wolf. "What is going on, my little mate?" I asked, trying to restrain my wolf from taking over.

"I don't know, my body is on fire still, it's better, but it hurts," she whined.

"I am going to call the doctor in to look at you. You will behave, do you understand me?" I said, unleashing my alpha authority. She huffed her displeasure but allowed the doctor to enter. I held her tightly as Rebecca examined her. Jasira went back and forth between growling and apologizing.

"I know what is causing this. Jasira is approaching her first heat," she concluded. My mouth fell open in shock. Usually, this doesn't happen so suddenly after the first shift.

"She just shifted, that shouldn't be happening yet. Right?" I asked, hoping the doctor could explain.

"Not typically this soon, it usually happens three months after a female finds or claims a mate." She paused, clearly thinking. "I think this is because she has kept her wolf at bay for so long. Usually, a female wolf starts puberty around sixteen elemental wolves or not. That is when mood swings typically begin to present themselves. However, they increase right before her first heat cycle. If a she wolf finds her mate before or around eighteen, they usually have their first cycle three months later. If not, it can be six months before she presents." She states.

"Why now, after everything she has already been through?" I question, holding Jasira tighter as she jerks in pain.

"I wish I could tell you, but I suspect it is due to the supermoon being so close. I do know that with it being her first time in heat after being marked, it will be hard on her. The pain will only get more intense until the cycle finishes. You can certainly provide her with relief." She finished and then turned, leaving us.

All Jasira could do was whine at this point from the pain, I couldn't stand to see her like this.

"Please help me," she pleaded, her beautiful violet eyes filled with desperation. Her arousal was thick in the air, making my wolf go mad. I laid her down on the bed, my hands traveling every curve of her body. She arched her back, letting a gentle moan out in response. I spread her legs, admiring her perfection, before I drove myself into her. She cried out, begging me to keep going. I knew exactly how to provide her with relief. I picked up my pace, driving deeper, letting her feel my entire length.

"What a good little mate," I praised. I could tell she was close as she clawed at my back, wrapping her legs tight around me. She found her release screaming my name, sending me over the edge as well.

Her eyelids were heavy with exhaustion. I lay next to her, pulling her close and purring. She instantly relaxed into me, her breathing soft. I kissed her head before untucking myself from her. I would not go that far again while she was still dealing with this. Who knew when another wave would hit. I mind-linked our Betas and Deltas, asking everyone to meet me in the living room, then quickly jumped in the shower to wash off. I wanted to get an update on the plans for the next few days and ensure that Jasira had the least amount of stress.

After my shower, I dressed quickly, checking on Jasira before leaving the living room.

"Is she better? Valentina asked immediately. Everyone looked in my direction, clearly wanting to know the same thing.

"I think so. She was sleeping peacefully, but I won't be going far from her." I replied.

"No one expects you to. I remember my first heat. It was horrible but, luckily, lasted only three days." Liana added.

"It was hard seeing you that way." Declan looked at his mate lovingly.

"After that, it becomes easier," she assured me. I nodded my agreement, thankful for my friends.

"I did call you all here for a reason. I want to be sure that we are on track with everything. Jasira needs me by her side with as little stress as possible," I insisted.

"Gina and I made our way out to the border after you were pulled away this morning. Gina did patrol while I set up magical barriers. They will help conceal us better and alert us if someone comes too close." Valentina declared.

"I have been working on the ceremony with both of your aunts. Everything is in place for the night before the Supermoon Festival." Liana added excitedly.

"Before Gina was called away, she was helping Gage and me prepare the route for the pack to the festival," Declan stated. Relief filled me knowing that they handled everything. All I had to do was take care of my little mate.

20

JASIRA

I woke up with a start, quickly checking in on my body to see if the agonizing pain was still there. To my relief, it had passed, but disappointment quickly trickled in, noticing my mate was no longer here. I reached out through our mind link, hoping he had not returned to the border.

"Felix?" I let his name ring in my mind. A pulse of love filled me as our connection opened, and he responded.

"I am on my way back to you right now, my little wolf. I thought you might be hungry, so I ran to the kitchen briefly." On cue, my stomach rumbled, informing me that he was right.

Moments later, he came into our room carrying a tray full of different foods. He placed it on the bed in front of me and then took his place next to me. As hungry as I was, his scent was what made my mouth water. He reached out, caressing my cheek, his touch sending calming waves through me. My stomach rumbled again, making him chuckle. I turned my attention to the tray, making sure to try everything.

"How are you feeling?" He asked with concern evident in his voice.

"I am fine now. I am just a bit embarrassed about how I acted," I murmured, pushing my food around on the tray and not looking at him. He clucked at me, grabbing my chin.

"You have nothing to be embarrassed about. What you are going through is what every she wolf does. Well, except not usually this quickly after they find their mate." he assured. No matter how he assured me, I still felt I owed some apologies. I could see the fear in Dr. Rebecca's eyes before my mate arrived. Then there was Kai. Ugh, how I acted around toward him. I pushed the tray away, no longer hungry. Felix glared at me with displeasure at my sudden apprehension to eat.

"I would really like to go take a bath right now." I started, getting up from the bed before he could protest. I made my way to the large tub without another word. My mind was overwhelmed with everything I didn't want to talk. I couldn't, if I did, I might lose myself in a dark hole. I had felt this way before so many times. I questioned why I was even alive because I was nothing. Even now, knowing why I was born, knowing people loved me. That darkness was trying to take over the light I had found. I pushed it back, refusing to let it win.

I leaned over the tub, turning the nozzles to begin filling it. When I stood back up, Felix was behind me, his body pressed against me. I leaned into him, his solid body grounding me. He wrapped his arms around me, placing kisses on my neck while nipping at my mark. I relaxed, grateful for my mate's affection. He stripped me off my clothes, then proceeded to scoop me up, placing my body gently in the tub. I sighed as my body hit the steamy water. He washed my hair and body without a word, sending love through our bond the whole time. How did he know this was precisely what I needed? I thought to myself, closing my eyes.

By the time I had finished my bath, my spirits were much higher. Felix stayed by my side the whole time, his presence keeping me steady.

"I would like to go speak with Kai," I said while I was dressing.

"We can do that," he replied in agreement leading the way.

We walked holding hands in silence. Felix was allowing me time to process clearly, sensing my inner turmoil. This only made me love him more. I decided it was time to break the ice, feeling guilty for not talking to my mate this whole time.

"Felix," I uttered, drawing his attention to me. "I never really had anyone to teach me about going into heat. How long does it last?" I questioned, my cheeks flushing with slight embarrassment. Not because of him either but because I had to ask something I should have been taught. I was never allowed to go to school after I was forced by the Alpha to live outside of the packhouse.

"The bad stuff usually only lasts a few days, but you're technically in heat for around 10 days. Most she wolves only notice their peak, which is a couple days before it finishes. I would say that your heat began immediately after I marked you or only days after." He claimed. I couldn't believe all of this was happening so fast. We had an official mating ceremony and then the Super Moon Festival. I gasped, thinking about being in heat during the festival. "You should be done with your heat on the day of our mating ceremony." He assured, a wicked smile on his face. That smile said he knew something I didn't.

"What are you smiling about, mister?" I said pointedly.

"Well, my little wolf, that will be the worst of the three days. You will want me to fuck you all day," he winked. I blushed in response, but what surprised me more was my wolf speaking up saying to him.

"Seems like the perfect mating ceremony."

Felix's eyes glowed, hearing my wolf's response.

"Naughty mate," he chuckled. He pulled me to his chest, claiming my mouth. I parted my lips, allowing him access, loving how he tasted. He pulled away abruptly, making me whine slightly. "Jasira, if you want to go see my father, we have to stop, or you are not going to make it out of this hall," he growled, his wolf still at the surface. He was right, even if I liked his promise to take me there. I needed to get this guilt off my chest, so I conceded.

Facing Kai was more complicated than I thought. My guilt made my stomach twist, threatening to purge all the lunch I had eaten. We found him in the restricted part of the library, focused intently on what he was reading. He looked up as we entered, offering us a kind smile. I looked down, unable to bear his kindness right now.

"My two favorite people," he announced cheerfully.

"I am sure that is not the case," I whispered.

"What do you mean, Jasira? What is on your mind?" He questioned, his voice gentle.

"I...I am sorry," I wailed, feeling myself break. "I am just so sorry for how I treated you, you must hate me. I don't blame you." I was spiraling again, the darkness clawing at me. Strong arms wrapped around me, holding me tight.

"I don't hate you my child, it's okay shush now." Kai soothed. He pulled back, holding me at arm's length, "You are in heat. You weren't yourself. I hold nothing against you." He explained, gently touching my cheek and wiping away the tears. "I have loved you since the moment your mother put you in my arms. There is nothing you could do to make me hate you, pup." he crooned. I cried more now, but this time, it was because of his love for me. My mate purred behind me, a calming blanket that wrapped around my body. I wiped my tears, thanking them both for being there.

"Would you like to know what I was reading before you both came in here?" Kai commented. With a final calming breath, I followed Kai to the table he had been sitting at. My curiosity is now at the forefront. Kai sat down, gesturing for us to follow suit. "The last time you spoke with your mother, you said that she mentioned that our wolves were different," Kai stated.

"Yes, that is true. She briefly explained about the curse." I acknowledged.

"Well, I have found several stories written by the four elemental lines. They all talk about how those wolves' curse can be lifted." He paused. I gestured to him to continue, eager to hear how that was possible. "It says here that if a goddess blessed wolf and a cursed wolf are true mates once they mark one another accepting their bond the curse will lift revealing that wolf's element. There are only rare cases of this because the goddess only allows a worthy wolf to be freed." He explained.

I reeled back, needing a moment to process this. I stood up, beginning to pace. This is why I felt so strongly about the Super Moon Festival. If you meet your mate there, I have heard it is almost impossible not to mark them. This may mean that we will be coming home with more Elemental wolves. It also means we will have ties with the families in other packs, making them less likely to want to help whoever is behind the attacks.

I spun around, facing Kai and Felix, who patiently waited for me to process the information.

"Do you realize what this means?" I squealed quickly, explaining my thought process.

"I see the importance of going to the Super Moon Festival, but I still don't like how exposed it will leave us. Especially you," he grumbled.

"This is true, son. However, doing what we have been doing would be more dangerous. The pack has been dwindling in numbers for a long time." Kai refuted.

I laid my hands on Felix's back, rubbing gentle circles, trying to soothe him. I could feel his turmoil through the bond. The tension eased in his body but not in his mind. A thought suddenly came to me if this information was in all these books. Wouldn't there be information on who started the fighting?

"Kai, are there more books like these in this library?" I inquired. His eyebrow raised in curiosity at my question.

"Well, yes, we have had several Elders write their history, important events that happened, and personal knowledge they gained," he replied.

"Do you know who the elders were when the attacks started?" I questioned, hoping that this could give us a clue. Something clicked for Kai, he realized the path I was going. Felix realized my thoughts as well.

"You're thinking that those Elders might be able to give us an idea on who started the war. That's a genius idea," Felix beamed. I blushed at his praise, he stood giving me a quick kiss. Kai stood as well, leading us to the section of journals.

"I can't believe I hadn't thought of that. It probably is the same bloodline that has been organizing this. The hate spilling down from Alpha to Alpha," Kai guessed.

"We should start with our great-grandparents, they were the generation before the big attack," Felix proposed. Kai made quick work grabbing four books. He laid them all out on the table in front of us.

"These are the four Alpha's. Each child born that will be the next Alpha has the same element as the previous one." He explained. "My father, his father before him were all Earth elements. Your father's line was the Alpha of Air, and your mother's was the Alpha of Fire." He gestured to me but continued, "Alpha Marlen water, Alpha Silas earth, Alpha Edith fire, and Alpha Victor air." He finished touching each book as he told me whom they belonged to.

I began processing everything he had just told me, but something nagged at me.

"If every Alpha was the same element as the previous, why was Felix water? Did I miss something?" I blurted. They looked at me confused but waited for me to elaborate. "Felix, you're not Earth," I stammered, a bit nervous about what I had just said. Kai chuckled.

"Ah yes, our Felix here took after his mother. Don't you see, Jasira, it was never meant for our packs to be separated. Felix, being your mate proves that. I knew he was special the moment he was born," he beamed a proud father. I looked at Felix, taking his hand. He certainly was special. I thought, feeling blessed once again for being given such a fantastic mate.

We each began reading through the books, determined to find some kind of answer. Hours passed, and the burning ache from my heat increased. I pushed it aside, not wanting to be distracted. It worked for a while, us pointing out small details within the book that continuously led us back to one problematic pack. The pack was called Black Water, but no one seemed to recognize the name, even though Kai said it seemed familiar. As my frustration grew, so did the pain.

Beads of sweat trickled down my face as I tried again to ignore what my body needed. Felix looked at me, sniffing the air.

"Jasira," he warned. My arousal was heavy in the air, clearly giving away my predicament.

"I am fine," I grunted, trying to play it off.

"You are not," he growled, his eyes glowing. Kai got up slowly, backing away from the table and taking the books with him. Felix let out a menacing growl at his father.

"I am leaving. Your mate is safe. I have no interest," he declared, backing towards the exit. I couldn't help the whimper that escaped out of my mouth, drawing Felix's attention back to me.

"Naughty mate," he tsked disapprovingly. He stood behind me, bending me over the table. He lifted my skirt, revealing my panties. His hand gently caressed my bottom. I whined, begging him to touch me. His hand landed against my ass with a hard slap making me yelp in surprise before he began rubbing the cheek again. He spanked me again, repeating what he previously had done.

"Felix," I protested, even though I was enjoying it. He grabbed my hair, pulling me up to his chest.

"You will tell me the minute you feel the heat coming on next time, little wolf, or I will have to punish you again. You may be protesting but your body tells me you love it," he hissed reaching between my legs feeling my slickness. He pushed me back down, so I was bent over the table again. He ripped my panties, making me gasp, then proceeded to spread my legs. He positioned himself, slamming into me. We quickly became lost in one another, not leaving the library until we both were fully sated.

After our Library experience, we made our way to the dining hall. We were both starving at this point. I was exhausted, but my hunger wouldn't be ignored. Once our food was ready, I quickly ate. My eyelids grew heavy as the food set in.

"What a tired little mate," Felix crooned. He scooped me up, carrying me towards the bedroom. My eyes grew heavier as we made our way. I drifted to sleep before we could even reach the room.

I woke slightly as he laid me in the bed, mumbling my objections, not wanting him to leave me. He quickly climbed into the bed, wrapping his arms around me, and pulling me against him. His scent wrapped around me, lulling me back to sleep.

***

We both woke up startled by none other than Liana jumping on our bed. Felix growled about being woken up while all I could do was laugh at her shenanigans.

"Liana, you have no boundaries. You do realize I am your Alpha?" Felix grumbled. Liana just shrugged in response.

"Today is the day we go pick out your dress. Now get up. Your Aunt and V are waiting for us," She squealed excitedly. I quickly removed myself from the grumpy Alpha, who was even more outraged that I had to get up.

"I don't know if it's a good idea if you go, what if your heat happens. I don't want other unmated males around you." Felix protested.

"I have arranged for Gina to go with us as added security," Liana quickly jumped in. I reached back in bed, caressing Felix's cheek.

"I promise to mind link you if I feel anything at all. This is important for our big day." I assured, giving my best puppy dog eyes. He growled, nipping at my hand, making me giggle.

"Fine but you take Declan as well, Gina will want to be a part of the dress picking. Declan won't be distracted," He conceded. I nodded excitedly, turning to Liana, who grabbed my hands, jumping up and down, both of us now squealing. This earned me a smile from Felix.

We all made our way across town to the dress shop, talking about all the different styles of dresses. I had never pictured myself getting married. That dream had seemed so far. Now that it was happening, I didn't know the first thing about what I wanted for a gown. All the ladies had comforted my fears that we would find the perfect one. As we walked into the boutique, I paused in wonder. It was beautiful, almost like a wedding itself inside. Flowers were everywhere, and decorative chandeliers lit the expansive showroom.

I was quickly pushed forward as a thin blonde woman approached me. She was beautiful, but a glint in her eyes made me think she could be cruel. I learned long ago not to judge someone before knowing them. I ignored the gut feeling about her not willing to jump to any conclusions.

"This must be our future Queen," she announced. I wasn't sure how to feel about the way she greeted us, but I probably was imagining things. My nerves were putting me on edge. That was probably it. Gina growled towards her.

"You will show respect to Queen Jasira," she said harshly.

"It's okay, Gina, just let it go," I said through our mind link. The woman smirked.

"I apologize, Queen Jasira," she emphasized the Queen part, "Come right this way."

I didn't like this woman's attitude, but maybe she was just coming off wrong without realizing it. We all followed her into a large private dress area. There was a stage surrounded by mirrors for the bride to walk out to display her gown. Butterflies grew in my tummy, along with excitement.

"Why don't you have a seat? I will be right back. I will get my assistant." She waved nonchalantly towards the chairs. Once she disappeared, I sat quietly.

"You are not going to continue to let her treat you that way, are you?" Declan asked, surprising me.

"I am not sure what you mean," I murmured, not looking at him. He grunted his displeasure, Liana was quickly by his side giving him a look. Gina approached me, crouching in front of me.

"You know what he means." She lifted my chin. I sighed, unwilling to confess, so I waved her off instead.

"It's fine, let's just enjoy ourselves," I said brightly, trying to change the mood. I turned toward my Aunt Amelia, "Thank you for coming. I feel like we haven't had much time to get to know each other," I said, smiling warmly at her.

"Yes, of course, I wouldn't miss it, darling," she replied shortly, seeming distracted. I could understand that with all the ceremony planning, she probably had a lot on her mind.

The blonde returned with a brunette woman whose eyes were glued to the ground. She looked sweet but shy.

"Mindy will show you to your dressing room while I gather information on what dress we are looking for." I followed Mindy back. She was reticent the whole way.

"Here we are, my Queen," she whispered, opening a large dressing room.

"Thank you, Mindy," I offered, walking into the room. She stood at the entrance, still looking at the ground, nervously fidgeting with her fingers. "Mindy, you don't have to keep looking down," I implored, hoping I could coax her from her shell. She quickly looked up, then retreated to her previous stance. I approached her gently, bringing her chin up so our eyes met. I tried to send comfort and kindness through my aura, hoping it would help ease her. "You have nothing to fear from me," I assured. I stepped back, offering her a smile, which she returned.

"Now tell me, what do you think I would look good in for a gown?" I inquired, still using a gentle tone. Mindy blushed.

"You're really asking me." I nodded, excited to hear her thoughts. Mindy had a fantastic aura, and I was excited to get to know her.

"Well, why don't we see what Nadia brings in then? If you're not happy, I have one in mind," She insisted. I agreed only because I didn't want to push her. She grabbed the undergarments I would need and helped me put them on so that when Nadia came in, we would be ready.

Nadia came in a moment later, bringing several gowns.

"Get these on her, girl. I don't have all day," she snapped. Mindy quickly compiled her eyes cast down again. Okay, now I really do not like this woman. Mindy had done nothing wrong, but she treated her like trash. Mindy touched my shoulder, pulling me from my thoughts. I stepped into an A-Line gown. It was very plain, and the fabric was heavy. I looked in the mirror as Mindy zipped the back, her dislike for the dress evident. I looked at Nadia. She stood there smiling, but there was no kindness.

"This gown is an A-Line made with taffeta. It is a clean, modern gown. I think it looks stunning, don't you think Mindy?" She eyed her as she asked the question.

"Yes, Ma'am," Mindy responded, eyes not meeting mine.

"Come now, let's show your friends," Nadia insisted. I walked out knowing already that this gown was not for me. Everyone was anxiously waiting, but their faces fell, seeing my reaction to the dress.

"What is this?" Valentina quickly pipped up. Nadia looked insulted almost.

"Well, it is one of our finest gowns. Don't you like it?" She defended.

"Why don't I try on another? I don't think this is the one," I stated.

"Fine, let's go." She sighed, exasperated. Once back in the dressing room, I put on three more gowns. Each one was clearly not picked with my curvy body in mind. They were all very bland as well. It's not that I wanted to be covered in sparkles, but something was missing. The girls quickly sensed my distress. There was one more to try on. Nadia continued her attitude throughout, but I was unsure why. I tried the last one on, nearly in tears. Mindy wanted to comfort me, but she clearly feared Nadia's wrath.

I walked back out to the showroom feeling defeated. I didn't want to look at everyone's expressions, so I kept my eyes down as I approached the stage. Until I smelled a tantalizing scent, I would recognize anywhere. My mate stood behind all my girls. His hands balled into fists, shaking with anger.

"What is the meaning of this?" he boomed, now drawing Nadia's attention.

"Alpha," she stuttered out. 'I didn't know you would be joining us, please have a seat. Would you like any refreshments?" She said, trying to sound sweet.

"What I would like is for my mate and your Queen to find the perfect gown." He growled.

"Of course, we have tried several on. She just can't seem to decide." she quickly said. I felt love pour through our bond.

"What is going on here, my love?" He asked through the mind link. I hesitated, not wanting to make a fuss. "Do not hide things from me, little wolf," he warned through the bond.

I told him how Nadia had been acting, how I thought she was giving me awful dresses on purpose. His anger was burning through our bond, but not at me. He was infuriated with Nadia.

"Mindy said she thought she might know the perfect gown, but I am discouraged now," I confessed.

"Go tell Mindy to get that gown, try it on. If you don't like it, then we will leave. If you want to show the ladies, I will step outside, so I don't ruin the surprise," Felix demanded. I turned to Mindy, smiling.

"Mindy, you're up," I said. She smiled at me but quickly cast her eyes down when Nadia glared daggers at her.

"What do you mean Mindy is up?" She shouted. Declan came in at that moment, escorting Nadia out. I followed Mindy back to the dressing room. She quickly took off, asking me to wait there. I was excited but anxious to see what she would come back with. She brought in a dress bag, clearly nervous to show me.

"I hope you like this. I made it myself," she explained shyly.

She unzipped the bag, revealing the most beautiful gown I had ever seen. I couldn't help the gasp that escaped my mouth. She made quick work of pulling it out of the bag. Both of us were eager for me to put it on. I stood in the mirror, my eyes welling with tears.

"I didn't know who I was making this for when I did until I saw you" she whispered. I choked on a sob, knowing this was the one. The sleeveless gown had a sweetheart illusion neckline. The overall dress was a faint lavender, the intricate beading with the lace was white making it stand out. It hugged my curves in a trumpet style, flowing out mid-thigh into a long train. I mind linked Felix to leave because this time, when I walked out, I felt like a queen.

Everyone gasped as I approached the stage. I couldn't stop smiling as I spun around. Mindy rushed over, arranging the bottom of the gown so everyone could get a full view.

"You look breathtaking," Valentina gushed.

"Oh, my goddess, this is the one," Liana Squealed excitedly. Everyone fussed over the dress and how I looked in it. I felt so beautiful I couldn't help but smile. I turned my attention to Mindy, feeling incredibly blessed by the goddess for bringing her into my life.

"Mindy, would you like a job as my personal stylist." I asked. Mindy's mouth opened, then shut, then opened again, words failing her. "I will take that as a yes. "I chuckled.

I returned to the dressing room, changing back into my regular clothes. Mindy took the dress from me, carefully placing it back in the dress bag. I asked her to follow me, wanting to take her to the packhouse. I feared the wretched woman might do something if I left her with Nadia. The other ladies had already left in a hurry. Apparently, they had several things to do before the ceremony tomorrow. Felix waited patiently outside the boutique. He pulled me into his arms, immediately breathing me in.

"I heard you found the dress," he whispered in a low voice. A shiver ran up my spine.

"I certainly did," I sang back my body, starting the familiar burn of the heat. I took a step back briefly, almost forgetting that Mindy was waiting.

I cleared my throat, the distance from my mate allowed me to calm down momentarily. Damn, if he wasn't so intoxicating. He held my gaze, a knowing look in his eyes and a wicked smile on his face.

"I have offered Mindy a job as my personal stylist. I would like her to come stay at the packhouse with us." I informed, trying to sound unaffected. Felix turned his attention to Mindy, offering her a genuine smile.

"Thank you for helping my mate find the perfect dress. Let's get you to the packhouse, I will have the staff ready accommodations for you." He proclaimed.

Mindy was still in shock. All she could do was thank us for our kindness. I could tell she was shy from the beginning, but I was determined I would bring her out of her shell. I put Naomi to the back of my mind as we headed home. I thought that having Mindy with me would eliminate any future encounters with the woman.

Once we reached home, we gave Mindy a quick tour. The staff were already setting her accommodations up. We also sent a guard to retrieve her items from her small apartment. I had spoken with her about the ball on the walk back. She had just the design for me that she had already started working on. After seeing how beautiful my wedding dress was, I completely trusted in her ability to make me something for that special event as well. I was able to talk her into coming with us. Maybe she would find her mate.

I sighed in complete bliss with Today so far. The heat chose to rear its head up again, even stronger this time, making me clench my thighs together. Felix promptly scooped me up, taking us to our room. I giggled at his eagerness, happy to have such an attentive mate. My heat was in full swing when we reached the room, making me pant. He brought us both to the shower, turning the cool water on as he stepped in fully clothed. It helped ease the fire that burned momentarily.

"Don't worry, my little mate," I have cleared our schedules. He promised in between kisses. "I plan to satisfy your heat for the rest of the day," he growled, continuing to kiss down my body. My inner wolf howled, clearly on board with his plan.

"Promises, promises," my wolf tsked at her mate's actions speak louder than words she challenged. Felix's eyes glowed, his wolf coming to the surface. He growled a warning as my wolf challenged him.

"Naughty little mate," he nipped. "Someone clearly needs to be taught a lesson," his voice deep with desire.

With that, there were no words exchanged. Just the sound of our pleasure filled the room. He kept his promise, fulfilling my every desire well into the night hours. With our bodies fully sated, we lay in each other's arms.

21

JASIRA

We eventually had to leave the bed because my stomach would not stop protesting. Felix would not just ignore my hunger, he demanded we go eat. He chuckled at me as I complained about my body ruining our cuddles. We walked hand in hand down to the kitchen. As we walked in, the staff stood bowing their heads in respect. They had put plates aside for us, for which I was grateful. A hot meal was laid in front of me moments later. I devoured every bite, sighing in contentment.

"Do you feel better?" Felix smirked.

"Yes, but I am not happy about leaving the bed still," I grumbled, trying to hide my smile. He placed a gentle kiss on my neck as he stood behind me.

"You poor thing, did you not get enough snuggle time with me?" he crooned. I turned, facing him, nuzzling into his chest. He purred, making every muscle in my body relax. I let it wrap around me as I yawned, exhaustion setting in. He scooped me up, cradling me as if I were fragile.

At that moment, I knew this man had every piece of me. I belonged to him, body, and soul. My heart was his to shatter, and my promise to never hope was gone. It scared the hell out of me, but it thrilled me as well. I felt safe in his arms for the first time in my life. I let all my emotions pour into him, my fear, my vulnerability. I could be fragile because he would make sure nothing could break me. He opened the bond as well, letting me feel his pain from the years of me being gone, his fear of losing me, his love, his strength.

By the time we reached the room, tears streamed down my cheek. He brushed them away gently, laying me in the bed, then immediately climbed in. He pulled me into his hard body, wrapping me in a protective cocoon with his arms.

"I love you, Jasira," he whispered. I turned slightly, looking at him.

"I love you too, Felix." I turned back, pressing my body against him, wiggling slightly. He kissed my head, purring for me. I sighed, enjoying this moment because we had to leave after the ceremony tomorrow. It meant the usual timing of the ceremony and reception would be much shorter, but that didn't matter. It was still going to be the most memorable day. I breathed Felix in again, letting his purr completely take hold and lull me to sleep.

I opened my eyes, the feeling of dread racking my body. There was a wall of bars in front of me. I needed to figure out where I was, yet I could not move. My chest tightened, increasing my terror. I reached for my powers, but there was a wall. My wolf wouldn't answer me either. She was in a deep sleep. I tried to steady my breath. You can still sense your wolf and powers, Jasira. This is a good sign. It means they are still there even if you can't reach them. I tried comforting myself. I called my mate, but that, too, was blocked. I knew he was alive, but that was it.

Ok, I need to stay calm. There is no way I am getting out of this if I lose my shit. I looked around, trying to take in my surroundings. My vision was fuzzy, making it hard to make out anything. I reached out with my senses. I took a deep breath in earthy, stale, damp, rust, metal, and blood filled my nose. I quieted my breathing so that I was able to hear as best as possible. I could hear mumbling, but it was far away, a heartbeat, shallow breathing, dripping of liquid. There was another person in the room with me. I turned in the direction of the person I knew who was watching me. My breath quickened as my fear spiked. A shadowed figure was sitting in the corner, purple eyes raised to meet mine. It was me, holy shit I was in bad shape.
"*Help me*" *is all the other me could croak out.*

A scream ripped out of my throat as I sat up in bed.

I fought whoever was holding me, panic still coursing through me. My wolf came forward bringing my shift, it had become second nature now only bringing slight pain. I snarled, biting at my capture, trying to escape.

"Jasira," a voice of authority boomed in my mind, making me pause. The breath whooshed out of my body as I was pinned to the ground, my mate now on top of me, concern in his face. "Baby, are you with me?" A gentler voice I now knew was his rang through the mind link. My wolf retreated, knowing I was safe. I am so sorry I sobbed as he picked me up.

"'Did I hurt you?" Another round of panic captured me.

"No, I am fine," his voice stern. "What just happened, and are you ok? Is my only concern?" He demanded.

I was still rattled by the nightmare but knew if I told him, it would just make him worry. I stuffed my fear away, telling myself it was just a bad dream.

"It was just a nightmare," I assured him, gently rubbing his arm, hoping it would soothe him. He wrapped me in his arms, rocking my body while purring. I felt safe as I nuzzled into him, relieved that he didn't press the issue.

He held me for a while, chasing the nightmare to the back of my thoughts. His warmth called to me, making my heat flare. I shifted uncomfortably in his lap, the ache quickly becoming unbearable. He lifted me so I was straddling his lap, his hardness pressed against me. His eyes filled with heat as my slickness indicated how ready I was for him.

"I guess this means we will have to start our mating ceremony a little early today," his voice deep with desire. His words increased the burning in my body, making me a whimpering mess. I rose allowing the tip to slide in, he grabbed my hips slamming me down on him. I cried out my heat making me mad with the need for him. His hands tightened around my hips as I clawed and bit at him. My wolf took control, chasing her animalistic need to mate until finally, I exploded around him, making his release follow. I pressed my head against his, my wolf was content for now.

It's a good thing, too, because that was when Declan decided to bang on the door. I untangled myself from him, making my way to the shower as he approached the door. I heard him growl as I shut the door to the bathroom.

"Did I interrupt?" Declan snickered knowingly. I chuckled as my mate snarled. I stepped into the shower, quickly washing off as Liana busted into the room. I yipped a bit in surprise, but that quickly turned into laughter.

"Today is the day," she said, jumping up and down. "You will both be officially the King and Queen of the Moon Stone Pack," she clapped happily. Excitement danced along my thoughts as the reality of today played out in my head. I would have a pack, a forever home. I had a mate that loved me. It just didn't seem real compared to what I had been through before.

I stepped out of the shower, wrapping a towel around me. Valentina stepped in at that moment, joining the bathroom party.

"It just doesn't seem real, if I am being honest," I expressed. Valentina approached me, pulling me into a hug.

"Well, it is real, and no one deserves it more," she assured. I took a deep breath, willing myself not to cry.

"Let's get ready for a wedding then," I cheered. Liana squealed in response, making Valentina laugh at her.

We made our way to the large dressing rooms by the ballroom. Aunt Amelia, Gina, Madeira, Isla, and Deema were waiting for us to arrive. They popped champagne as we entered, cheering for me. I smiled, hugging all of them, thanking each one for being here. Madeira had told me a couple of days back that she, Isla, and Deema would be returning to their home. Madeira had confirmed what we suspected with the diaries. There was dark magic involved with the slaying of my mother and father. The pack that attacked had help from some strong magic wielders. Whether they were witches or not, we do not know. Madeira had to go and find out what was going on.

So, when she hugged me, I held on a little tighter for a little longer. She has shown me so much love in the short period of time I have had with her. I was hesitant to allow her to leave. As I pulled back, she reached up, taking hold of my chin.

"Now, don't you worry, child, I am only going for a few weeks to investigate. You will be wrapped up at the Super Moon Festival for a few days and then busy when you return. You won't even know I'm gone." She insisted. I nodded even though I knew that was not the case. I didn't want her worrying about me when she was the one going after dangerous magic folk.

The real fun began once we all had champagne in our hand curtsy of Isla. We all sat getting our hair and makeup done. I had a braid like a crown with soft curls framing my face and curls falling down my back. I wanted my makeup to not look too over the top. I knew we would only have a little time after the ceremony and reception. I did not want to spend that time removing the makeup from my face. Valentina, Gina, and Liana got into their bridesmaid's dresses while Mindy helped me into my gown. We had chosen to have our wedding at noon, hoping to be on the road for the festival by four o'clock. It took a day of driving to reach the sacred ground.

"It's time," Valentina whispered as she stood behind me, looking at me in the mirror. Butterflies danced in my tummy with excitement. The bridesmaids lined up with the groomsmen, preparing to begin walking down the aisle. Our ceremony was held in the garden, where I now love to sit and explore. A large door opened, revealing a small set of stairs. Then, it was a straight walk back, bushes lining the sides until you reached an arch. Then the garden opened. A large open area was surrounded by flowers and plants, allowing plenty of seating. Right in the middle of it all was the most romantic gazebo. That's where we would say our I do's.

I waited patiently, standing back out of view. A hand gently laid on my back, making me turn slightly. Kai stood there, tears in his eyes.

"You look breathtaking, my daughter." I could feel the tears threatening to ruin my makeup.

"Stop it, Kai, you will make me ruin my makeup," I choked out. He cleared his throat, wiping his face quickly and putting on a serious one.

"I'm sorry, we can't have that," he apologized. I chuckled at him, gently wiping the dampness from my eyes with the tip of my finger.

"Thank you for walking me down the aisle. It is truly everything I ever dreamed of." I beamed, kissing him on the cheek.

"The honor is mine," he said, bowing. "Now I think we're up," he gestured to the music playing. I nodded, taking his offered arm, and allowing him to help guide me down the stairs. I couldn't help but hold my breath as Felix came into view. He looked incredible. His blue suit fit just right, displaying his muscular body. His hair was swept back slightly. I could tell he had run his hand through it several times. When his eyes met mine, that was it. He suddenly became the only one in the room, his eyes glowing a brilliant blue, capturing me in every way.

I was so grateful to Kai for keeping me steady, otherwise I would have fallen. As we reached the gazebo, Kai turned to kiss me on the cheek before facing Madeira. She was the one officiating the ceremony.

"I, Alpha Kai Dunamis of the Emerald Pack, present Alpha Jasira Selinofoto," Kai announces to the crowd. I climbed the couple of steps up to the gazebo platform to stand by Felix. He has tears in his eyes as he takes me in up close.

"You look breathtaking," Jaz, he whispers. The heat in my face began to rise. It still felt so surreal to have someone adore me in such a way.

"You look pretty hot yourself, mate," I tease quietly, drawing a soft chuckle from him. Madeira smiled at us both.

"All right, you two, let's begin," she chides playfully. "We are gathered here to begin a new pack. Typically, we are just accepting one wolf into another pack, so this is a special occasion," she bellows out to the crowd. Will all of our pack Elders please rise?" She gestures toward our guests. "As the three of you rise, you take responsibility for your packs, the four elements. I will have all three of you step forward," they do as Madeira requests, standing in front of Felix and me.

"At this moment, we pledge our allegiance and trust in the Moon Goddess. Do you accept Alpha Felix and Alpha Jasira as your King and Queen to unite the packs as one under the Moon Stone pack? Alpha Kai of the Emerald pack, do you accept?" Madeira asks.

"I do," he proclaims. Madeira reaches for his hand, making a small cut along his palm.

"As the blood drips, she takes a glass cup under the drips, catching just a little within it. Alpha Amelia of the Amber pack, do you accept?" Madeira asks.

"I do," Amelia proclaims, allowing Madeira to reach forward and slice her hand.

"Alpha Theo of the Amethyst pack, do you accept?" She finishes.

"I do," he proclaims. Madeira makes the final slice and then turns to us, smiling.

"Alpha Felix Dunamis, do you take Alpha Jasira Selinofoto as your true mate? I ask that you enter this with special care, as your souls will be tied together under the moon goddess for eternity." Felix's eyes meet mine, a smile on his face that instantly warms my heart. He reaches for my hands, holding them tightly.

"I do," he vows. Water ripples out of Felix's hands, wrapping around mine. It surprises me but in a pleasant way.

I feel my eyes water as Madeira turns to me, reciting the same question about Felix.

"I do," vowing as Felix did, tears streaming down my face. I feel a jolt running through me, gasping in shock. All four of the elements spring to life, tying themselves with Felix's water. He is also shocked, gaping down, watching them wrap our hands and arms. The crowd gasps, but when I look at Madeira, she simply smiles. Once they have thoroughly knotted together, I feel a tingling sensation begin. A purple stream of light joins the elements, making a final knot. Madeira turns to the crowd.

"The Moon Goddess has accepted this couple as one." Everyone cheers but quickly grows quiet as Madeira turns back to us. "Now for the final part," she says, winking. "Do you both promise to protect this pack with your lives, putting their needs above all others?" Madeira calls out.

"We do," Felix and I respond in unison. She holds out the cup for us both to take a sip of. Felix drinks first, and I follow, expecting it to taste horrible but knowing it has to be done. I was surprised that it tasted like each of their elements. I handed the cup back to Madeira. She raises it up.

"It is my honor to announce King Felix and Queen Jasira of the Moon Stone pack." A wave of energy blasts through the crowd, touching each pack member. I can feel them all, not like I feel Felix, but they are a part of me now. Everyone stands clapping and cheering. Madeira steps to the side, but not before kissing my cheek, telling me how proud she is. Felix pulls me, wrapping his arms around me. He dips me and then claims my mouth, leaving me breathless. He brings me back up, releasing me from the kiss but holding me steady so that I don't fall.

I laugh, allowing myself to feel this joy, this moment. I never thought this would happen to me. That I could mean anything to anyone. I pushed away the negative memories that tried to creep in. Looking into my mate's eyes, he wrapped his arm with mine, guiding me back into the ballroom where our reception would occur.

We entered the quiet space, going across the room back to the dressing areas. My heart chose that moment to strike.

"Felix," I whimpered, the ache unbearable, making me double over. He growled, dragging me into the dressing room and locking the door behind us.

"Don't worry, my queen, I will stop the pain." He was a man of his word because make the pain stop, he did.

After he fulfilled his promise several times, we finally made our way to the reception. I would be lying if I said I didn't consider not attending the reception. My heat was exhausting, but I also knew I would regret not going when I looked back on this day. Plus, Felix said it would be rude for us not to show up.

I put my dress back on with Felix's help, then checked my makeup, touching it up slightly. I had to mind link Valentina and Liana to provide entertainment for our guests. Most would just assume we were two love birds unable to keep our hands off one another, and while they were not wrong, I still felt terrible for not showing up when we were supposed to. As Felix and I were announced, nobody seemed to notice or care that we had been late. Everyone was so excited to see us. The ceremony was quick, so there was still time to enjoy the party, even with our excursion.

I felt like I was in a dream as I looked at the beautiful room, we were in. The ladies had done such a fantastic job with decorating. Flowers, silk, and twinkling lights made the room magical. I could feel the tears creeping in. Ugh, get it together, Jasira. Your heat is causing you to be emotional, I chastised myself. I caught Felix looking at me, a sweet smile on his face.

"What are you looking at?" I teased, poking at his chest. He laughed.

"Only the most incredible mate a man could dream of." His tone was warm and soft as he spoke.

"Stop that before you make me mess up my makeup," I said, trying to sound stern. Felix got up from his seat and walked behind me. He proceeded to nuzzle me, making me giggle.

"No chance of that happening," Felix murmured into my hair. Before I could respond, he grabbed my hand, pulling me up from my chair, a small gasp escaping my lips in surprise. He then began pulling me out to the dance floor. Where the music had just changed to something soft and slow. He spun me around before bringing me back to his chest, wrapping his strong arms around me. At this point, I couldn't stop giggling. He smiled down at me,

"I love that sound," he rumbled.

We danced through the next couple of slow songs. Once the music picked up, I waved out Valentina, Liana, and Gina. They, of course, had to drag out Kai, Declan, and Gage. Soon, everyone was on the floor dancing and singing to the music. By the time we were done, I was exhausted. We ate, danced, and had our cake. It was time to make the final announcement about the Super Moon Festival before we had to get moving. We stood at the top of the stairs so everyone could see us. Felix started by thanking everyone for attending and apologizing that we had to cut the party short.

"We will be leaving in just shy of an hour. Everyone that would like to attend, please have everything ready to be loaded on the caravan within thirty minutes." I announced, wrapping everything up. We had already packed, so we had put our luggage in the SUV before the ceremony. I was grateful for the extra time to shower and change. I needed to wash this hair, it was stiff and filled with pins. Not traveling hair, for sure. As everyone dispersed, Felix scooped me into his arms.

"My lady off to the shower with you," he jested. I laughed at his antics.

"I can walk, you know," I teased, knowing full well he was not letting that happen.

"Yes, you keep saying that, but we are on schedule. It will be faster if I just carry you," he retorted.

"Are you calling me slow? How dare you?" I accused. He smiled a cocky smile.

"Just slower than me," he poked. I crossed my arms, feigning anger, but I couldn't help peeking at him. Which made it so I couldn't stop smiling.

Once we reached the room, he gently deposited me on the bed, situating himself between my legs. He leaned down, kissing me thoroughly, stealing my breath. I could feel my heat kicking in. Come on, it hasn't even been that long. Then again, on a regular basis, I wanted to jump my mate. I mean, just look at him, pure perfection. Felix coughed, dragging me from my naughty thoughts.

"Good, you're back with me," he chortled.

"Sorry," I blushed.

"Come, my little mate, let me help you in the shower" he commanded, pulling me to the bathroom.

Just him mentioning helping me in the shower sent shivers down my spine. I became slick between my legs as my core throbbed. He turned the shower on quickly, making the room steamy. He turned me to face the mirror, kissing my neck as he pushed me up against the counter. He slowly unbuttoned my dress, kissing down my spine as he went. He slid the dress down my legs, gesturing for me to step out of it. I obeyed to, his approval. He stood up behind me, pressing his hardness against my now bare ass. Reaching around the front of me, he slid his fingers into my slickness, rubbing my swollen bud. I threw my head back moaning in pleasure, I was already so close. How does he do this? I thought to myself. He continued his assault until I was seeing stars at the strength of my release. He pulled away from me, taking his fingers and sucking my juices off him.

"You taste exquisite, Jasira," he hummed.

"Now, in the shower," he demanded. I did what I was told, still in a fog from the last orgasm. The hot water felt amazing. I sighed with pleasure. Felix stepped into the large walk-in shower as well. He made quick work of pulling my hair down. Personally, I don't know how Felix managed to find every pin. He shampooed my hair twice, massaging my scalp as he worked diligently. I was in heaven, my entire body relaxed against him. After rinsing the conditioner out, he turned me to face him. His eyes were lit with desire, he pushed me against the wall crushing his mouth on mine.

His tongue dove in, demanding me to open and receive him. I parted my lips, loving the fierceness of his kiss and how he tasted. He grabbed both my legs, pulling them up around his waist and slamming into me. He showed no mercy, each thrust harder and deeper than the last. I clawed at him, loving every second, needing something more. He lowered his head to my mark, biting into it once more. I cried out as I exploded around him. I could feel his magic, his lifeline within me now we were connected. This did not stop him, though he continued giving me everything. I was a whimpering mess, begging him not to stop feeling like I was going to peak again. I licked his neck, needing his taste in my mouth. I need to complete our mating ceremony officially. I sank my teeth into him, his sweet taste pouring into my mouth. At that moment, I had a flash of our bond, the true love he felt for me. I began to cry as we both found our release.

He pulled me into his arms, allowing me to sob into his chest. Purring to soothe me.

"That was amazing, I am sorry I'm such a mess" I sniffled.

"There is no need to apologize, Jasira," he comforted. "I felt it to my love. That was… well, I don't know how to describe it because it was out of this world," he exclaimed. I suddenly realized how long we must have been.

"Oh, my goddess, Felix, we are going to be late," I panicked.

"We are the King and Queen, plus we just had our mating ceremony. They won't expect us to be right on time." He explained, easing the rising panic.

We quickly finished cleaning up, my mind now entirely focused on the journey ahead. I raced to get dressed, Felix trying to calm me the whole time. I chose a dress with flats that would be comfortable. I gave myself a once over, happy with my appearance. I stopped for a moment to take in myself. Not because I was conceited but because so much had changed. I used to look in the mirror and see a girl who was too skinny for her curvy body, pale skin with sunken eyes from being tired, tangly hair that most often was tied back because there was nothing I could do. Now my skin glowed, I had put on weight, making my curves fill out nicely, and my hair was shiny, the natural waves smooth because I was able to care for it. I was in awe.

Felix came up behind me at that moment, wrapping his hands around my waist. He breathed me in, kissing the top of my head.

"You are so beautiful," he marveled. I closed my eyes, letting his scent wrap around me, soothing my soul. I basked in this moment of peace but quickly sighed.

"Let's go on a road trip," I stated. He nodded, taking my hand in his as we walked down to the transports.

When we arrived, everyone was already seated on the bus. There were more pack members than I had expected that would be coming with us. This was great news, I was so excited hoping these wolves would find their mates. Dr Rebecca rushed up to us with a big smile on her face.

"We are ready to go," she chirped excitedly.

"That is wonderful, Dr. Rebecca, but I didn't know you would be coming with us," I asked, surprised.

"Well, with you being newly shifted and your surprise heat, Felix thought it would be wise I attend. Plus, I have no mate, so I figured, why not?" She shrugged. I looked at Felix. He simply raised his eyebrow, daring me to say something. I turned away, rolling my eyes.

"I saw that, my naughty mate. "Don't think I won't remember that later," he growled through our mind link. Shivers ran down my spine in anticipation. I hoped he did remember.

Valentina, Evander, Gina, and Gage piled in the SUV with us. I hadn't had much time to chat with V about Evander, but I knew she was still trying to fight against the bond. Evander, however, was patient and would not just let Valentina get away. I knew he was the perfect fit for her just for that reason, so I was secretly cheering him on. Liana and Declan stayed with the rest of the pack, ensuring everything ran smoothly in our absence. It made it slightly easier to relax, knowing our people would be safe. Our people, wow, Jasira, we have a pack.

"You are a literal queen." My wolf rolled her eyes at me, clearly not impressed with my thoughts. I looked out the window back at my home as we pulled away. Watching it fade out of view, I was thankful we would only be gone for four or five days.

22

FELIX

I watched Jasira as she stared out the window. I could feel the ache of us leaving through the mate bond. I place my hand on her thigh, sending waves of comfort through the bond. I knew this was hard on her, she finally had found a place she could call home and we were leaving. Although the leaving part was her idea, she certainly was a stubborn she wolf. Once she had her mind set, nothing would change it. This was one of the many qualities I loved about her.

We drove for about two hours before we reached the border of our protected lands. Reaching the main road did allow for a smoother ride, and as I looked at my mate, I noticed her eyelids were heavy. I pulled her to my lap, nuzzling her,

"Sleep, my love, you are clearly exhausted," I whispered. She tried to protest unsurprisingly, so I began purring, knowing that she wouldn't be able to resist it.

"You're evil," she grumbled through a yawn. I chuckled at her, loving how spirited she was. Her body betrayed as her breathing became softer as she drifted to sleep.

I held her close, mainly to comfort myself. My nerves were shot thinking about going to the festival. There were too many pieces I could not control. I knew it was on sacred ground, so no one would dare to attack, there at least. But what about after I had lost her once. I had known then that she was something more to me, even at the young age of six. My wolf had started to appear around then. My wolf and I were both infatuated with her. I tried to tell my father about the bond I felt, not fully understanding what it meant then. He wouldn't budge about sending her to Trenton. He had said it was the Goddess's decision.

My guilt for letting her go still consumed me, but I would be damned if I let her go again. On top of that, we may see Trenton or Liam. The thought made my blood boil, and rage began to consume me. Jasira shifted in my lap, letting out a little whimper. I took a deep breath, relaxing, knowing she probably felt my anger through the mate bond. I looked up, feeling eyes on me. Valentina was staring at me like she was trying to read my thoughts.

"I hope all that anger is directed towards Alpha Trenton and Liam." I opened my mouth in shock. How did she know that? She smiled.

"Felix I can see aura's, and yours is a gray mixed with a dull red right now." Valentina explained.

"Does it look like that all the time?" I asked, concerned I was holding too much anger in.

"No, the aura I saw was just a powerful flash based on emotion." She explained simply. I nodded, comforted by her explanation.

"I am scared and angry, too," she said. I was surprised by how openly she was sharing. "Jasira is powerful, but she is only one wolf. She hasn't had the chance to hone all her powers yet. But there will be others there ready to hurt her." She continued. I tensed, knowing the truth of her words. Seeing her lying in my lap, she looked so fragile. My fear rose, but so did my determination. I would be damned if someone took her from me again.

The car was silent for a long time after that. The others drifted off to sleep, leaving me with my thoughts. I smiled, thinking about how Valentina had tried to lay away from Evander, but the minute her body was relaxed with sleep, she had cuddled up to him. Her stubbornness reminded me of Jasira, which is probably why they were so close. My eyes grew heavy as I listened to Jasira's soft breathing. I breathed her in as I held her tightly in my arms. I let sleep take me, knowing I would need to be fully alert to protect my mate.

23

JASIRA

Warmth cocooned my body as I snuggled into my mate's embrace. Everyone was still sleeping, including Felix. I couldn't help but stare at him. He was mine. His face was still beautiful, even with the worry that was clearly displayed on it. Even in his sleep he worried, I sighed wishing I could wipe away his fears. I quietly lay there, not wanting to wake him up. He needed his rest. I snuggled back in, letting sleep take me once more. This time, my nightmare found me once again.

I stood in the same cell once again, the fear that gripped me before still trying to consume my every thought. Not this time, I thought to myself, this is just a nightmare. Breathing deeply, I tried to calm myself, letting this dream world come to me. There had to be a reason I kept being pulled here. I centered myself as madeira had taught me, focusing on my senses alone. I turned to face the corner that the other me had sat in before.

"I know you're there. Tell me why you keep bringing me here?" I demanded. A small whimper came from the darkness as the other me stood, walking towards me. I could see more clearly this time, so I quickly tried to take in the surroundings. "Please speak to me. Tell me where we are. What is going on?" I pleaded.

"You are in danger, remember to leave a trail. Don't panic, and don't worry about your magic. Leave a trail. Your life depends on it." Her voice was weak and raspy.

"Can I stop this?" I asked. *If this was a vision of the future, telling me how to change things, then I must be able to.* She shook her head repeatedly.

"The one before me tried to say that the result was his death. Don't tell anyone, leave a trail and he will come." Her voice was filled with warning and fear. *"Go there coming,"* she whispered.

I jolted upright, my heart pounding out of my chest. I tried to catch my breath but couldn't. I was still in Felix's arms, but he was very much awake now. I needed air like now, as if sensing as much Felix shouted for the driver to stop the car. The car came to an abrupt halt, but Felix held me tightly. He opened the door and carefully held me as he climbed out of the vehicle. He sat me on the ground, letting me feel the earth beneath me. I pulled my knees to my chest, trying to gather my thoughts. I allowed the earth to ground me, the wind blew, and I allowed it to ease my fear. Felix reached up, taking my face into his hands. I felt the power of his water element, making me calm and cool. I sighed, looking into his eyes.

"How did you know that's what I needed?" I smiled already, feeling better.

"Maybe because I know my mate," he replied, smiling back at me. Another nightmare, he questioned.

"Yes," I responded quickly, thinking about the warning she had given me. I couldn't tell him, I would rather end up dead than risk him. "I'm okay now, really. Let's keep going," I insisted. I knew I couldn't tell him, but I also was horrible at hiding things from him. He raised an eyebrow, giving me a suspicious look as if he wanted to say something. I did the only thing I knew that would distract him. I grabbed his face, pulling his lips to mine, claiming his mouth. He hesitated for a moment before deepening the kiss. We were both breathless when I pulled away.

"We will talk about this later," he demanded, standing up and holding out his hand. I reached for it, letting him pull me up. I winked at him as I climbed into the car again. He shook his head clearly, not happy with my diversion techniques. He slid in beside me, closing the door so we could continue. Valentina looked at both of us, unsure of what had just happened.

"Everything okay?" She asked, her voice still soft from sleep.

"Just a nightmare. I am fine now," I assured her. She nodded clearly, understanding that I was not open to talking about it. V always could read me, even when we were kids together. She would allow me time to process the nightmares and things that happened to me. She would be there every second she could, soothing me, waiting for me to be ready to talk. I did need time to think this through. No matter what I saw, I knew I would never spill a word. My mate would try to protect me with his life. That was not happening. I looked at Felix. He was staring at me intently, watching my every move. I reached out, caressing his cheek and offering him a reassuring smile. He kissed my palm, taking my hand in his.

We continued to ride in silence, which gave me time to think. My mind was all over the place, trying to remember the surroundings of where I had been. I wasn't even sure when this would happen. All I knew was that I needed to figure out something before it did. I needed to take a break, thinking about this was driving me crazy.

"Is anyone else starving? "I blurted out. Everyone chuckled before agreeing with me.

"We should reach Silveroake City in the next 45 minutes. There will be something that can accommodate all of us." Felix chimed in.

I had heard of Silveroake before, it was a large city where humans and nonhumans coexisted. I had thought maybe I would live there someday since I did not have my wolf. That, however, was not the case now, but I was still excited at the possibility of seeing it. I watched out the window intently as the skyscrapers came into view. The morning sun gleamed off them as it rose. I couldn't believe we had already been driving for Fourteen hours. No wonder my stomach wouldn't shut up.

We pulled into a breakfast diner we had been riding for so long and were eager to stretch our legs and eat. I looked around at all the pack members exiting the bus. There were so many of us, it was wonderful to see but sad at the same time. They were here to find their mate, something they had been deprived of because of fear. There were so many familiar faces that I hoped the Goddess would help our people.

One of the faces among the pack made me pause. Nadia was within the group. I guess even mean bitches deserve a mate, maybe it would make her more likable. Mates did bring out the best in each other. I brushed it off, putting her in the back of my mind. I was not letting the likes of her spoil our trip.

The diner was quite still, which was perfect since there were so many of us. Felix gently placed his hand on my lower back, guiding me to our booth. Valentina, Evander, Gina, and Gage joined us. I looked out the window, admiring the world around me.

I watched in awe as we drove past buildings of all shapes and sizes. The city had just started to wake up, which meant we missed the morning traffic. As we left the city limits to go to a diner Felix was familiar with, I couldn't help looking back. I had never been allowed to leave the Cross River Pack lands, but seeing the city made my curious soul want to explore. I had heard of the town I had dreamed of going. To be accepted, to be where no one would judge who you were.

"One day, I would love to come back and actually explore the city," I whispered, leaning into Felix. He kissed my head.

"I would be happy to show you around," he agreed, staring at me.

"What? Why are you looking at me that way?" I asked.

"You are so beautiful, I just can't believe you are all mine" he reached out taking my hand in his. I felt the heat rise to my face. I was still not used to receiving compliments. The waitress approached our table at that moment. She did a once over Felix, practically drooling.

"Hi there, handsome, my name is Sam. What can I get for you?" She batted her eyelashes at him, clearly not caring about my presence.

"Are you just going to let her talk to our mate like that?" My wolf shouted.

I rolled my eyes, "we can't fight every female. Have you seen our mate? He was definitely drool worthy." I countered back at her. Felix didn't seem to notice the woman was flirting with him...

"Jaz, you go first," Felix turned to me. I smiled up at the waitress. Ha ha, take that. She never took her eyes off Felix as I ordered, making my anger bubble up again. She moved on to Evander, making eyes at him.

"Wow, I really hit the Jackpot today. I have never seen so many attractive males at once." She giggled. Valentina let out a low growl, and the waitress gulped slightly. I tried my best to stifle a snicker.

All this talk about not wanting a mate, yet here V was, growling at our waitress. I was going to tease her later. The waitress finished the orders, hurrying off. I relaxed slightly now that she was gone. I nudged Felix gently.

"I need to use the restroom," I said. He moved, so I was able to stand up.

"Me too," Valentina chimed in. Gage slid out from the end as well. Valentina and I made our way to the other side of the diner. I listened as we walked by our pack, wanting to ensure everyone was happy. Even though many of them were groggy, there was a buzz of excitement. I smiled as we reached the ladies room. Valentina chose the stall next to me.

"Can you believe the nerve of that waitress?" she huffed. "I mean it is one thing to admire and is another to hit on them with us sitting right there." I could hear the anger in her voice. She felt the same way I did. Which could only mean that she did have feelings for Evander.

"I can't believe you", I teased. She sighed as we both met at the sink.

"I tried to fight my feelings, I am your protector. I only should focus on you, but I can't fight this." I stepped back a moment, shocked. Was I the reason she had been fighting this?

"I would never ask you to fight your feelings for your true mate V. You are my sister, you deserve happiness just as much as I do." She had been looking down, not willing to make eye contact. "Valentina, look at me," I commanded with my Alpha authority. I could see her struggle against the command for a moment before her eyes met mine.

"We are always stronger with our true mate. The same goes for you. You will not shut your feelings away to protect me." I released some of my alpha power so she couldn't fight it. She opened her mouth to protest but closed it back, pulling me into a hug.

"Thank you, Jasira," I smiled, knowing she needed this from me.

"Alright, let's go back before they send a search party." I pushed open the restroom door, rounding the corner.

I looked across the diner, my blood immediately boiling, stopping dead in my tracks. Valentina bumped into me.

"Jaz, why did you?" Her words stopped as she looked at the table, a low growl coming from her chest. The waitress was over there with our men. She was leaning over, poking out her breasts, laughing. She gently touched Felix's arm. My wolf snarled. No one put their hands on our mate. I stalked across the diner, Valentina in tow, her anger radiating off as much as my own. I released my aura, allowing the waitress to feel it. I would tear this woman to pieces for touching what was mine. Felix was by my side instantly, wrapping his arms around me. I shook with anger.

"Mine," I growled. The waitress cowered, backing away slowly as Felix held me in place. "You have to calm down, baby," he soothed, not letting me go. I nuzzled into his chest, breathing him in. My anger cleared, and I looked over to Valentina. Evander had her in his arms, soothing her wolf as well.

"Come on, let's eat," Felix gestured towards the table filled with food. My stomach growled in response, reminding me of how hungry I was. I sat with my mouth watering. I dug in immediately. Gina excused herself from the table, but I was too hungry to find out why. She returned several minutes later, eating her meal as well.

We gathered the pack, getting everyone back on the bus. We all felt better now that we had stretched our legs and ate. It was Eight in the morning, the day's warmth already starting. I climbed into my seat next to Felix, there was eight more hours to go before we reached Gaea. A rush of excitement coursed through me, I had heard about Gaea while listening to several pack members. They had whispered of its beauty, how you could feel the magic coursing through you. It was a sacred ground, protected by the Goddess herself. Fighting was strictly banned, meaning I was at least safe while on the grounds.

It also meant my people would be safe, making it the perfect place for the Elemental wolves to come out of hiding. The event was three days long, the length of time the Supermoon would stay in the sky. I was eager to learn more about the different events that took place. I knew mainly about the dance.

I reached over, grabbing Felix's hand as a shiver ran through me. My dream kept creeping up on me, an overwhelming feeling of helplessness settling in the pit of my stomach. Having Felix close was the only reason I wasn't losing my shit. He kept me steady, his warmth washing over me. I sighed heavily.

"What is on your mind, my little mate?" Felix was now staring at me, searching my face.

"Oh, well, I am just nervous," I couldn't help but stumble over my words. I was horrible at lying.

"Get it together," my wolf growled. "We must protect him." He cocked his eyebrow at me, why could this man see through me. Ugh, it was so frustrating.

"Nervous, Jaz, really?" he shook his head, chuckling. He didn't believe a word.

"Yes, nervous," I said haughtily, "I don't know what to expect for the events at the Supermoon Festival, and it's a bit overwhelming." His gaze never left me, but he decided not to push.

"I am sorry I didn't realize you didn't know what the three days entailed." He ran his hands through his hair, a flash of guilt passed his expression briefly. I wasn't trying to make him feel guilty either, damn it.

"It's okay. I should have just asked, but I would love to hear about it now," I reassured him.

"Well, when we arrive late this afternoon, there will be a brief meet and greet with all the Alpha's. Tonight is the Moon Run. Each pack shifts, and then we all run together in the forest. Many will meet their fated mate. Their wolves will lead them to one another. Already mated wolves can participate as well. Once everyone finds each other, they mate under the Supermoon," he explained.

"I like the sounds of that," I wagged my eyebrows at him, drawing a laugh from him. His face changed right after darkening with hunger.

"It certainly will be. I can't wait to chase you down and take you," he growled. A shiver ran down my spine in anticipation. Tonight, would be fun.

"The second night is the actual ball, and the third night the feast," He finished explaining. I processed everything he just told me.

"Wow, is it as incredible as it sounds?" Felix shrugged.

"I have no idea. The whole Festival is supposed to focus on our relationship with the Moon Goddess. I imagine its powerful, but I have never been." He looked at my confused expression.

"Why?" I whispered.

"First of all, I have always known who my mate was." He gently took my chin in his hand, his eyes filled with love. "Secondly, we have all been in hiding. I have only seen the cities because of business and trying to find you."

The last part of his statement raised more questions.

"Find me? What do you mean?" He shook his head again, trying to chase a bad memory away.

"Yes, Jasira, I told you I would find you. I looked everywhere, even though the protectors told me this was the wish of the Goddess. Whether it's your mother or not, I still have not forgiven her. I tried everything, I was in a dark place willing to do whatever it took." my chest constricted with the pain he had gone through. I didn't realize I was holding my breath until it whooshed out of me. He really had loved me all this time. The boy of my dreams had always been mine.

My heart felt so full as I gazed into his blue eyes. His thumb brushed a tear from my cheek. I hadn't realized I was crying, but now I could feel my cheeks dampened by the tears of joy.

"Please don't cry. It kills me," he crooned. Breathing deeply, I gathered myself and wiped my face.

"I love you, Felix," I whispered, resting my forehead on his.

"I love you too, Jasira."

We were only thirty minutes away when I felt the shift of energy. We had been off the main road for two hours, and now we were surrounded by a heavily wooded area. The rest of the trip was lovely. We all had the chance to talk. Joking around like this was just a regular everyday trip. Now everyone was silent, they could feel it too. My skin buzzed with energy, making my soul feel electrified. My wolf could feel it as well.

I felt different the closer we became. My powers shifted inside me, the strongest being the one I now knew as ether. Madeira had told me that this power was thought to be lost except, of course, with some gods and goddesses.

"Shit, Jasira, are you okay?" Gage asked. Everyone was staring at me.

"Umm...I feel a little weird, to be honest, but I am fine. Why are you all staring at me?"

"Well, you're kind of glowing," Valentina chimed in.

"What?" I squealed. Gina pulled a small mirror from her bag and handed it to me. Purple glowing tendrils wrapped around my skin, I was baffled.

"It's okay, baby," Felix soothed. "This place is full of magic, I feel it too. My element is pressing to the surface the closer we get." I took a deep breath, calming myself. I felt better knowing that he had the same feeling. Well, there was definitely not going to be any hiding me. I wasn't going to just display that I had magic right away in fear of the response from other wolves. *Mom, I hope you know what you're doing here*, I thought, sending a silent prayer to the moon goddess herself.

When the vehicle stopped, I darted out of the SUV. I was trembling at this point, the energy racking my body. I began to run, I had no idea where, but I had to. I heard shouting behind me, but it was muffled by the buzzing in my ears. I was a bomb about to explode, and I would be damned if I hurt anyone. My clothes felt constricting, my body burning up inside. I was wearing a summer dress, so I quickly ripped it over my head, tossing it as I pressed forward. I had no idea where I was going, so I allowed my instincts to take over. I heard the heavy splashing of water before I saw it. All my senses were heightened. I came to a stop, a large waterfall pouring into the most beautiful blue water. I trampled into the water, diving when it was deep enough.

Only then did I let go. I felt the earth tremble around me, the water erupting, sending me back to the surface. I crested the water with a scream, a blast of energy flowing out from my body. I panted as I swam to where I was able to touch. Relief filled me as I felt the sand between my toes. Felix was in the water, pulling me into his arms. He pushed my hair back, checking my body to ensure I was okay. I could see the fear in his face as he held me.

"I am okay," I smiled. I was okay, I felt amazing actually. He continued his inspection until he was satisfied, his hands returning to my face. He claimed my lips fiercely. I parted my lips, allowing him entry, relishing in the taste of him. He groaned in approval as our tongues explored each other. His hands slid down my body grabbing my ass. I wrapped my legs around him, feeling his erection pressing against my naked body. Our kisses became more desperate as the heat grew between us.

"I need you, Felix," I whimpered. He reached down, undoing his pants and releasing himself. A soft moan escaped me. Just seeing him like this made me feel like I was on fire. He slid into me, giving me his entire length. I cried out with pleasure.

"Please don't stop," I begged. Felix nipped at my skin, his fingers digging into me possessively.

"You feel so damn perfect," he hissed as he drove into me, picking up his pace. I climbed higher as he continued giving me every part of him, and then I was falling. I saw stars as I exploded around him. My release brings him as well. I laid my head against him, taking in the moment. He kissed me gently, carrying me out of the water, my body still wrapped around him. He put me down, handing my dress to me. I couldn't help but take him in as he zipped his pants up. He was so fucking hot with the water dripping down his chest. I couldn't believe he was all mine, I thought, smiling to myself.

"Are you sure you're okay? He chuckled, clearly catching me staring at him.

"Yes, I promise, I just don't know what happened." He nodded, running his hand through his hair. I loved it when he did that.

"I am not sure, but nothing surprises me when it comes to you. I do know that everyone knows we are here now." He grabbed my hand as we began to walk.

"What do you mean everyone knows I am here now?" I blanched. "Did everyone really just hear what we did? Was I that loud?" He laughed, a true happy laugh that pulled at my heart. But I wasn't going to let him know that. I stopped, putting my hands on my hips, glaring at him. He laughed more. He was infuriating.

"I wasn't referring to what we just did, Jasira. Although we are amongst shifters, I would not be surprised if they heard you." He shrugged a smile on his face. "When you released that energy, you dropped every wolf to their knees, demanding their submission." His face was now serious. My jaw dropped.

"I didn't even know that was possible." Felix reached for my hand again, and I allowed him to take it, needing to feel his touch.

"It will be fine, we will figure it out together," he cooed. We continued walking, but I still had no idea where we were going. I knew our pack was close, so I assumed we were headed that way. As everyone came into view, I saw Valentina pacing. She ran to me, throwing her arms around me.

"You scared the crap out of me," V whispered.

"I'm sorry, I'm okay." She held onto me for another moment, then pulled back. Evander came to her side, rubbing her back. I smiled, knowing my friend had someone.

"We should go get cleaned up. We need to meet the rest of the alphas in a few hours." I nodded my agreement. I would kill for a shower right now. He led me forward, a cabin stood in front of us.

"Each pack has one of these cabins, it sleeps up to fifty people," he explained. Wow, could this place "get any more beautiful? I was excited to explore further. We made our way inside, the rest of the pack in tow. Everyone was exhausted from the long trip.

Walking into the kitchen, a display of food had been laid out on the large island. The kitchen quickly became filled with hungry wolves. I smiled, watching my pack eat and chat happily. My stomach growled at that moment, but Felix was way ahead. He stood in front of me, holding a plate. He winked at me as he handed it to me. I shook my head, smiling at him. How did he know me so well? I thought to myself. I quickly ate so we could make it up to our room.

The room matched the cabin in its beauty, earthy tones decorated the room. Giving the room a calming vibe. Felix wrapped his arms around me, lifting me from the ground and kissing my neck. I squealed in delight as he dropped me on the bed. I giggled at him as he pounced on top of me, but I was quickly silenced as he claimed my mouth. His kiss was hungry, a need behind it. He pulled away reluctantly, nipping at my lip.

"I have to go call Declan to check on the pack." He sighed. I reached up, caressing his cheek.

"I know, my love, I would like to go for a walk anyway." I said. He looked as if he was going to protest, but I held my hand up. "I will stay in sight of the house. If I am to prove myself to everyone, I can't have babysitters all the time. How will they trust me to protect them if I can't protect myself." I asserted. He growled, knowing I was right.

"Don't be long." I jumped up from the bed, kissing his cheek and giving him a wink as I left to explore.

As I walked outside, a gentle breeze caressed my skin. This provided some relief from the heat of the day. There was a pathway to the woods near the house I wanted to explore. Colorful flowers lined the beginning of the path. There was a strong fragrance lingering in the air as I continued. I stopped abruptly, a scent in the air that did not belong to the forest. I inhaled deeply, and the smell of citrus and Cedarwood teased my nostrils. Why was this scent so familiar? I pressed forward, drawn towards it.

Suddenly, the scent shifted. What the hell? Where did it go? I heard the shift above me too late before someone jumped down behind me from the tree above. I turned around swiftly, trying to gain my bearings of the opponent in front of me.

Hudson stood there holding his stomach in laughter. Once my shock passed, I couldn't help the smile that I felt rising to my face. Even if I wanted to be mad at him for scaring the shit out of me.

"What the hell, Hudson?" I exclaimed, swatting at him. He wiped tears from his eyes, trying to pull himself together.

"I'm sorry Jaz, I couldn't help myself." He pulled me into an embrace that I returned. I breathed him in, memorizing his scent. I guess my wolf had made a difference. His smell was now more in-depth, which is why it felt familiar, but I couldn't place it.

I allowed us this moment as we held each other. I hadn't realized how badly I missed Hudson. When he had left before, I cried for a month. As if I was grieving the loss of my family. Something was different now. With my wolf released, I could feel a stronger connection between us. A tear slid down my cheek as he pulled back, holding me at arm's length.

"Please don't cry," he whispered, swiping the tear away.

"I have missed you, Hudson. I am so glad you are here. But how did you find me?" I questioned.

"Well, you didn't make it hard, that's for sure. We all felt the ripple of power, but I knew it was your aura the minute it hit me. Plus, didn't I tell you I would find you?" He smirked. If he knew, does that mean that others in the Cross River Pack knew as well? I chewed my lip, anxiety brewing in my stomach. Hudson placed his hand on my shoulder. "Hey, now I know that look. Don't panic. I am the only one who recognized you." he assured. I sighed in relief.

"We have so much to catch up on. A lot has happened since I last saw you." I was excited to tell him I had finally shifted and found a pack. But my excitement dimmed as I thought about losing him again. We were so far apart at this point. I would never be a part of his pack, in fact I wanted to take that pack down.

With everything that was going on, I had been pushing the pain of not having him around away. Burying it deep so that I didn't have to deal with the reality of it.

"Hey, what's bothering you?" He stared into my soul like he always did, making it impossible for me to hide anything. I had to tell him how I felt about him, this may be my only chance. I had thought for the longest time that having family or a mate wasn't in the cards for me. Now that I had it, I knew I would not be complete without him.

I looked down at my hands but let everything out.

"I finally have shifted, which is wonderful. I am the daughter of Selene, I have elemental powers, and I am meant to be the Queen and join the packs together. I found my fated mate, a pack that accepts me. Yet you are missing. Maybe I am tempting fate or being too greedy. I need you. Since I arrived on the pack's doorstep, you have been my best friend, protector, and brother. You have a piece of my heart, there was a time I even thought if I ever shifted you would be my mate. I am sorry for laying all this on you. It is not fair. I just needed to say this in case I never get the chance." I dared to peek up at him, and he stared at me with an unreadable expression.

He was silent for several moments, I felt as if I was dying inside. I looked back down, fearing what I might see on his face. He gently reached out, raising my chin.

"Jasira, you should know I feel the same way" about you. I have been losing my mind since I haven't heard from you. I thought," he shook his head as if he was willing a bad thought away. He reached for my hand, squeezing it tightly.

I felt him before I saw him. I could feel his power radiating off him before the growl sounded from his lips. I turned to see my mate coming up the path, great now here goes the cock fight. Goddess help me. I felt Hudson's power flair out as well. I never realized how much he hid it as it swept across my skin. Hudson returned Felix's growl, pulling me closer to him. Not exactly a good idea on his part, but he thought he was protecting me.

"Enough, you two." I released my power briefly, shocking both of them. I had been practicing holding it in with Madeira so that I could shake the Alphas. I removed myself from Hudson, but not before I saw the flash of hurt in his eyes.

I went to Felix because this is what my Alpha needed. He needed reassurance that I was safe. I wrapped my arms around him, allowing him to breathe my scent. I felt his body relax slightly before I pulled back, turning to Hudson.

"Felix, this is Hudson. Hudson, this is my mate." Both of their faces held understanding. I held Felix's hand as I pulled him towards Hudson. I could tell Hudson was thinking about everything I had said. "Felix, being here does not change what I said before. I need you by my side as well, you are my pack." I shared my feelings for Hudson with Felix through our mate bond. I wanted to reassure Felix that he had nothing to worry about, but I needed this. Felix stretched out his hand to Hudson.

"It's nice to meet you, Hudson." Hudson paused but only briefly before he took his hand, giving it a shake.

"Jaz, it's always been you. Since you left, I realized the pack is not mine without you. I will follow you anywhere, sunshine." My heart felt so complete. Honestly, I couldn't believe this was happening. Now came the hard part. How would he explain it to his pack? Trenton was going to lose his shit.

"We should probably get back to the house to get ready for the meeting of Alpha's." Felix chimed in, breaking me from my thoughts. I nodded in agreement, this would have to wait I had some Alpha's to get into line.

We all agreed it would be best for Hudson to return to his pack and not raise any flags yet. We decided to meet up tomorrow morning. Tonight was the first night of the celebrations. The moon being full increased emotions and our sex drives. Most mates stayed together, basking in their bond. This moon was different, it was stronger. Then add in the magic this place held. It just amped everything up. A lot of fated mates would find each other tonight underneath the moonlight. Even though I had mine, I couldn't wait for him to chase me down and claim me under the night sky.

Our walk back had been quiet. We were both stuck in our thoughts. I could feel that Felix was on edge, even though he tried to mask it. I turned to him as we entered our room, wrapping my arms around his neck. A low growl escaped his lips in satisfaction. I kissed his lips hard, allowing my need for him to rush through our bond. He matched my fierceness, his lips parting and our tongues tasting one another. He guided us further into the room, his lips never leaving mine. The back of my legs hit the bed as his hands slid down my body.

He spun me around, pushing me down so I was bent over the bed. He yanked my pants down abruptly, making me gasp. He began caressing my ass cheeks, my anticipation growing. I needed him just as much, and he knew it.

"What a naughty mate I have, disobeying her Alpha's order." I shivered with the authority in his voice, my panties becoming drenched with my need.

"I think you need to be taught a lesson," he purred as his hand came down on my bare ass cheek. It stung at first, but his hand returned, caressing the spot.

The pain mixed with pleasure had me whimpering. Felix spanked the other cheek and then caressed again. He continued alternating back and forth several more times. I begged him to give me what my body was so desperate for. His hand slid from my ass to between my soaked folds, his fingers finding my throbbing bud. One caress is all it took as I exploded. He pulled his fingers from me, sucking my juices from them. You taste delicious, mate he hummed his approval. I panted, I still needed him.

"Yes, Felix." I pressed my ass back into his hardness, rubbing against him, allowing my slickness to coat him. He groaned, grabbing my hips as he slammed into me, giving me his entire length. I moaned, the feeling of him inside of me bringing me to the edge again.

"Damn baby, I just can't get enough of you." He hissed.

There was nothing slow or gentle about how he drove into me. We both needed this. I shattered around him first, crying out his name with my orgasm. He followed as I clamped down around him. I ached for him as he slid out of me, turning and facing him. He caressed my cheek, his eyes filled with love, I kissed his palm. Holding his hand in mine.

"Thank you for understanding," I whispered.

"Anything for you, my Queen, now go shower. We have a meeting to get to."

24

JASIRA

We walked hand in hand down the path to our meeting, my stomach fluttering with anxiety. A large building stood in the center of the land, a way to each pack leading here. I kept a tight rein on my aura, not wanting to show my power to any of them. I could hear several voices as we entered, at least they sounded happy. We followed them, finding our way into the conference room. Felix made no attempt to hide his Alpha aura, which drew attention immediately.

Several Alpha's and Luna's approached us with interest, smiles on their faces. We shook hands, introducing ourselves and passing pleasantries. No one seemed like they hated us, they were shocked but that was to be expected. They thought the same as I had that Elemental wolves were gone. Another couple approached us.

"Hi there, I am Alpha Ezra, and this is Luna Briana of the Thundercrest Pack." Alpha Ezra said, shaking our hands.

"I was excited to come over here. You're special, I can tell," Luna Briana whispered as she took my hand. Surprise coursed through me. How did she know I was keeping a tight hold on my aura? She smiled knowingly, "Don't worry I am the only one to notice, I am part witch." This could be a good thing if another pack accepted magic. We could have an ally in the upcoming battle.

"It's lovely to meet you Luna Briana, I am Queen Jasira of the Moon Stone Pack." She was not surprised by my declaration. I had a feeling that not much surprised her. She had a look in her eyes like she knew things others didn't. We chatted as more Alpha's arrived. I learned their pack wasn't far from here, only five hours away. They were the closest pack to this sacred place and took it upon themselves to protect it.

I spun quickly toward the door the minute I sensed Trenton entering. Felix's hand rested on my waist, pulling me to his chest to comfort both of us. I felt his wolf coming to the surface, demanding retribution. Trenton's gaze assessed the room, finally landing on mine. He squinted his face one of anger, and he stomped toward us. Luna Briana stepped in front of me at his approach, Alpha Ezra on his mate's tail.

"Isn't it nice to see you again?" Luna Briana interjected, blocking Trenton's way. I could see the debate on his face, but to him, appearances were everything. How poorly would it look if he was rude to Luna? The packs held the Luna as the most crucial role. His face twisted into a smile if that's what you could call it.

"You look lovely as ever, Luna Briana. Is your pack well?" He politely responded. She held him in conversation as Felix, and I moved away. His eyes followed my every step. I was grateful for Briana I could tell we would become friends. The Elders came in, bringing silence to the room just in time.

"Good evening, everyone," they greeted, waving for us to take our seats at the many tables scattered across the room. Elder Mason took the stage, the others following him.

"Every year, we celebrate and help our kind find their fated mates as the Goddess intended. It is a great honor to host this event and bring our packs together. Let's have a great Super Moon Festival." Everyone cheered for Elder Mason. I had never met the man but knew of him as the pack spoke of him. He was old but powerful and wise. His eyes landed on me, an eyebrow raised. "I believe we have a newcomer or two. I would love for you to come introduce yourself." His face was filled with kindness, a glint of knowing passing in his eyes. I hesitated momentarily, but this was the moment I wanted. Wasn't it?

I felt eyes on me as I approached the stage, Felix at my back, tension rolling off him in waves. I could sense his apprehension through our mate bond. I knew he hated how exposed I was in front of everyone. As I approached Elder Mason, he turned to me, taking my hand. I felt a surge of energy asking for permission as we touched. I opened myself up to it, allowing the connection to happen.

"I knew your mother," he said in my head. Holy shit, we had just mind linked through touch. I know why you are here now. I have stayed quiet all these years since the death of the Elemental wolves, but I will support you. Many will bow." He let go of my hand, gesturing towards the podium. My mind was still blown by what had just happened, but I smiled at him, feeling more confident.

"I am Jasira, daughter of the Moon Goddess. I am an elemental wolf, and I am the rightful Queen. I intend to bring our kind together in peace." The room was silent as they looked from me to Elder Mason.

"What she says is true," he boomed. "These two are fated to bring peace to our kind." Alpha Ezra and Luna Briana stood up from their seats and then took a knee.

"We should pledge our allegiance to you?" Alpha Trenton scoffed, "You expect us to bow to this simple girl. She is weak, not to mention she can't shift. How dare you come here?" he bellowed. Elder Mason was about to protest, but I held my hand up.

"It's ok. I understand his confusion. Let me ease your fears, Alpha Trenton." I slowly released my aura, not letting its full power unfurl. I wanted to save that for him. I leapt off the stage, shifting into my giant black wolf that clearly stated I was an Alpha. Ripples of purple flowed through my skin, displaying my Aether element. I prowled towards him like I was on the hunt, releasing more and more of my aura as I shifted back directly in front of him. I stood face to face with the man who had allowed so much cruelty to happen to me. He shook with anger, his face red spittle on his lips. He tried to fight kneeling before me, but we both knew he would lose. I looked around, everyone else was kneeling before me. I shielded them from the harsh pressure of power but would not shield Trenton. I released the last bit, making him collapse to his knees. I bent down to whisper in his ear.

"You may think you broke me, but here I am, stronger than ever."

I turned, making my way back to my seat, reeling all my power back in. Felix approached the podium as everyone sat back in their seats. He released his water element, allowing it to swirl around him. Watching it move across his skin, being one with him with such grace, was incredible.

"The Moonstone pack is made up of Elemental wolves we were forced into hiding. But we will hide no more, we have brought our pack members here hoping to find their fated mate. We ask that you show us kindness, we miss all our people." Felix announced, then returned to his seat. Elder Mason stood at the podium once again. A smile on his face as he looked around the room.

"I know this is hard on some of you. I had hoped I would be here to see this momentous day. Let us embrace each other and become stronger as wolves. There are other forces that care not about what kind of wolf we are but seek to destroy shifters. Now, enough formalities. Let us enjoy the festival." With that, he departed the stage.

I held tightly to Felix's hand, wondering now if we would be embraced or if others would turn against us. Luna Briana made her way through the crowd toward us, a force to be reckoned with. I hadn't seen it before, but her aura was a combination of magic, beauty, and strength. I was so focused on not showing mine I missed hers. I knew now more than ever I was grateful to have her on my side.

"Queen Jasira, let me be the first to say I knew you had power under there, but girl, you are fierce." I chuckled, thanking her.

"We would like to invite you to visit our pack sometime. It would be a great honor to have you both. You might also be surprised to see not all packs shun magic." Alpha Ezra said warmly.

"We would be honored to visit you," Felix agreed. Ezra and Felix started chatting about their packs, but I had questions for Briana. I pulled her aside for a moment.

"Luna Briana, can we chat a moment." She nodded.

"Of course, my Queen, but please call me Bri." I smiled.

"Only if you will call me Jasira." We both laughed, clearly hating formalities. I didn't want to be blunt, but I had to get to the point. I could see others wished to speak with us, and I couldn't afford to close off to them after everything we just did.

"Did you know who I was or that I would be here?" I inquired. She understood what I wanted to know even if I wasn't asking directly.

"What I knew isn't what you want to know. It's more the how. I have the power of foresight. Sometimes, I call upon it, and other times, it comes to me. This is not the place to talk though, I can see you are filled with questions. I am sure we will find time to chat soon." She patted my shoulder, then turned and grabbed her mate, ushering him away. Leaving me with a wink and a million more questions.

Felix's hand brushed my lower back, pulling me closer to him. I pulled myself back to the room, knowing I needed to focus on the people here. Most of the Alphas seemed receptive to us, so we assured them that we had no plans to take over their packs just to help keep us all safe. Build a stronger community amongst our people. This eased a lot of concerns. I mean, I got it. If someone came in like we had, I would fear for my family and pack members. I knew there were packs out there that treated their people unkindly, amongst other things. Those are the ones who should be scared.

I wanted to stop anyone from being treated how I had been. Even worse, being sold off as property or a sex slave. We would show no mercy to those who participated in such horrors. As we got lost in conversation with several of the packs, I took note of the three Alphas that stayed talking with Trenton. They never came to see us, just left the conference room. We would need to find out their connection to him as soon as possible.

After spending an extra hour chatting with everyone, the room cleared out. Elder Mason sat on the stage quietly, waiting for us to be the only ones left. He radiated a warmth that made me want to trust him instantly.

"I'm sure you have questions, dear," Mason chimed, breaking the silence. He walked off the stage, standing before us, gesturing for us to have a seat at the nearest table.

"I have a short story to tell you that will give you some insight." I gave him my full attention, eager to learn what this man of wisdom knew.

"Before my time, fifteen elders were making up the council. Four of which were elemental wolves. They lived here together, protecting the sacred ground and calling upon the goddess for guidance. Of course, they also stayed close to their original packs, returning to their roots, and providing the alpha with wisdom."

"a few elders seemed to pull away from the peace we had created. They began to cause strife with the other elders and encouraged their packs to do the same. The divide became more apparent as time went on. They were targeting the elemental wolves and anyone who supported them. The elders fought against them, wanting to hold on to the peaceful life they had created because we were stronger when united."

"Eventually, a war broke out among them. From journals I have read, the other elders were using some type of powerful magic. I was but a baby when the slaughter happened, so I don't know much else. Your grandparents were babies as well. Fortunately, two elders saved the children, bringing them here where no one dared to attack. They stayed here protected until they were old enough to return to the packs they came from. There are only five of the original elder bloodlines left from those children. They sat here with me today."

My chest felt heavy, how could someone hurt their own people in such a way. I couldn't understand it. The hate that drove those Elders was unthinkable. I reached out for Elder Mason's hand, trying to provide him comfort.

"Thank you for sharing that story with us, I am sorry for those that were lost." He placed his hand on top of mine.

"I shared that story because you are the only one who can stop what is to come. The other Elders and I have felt the blackness again, the powerful magic killed so many before is back. Reach out to the world, my Queen. You will feel it, too," Mason encouraged.

I wasn't quite sure what he meant, but I gave it my best. I closed my eyes, reaching down inside of me for the swirls of magic that lived there. They bounced excitedly, ready to answer my call. I imagine them spreading out of me, feeling the aura of the world instead of just a person. It was exhilarating, everything sprung in rainbows of color. The natural beauty of every living thing was breathtaking. I spread myself further, leaving my body behind and joining the Aether as it showed me all the pureness of the world.

That's when I felt it. There was a blackness. It was a sick weight pressing down on me, making my stomach roll. Its dark shadow tried to dim the light, feeding off the different colors. It may have been small now, but I could feel it fighting to grow. I tried to get closer to see the source, but it reached out for me as I grew nearer. Fear encased my body, a cold sweat forming over my skin. Its smokey tendrils tried to grab at me, but my Aether element shot out, shielding me from it and sending me flying back to my body.

The room spun as I opened my eyes, the fear still gripping me. A fire burned up my throat as I vomited on the floor beside me. Cool, calming hands wrapped around me, a gentle purr easing my fear.

"I've got you, baby, I'm right here," Felix cooed. I wiped my mouth with a cloth Elder Mason held out for me. I understood now more than ever what was at risk. Not only had that thing tried to destroy my people. It was the same darkness I had felt in my dreams. The one I couldn't share with anyone, especially my mate. How was I supposed to fight this by myself? I was so fucked.

I paced around our room, my mind all over the place. Felix sat watching, trying to allow me the space I needed, except his concern was pouring into our mate bond. I didn't know where to begin with my own emotions. I couldn't deal with having his suffocating me as well. I stopped pacing, took a deep breath, and turned to him.

"I love you, Felix, with every fiber of my being, but I need space. I am going to go for a walk." He was going to fight me, I already knew it. Could I blame him? I wouldn't want him to run away from me if he were in this state. Yet that didn't matter, not this time. I could not share this with him, he was my heart. No matter what, I would not risk it. So, as he stood to protest, I held up my hand to stop him. "This is not up for debate. You need to respect my wishes." I saw the flash of hurt in his eyes, and anger flooded in.

Before he could say another word, I turned and walked out. I couldn't allow him to see how badly I actually did need him. This was the only way to protect him. I mind linked Valentina and Gina asking them to meet me at the front door. I was going to need help running interference.

They were waiting for me, worry on their faces.

"I need you two to make sure Felix gives me some space. I do not want him hunting me down." I commanded. They both wore shocked expressions, looking at one another rather than at me.

"Do you think you can handle that?" I said sharply, allowing my alpha aura to fill the air. They both nodded their agreement, their eyes drifting downward. I hated that it had to be this way.

I walked out the door assured that they would do their best, knowing Felix would only deal for so long. I threw up my walls, blocking all connections. The void reminds me of how alone I used to feel. I headed into the forest towards the waterfall from when we first arrived. The trees swayed with a warm summer breeze, filling the air with the scent of wildflowers. I listened as the birds sang, filling the space of silence. A calmness washed over me as I reached the waterfall, sitting on the grass.

I always felt at one with nature, it was once my only solace. I scooted closer to the water, putting my feet in. Letting the fear and anxiety wash away for the moment. I could finally think, it was time to formulate a plan. I knew I had to be careful how much I told anyone. I would write letters, that's what I would do. They would explain everything to Felix, except I needed to ensure he didn't receive them until the time was right. I would call Madeira, and maybe she could give me something to put on my body to allow a trail to be left. One I didn't have to use any of my powers for.

I didn't have to tell anyone about the dream, only what we were looking for overall. That may unknowingly lead them to the conclusion of who had me when this happened. Because I knew now that this was real. My dream would happen, it was just up to me to decide my fate. I was still lost in thought when I heard shuffling from the woods behind me. I sighed, waiting for my broody mate to come out, but when I breathed deeply, I realized it wasn't him. I couldn't help the smile that crossed my face as Hudson approached me.

"How did you find me?" I questioned, even though I was glad he did. He shrugged his shoulders.

"I will always find you, Jaz, but I was headed to see you and caught your scent this way." I patted the ground beside me, asking him to join. He came over, taking me in as he sat. He wrapped his arm around my shoulder, pulling me closer to him. It felt like home, I laid my head on his shoulder, allowing him to comfort me.

"What's wrong, sunshine?"

As much as I wanted to tell him everything, I would not risk him either. I had built a family, and he was a part of that. No one would touch it. I sighed again.

"I saw something with Elder Mason, something that is dark and threatens us all. I don't want to talk about it right now. I do want to try something if you are open to it?"

"Alright, what is it?" He raised an eyebrow in question.

"Do you remember when you asked me about what happened while you were gone? Well, I would like to try to show you." His eyes darkened, and his body filled with tension. He gritted his teeth but nodded his approval. I turned my body, now facing him. I reached for his hands, holding them tightly. He deserved the whole truth. I closed my eyes, opening myself up to him. I searched for our bond, knowing it was there. Even if we weren't mates or pack now, there had always been a connection between us. I grabbed hold of it, holding on tightly as I allowed my Aether power to surround it. The bond grew stronger and brighter. I let my memories flow forward, pulling us into them.

We were both standing in a warehouse, staring at me tied to a chair.

"What the fuck is this" Hudson exclaimed.

"This is right after you left. They waited for you to go, knowing you cared for me." His jaw clenched as beta Stephan pulled out a silver scalpel. Beta Stephan proceeded to cut into my body as I begged and pleaded. Liam stood watching the entire time, a darkness in his eyes. Eventually, my screams stopped as I passed out from the blood loss and pain. The memory faded, sending us into one with Liam and Ian. Liam was taunting me, Ian joining in. They shoved me back and forth between them, laughing as I stumbled. Liam sidestep, not catching me this time but allowing my body to slam into the wall. I crumpled to the ground, winded. Liam leaned over, whispering in my ear as he held me by the throat.

"Next time, maybe we won't have an audience, then we can really play." He stalked out with Ian, winking at me as he left. Several more memories twisted in of the pack's abuse.

They were quick flashes until we reached the one with Liam once again. I shook, knowing what was coming next, but Hudson's hand slid into mine, sending warmth through my frozen body. Liam was on top of me, pinning me down, and he slapped my face. I bucked at him, but he slammed my head against the floor several times. I struggled against him, even with my head screaming, begging him to stop. He ripped my top, exposing me, then yanked my sweatpants down. I couldn't watch it anymore. I turned, looking away from the scene unfolding in front of me. He began to unzip his pants, but then he was interrupted, allowing me time to get away. That was the only time I was ever thankful for Trudy.

We were pulled back from my memories, sitting still by the waterfall. I looked into Hudson's eyes, pain consumed them. Tears rushed down his cheek, and my chest squeezed.

"I am so sorry, Jaz. I had no idea." He grabbed me, pulling me into an embrace. I rubbed his back, trying to comfort him, his wound was fresh. He pulled away, then stood. Hudson offered me his hand, I took it pulling myself up beside him.

"I would like to join your pack because I am never going back there. Unless it is to kill my father and brother." Hudson stated. I looked into his eyes, seeing the pain still there.

"I did not show you that because I wanted you to leave the pack." A wave of guilt crashed down on me, his father did love him in his own way. I showed him because I had promised to share everything with him before I left but never had the chance. If something happened to me, I wanted to keep my promise. He shook his head.

"I know that wasn't your intent, regardless of that. What they did was unforgivable," he shook his head.

We headed back towards the house. I felt better after having some time to think everything through. I lifted the walls I had put up keeping Felix out, and emotions began to pour in. I could feel his anger at first, then panic and confusion. The most prominent of them was hurt, guilt stung my heart as his pain washed over me. As we entered the house, I saw V and Gina.

"Thank the Goddess, you are back. That man is insufferable." V grumbled, her arms crossed. Gina approached me, touching my shoulder.

"You should go to him before he loses control completely. We will keep Hudson company."

I took off up the stairs to our bedroom, his aura becoming stronger as I approached. I opened the door to our room in shambles, my Alpha was sitting on the floor shaking. I went to him, wrapping my arms around him and sending my love through our bond. His eyes glowed as he looked up to me, his wolf at the forefront. I nuzzled into him.

"Felix, please talk to me," I begged.

"You shut me out from our bond like it was nothing." His voice was so low I could barely hear when he spoke. I choked back a sob. Is that really how he felt?

"I can't lose you again Jaz, you have my heart. It only beats because of you. If you need Hudson too, I understand but please don't shut me out." I sucked in a sharp breath. My mate thought I wanted Hudson as well. How could I be so stupid not to see? Before I could interject, he continued.

"I know that's who you were with. I saw him follow you from the balcony, and I can smell him on you."

My heart broke that I made him feel this way. The desperation in his voice had my wolf whining inside.

"Felix, look at me." I grabbed his chin, forcing him to hold my gaze. "You are my mate, I love you just as you love me. I shut you out because that is the only way I could bury the fear that consumed me. I have only survived everything I have by locking it away. Hudson and I have a connection that I can't explain, but you are my heart."

Relief slid over his face, and his body no longer shook. His eyes returned to their normal glacier blue. I caressed his face, my fingers trailing down his neck to the mark I gave him. Hunger flashed in his eyes, my body shivering in response. He pulled me onto his lap, claiming my mouth as I straddled him. His kiss was hard and demanding. I loved every second of it, letting his need consume me. I moaned into his mouth as he grabbed my ass, lifting me in the air with him. He moved us to the bed, sitting at the edge, his hands exploring my body and under my shirt. He broke our kiss, watching me now as he took my nipple in his hand, rolling it between his fingers. I closed my eyes, relishing the feeling as he moved to the next nipple. I wanted him to continue, but I had other motives.

I pulled away, climbing off his lap, and spreading his knees. He cocked an eyebrow as I dropped down to my knees.

"I want to taste you," I purred at him. He slid his pants down, allowing his large member to spring free. I positioned myself eager to please him. I licked up his shaft before taking his tip in my mouth. He groaned, leaning back slightly on the bed. I moved my tongue around his head, teasing him before I pulled more of him into my mouth. At first, I set a slow pace, his moans encouraging me to take more. He reached out, grabbing my hair as I sped up. I pushed myself further, trying to take him all, his moans and heavy breathing driving me.

I felt him tense in my mouth as he groaned his release, his taste filling my mouth as I swallowed him down. He grabbed my arms, pulled me up, and threw me on the bed. I giggled at him, loving the devilish glint in his eyes.

"It's your turn now," he growled out. He sucked on my nipples, working his way down my stomach, and placing gentle kisses on my thighs.

He dipped his head between my legs, flicking his tongue across my swollen nub. I bucked into him, needing more, but he was quick to press my body down, not allowing me to move. He proceeded to tease me, his tongue moving in slow circles,

"Felix," I begged. He answered my plea, quickening his pace, then sucked on my pulsing nub. I shook as the orgasm racked my body. Before I could even come down, he slid into me.

"Mine," he growled out as he kissed my neck and nipped at my mark.

"Yes, I'm all yours," I panted, wrapping my legs around him. I need him, all of him. His thrusts quickened both of us, desperate for one another. I clawed at his back as he claimed my mouth, the fire between us all consuming.

I called out his name as I shattered around him. I poured my love for him through our mate bond, letting him feel what he meant to me. He groaned his release, pouring himself inside of me. His lips found mine, kissing me gently.

"I love you, Jasira." He mumbled between kisses. I smiled.

"I love you too, Felix."

We untangled our bodies, knowing we had to get ready. Tonight was the Supermoon Run, we had to show up. There were a few more hours until we had to go, but we needed to discuss some things. We dressed quickly, making our way downstairs, hand in hand. V, Gina, and Hudson were in the kitchen talking. The room went quiet as we entered a tension filling the air. I knew that it would take some time for Felix and Hudson to work it out, but hopefully, my reassurance would help Felix.

For right now, there are more important things to discuss. I needed to explain what I saw with Elder Mason. I wished the others were here as well, we were stronger together. Someone had to stay and watch over the pack while we were gone. I sat down at the table, Felix sitting next to me.

"We need to talk about what I saw today because if we don't stop this thing, it won't just be the elemental wolves that suffer. It will be all shifters. That is not where it will stop though, it will spread its darkness to other supernatural's. Consuming everyone in its path."

25

FELIX

I could see the wheels turning in Jasira's head as we walked to meet the others for our run. She had dark circles under her eyes, and her mouth was turned down. I fought back the urge to make her talk to me, worried about pushing her further away. I needed to speak with Elder Mason alone. Maybe he could give me a better idea of what this shadow was capable of. From what she told us, I knew it was coming from a supernatural being, and it hadn't smelt like a witch's magic. She wouldn't give us much else, which meant she was hiding something.

When we had pressed her for more, she pulled away, fear plaguing her face. So, we decided to move on with the night and discuss it later. Tonight was supposed to be filled with love, the sacred love for your mate. We should be enjoying ourselves, but as I looked around, it was clear it was more than just Jasira distracted. The others wore the same expressions. I turned, facing everyone, stopping them in their tracks before we met up with the rest of the pack.

"Listen up," I said, drawing everyone's attention. "I know all of us are distracted by the looming threat, but this is a special night and one we should all enjoy. I took Jasira's hands in mine, gazing deep into her eyes, "I need you to be here with me, especially now." I looked once again at everyone. We are not promised tomorrow. We need to live in this moment. Some of you could meet your fated mate tonight. That is something you don't want to miss because you are worried about what comes next." I felt Jasira's hand brush my cheek. I looked back at her, and she was now smiling.

"You're right, my love," she agreed. The tension in my shoulders uncoiled slightly as I saw her relax.

Once we reached the group, the excitement that buzzed in the air quickly consumed us. Our pack was here, about to run alongside all the other packs. Our people would find their mates as I had. My heart filled with happiness as I watched Jasira, admiring her as she spoke with several pack members. This moment was all because of her, she led us here. It would give our pack the chance to grow. Gage came up beside me, he was the quiet type but had been my friend since we were teenagers.

"She is special, Felix," he whispered as he patted me on the back. I smiled at him.

"She really is. I hope you meet your mate tonight, my friend."

Elder Mason made his way to the front of the pack, drawing everyone's attention.

"Tonight, we run as one, worship the Moon Goddess, and find our fated mates. I hope that the Moon Goddess blesses each one of you tonight. Call your wolves forward." I made eye contact with Jasira, giving her a wink. I allowed my wolf to take over, shifting with everyone else. Howls filled the night as everyone began to take off, hoping to find their mate.

I took a deep breath, my mate's scent filling my lungs. My wolf found his mark, stalking her, but Jasira would not let herself be caught that easily. She took off running, my wolf eagerly chasing. She was fast but not nearly as experienced in hunting as I was. We raced through the trees, weaving through them gracefully. I darted off her path quickening my pace, I was going to go wide and cut her off. I heard her pause, looking around for me. This gave me all the time I needed to get behind her. I leaped through the air, landing on her playfully, being sure not to put my total weight on her.

"I caught you," I exclaimed through the mind link, licking her face.

"You tricked me no fair," she pouted back.

"Poor mate doesn't like to lose, I see." I tsked at her. Her wolf growled, making me laugh. We both began to shift back, our naked bodies pressed against each other as we lay on the ground. My wolf howled inside me, the victory of having our mate beneath us. My body was burning with the need to take her right there. The Super Moon effects were in full swing as I claimed her mouth. Her soft lips parted, allowing me to taste her fully.

I slid my hand down her body, sliding my fingers along her wetness. She pressed herself onto my fingers, a soft moan escaping her lips. I answered her need, my fingers speeding up as they glide along her swollen nub. She cried out, her body bucking with her orgasm.

I swiftly settled between her legs, coating my length with her juices. She whimpered, wiggling beneath me. I slammed into her, giving her every bit of my length. She gasped in pleasure, opening herself to my size. I slowly started to drive into her, wanting to take this moment in. She was perfect and all mine. A new urge drove me, and I needed to claim her beneath the moon again. I quickened my thrusts, she was close I could feel her begin to squeeze around me.

I leaned down into her, finding where I had marked her, and sank my teeth in again. She called out my name as she exploded around me, her orgasm almost bringing on mine. She grabbed my neck, pulling me closer and marking me again, sending me over the edge. I placed gentle kisses along her neck and jaw, the need to have her again taking over my body.

She was just as ready as I was, her eyes darkening with desire. The supermoon was not done with us yet. We made love all night until the moon rescinded, and rays of light shone in the sky. I carried her home, heading straight for the bed. It didn't matter that we were both covered in leaves and dirt. We were both spent sleep claiming me as I tucked her in front of me.

26

JASIRA

I woke up with Felix's arms still wrapped around me. I slipped from his embrace as gently as I could, he needed sleep. I wish I could lay there forever, safe in his arms, but I desperately needed a shower. I tiptoed to the bathroom, picking leaves from my hair as I went. Last night was the most fantastic experience. I could feel my wolf's power still radiating through me, the supermoon keeping her close to the surface.

I looked myself over in the mirror, not surprised to see I was disgusting. My hand went to my mark, triggering thoughts of last night. Hot, tantalizing thoughts of my mate. My heart rate quickened, and the room suddenly warmed. Girl, you need to calm down, I chastised myself. I shook my head, clearing my thoughts as I climbed into the shower.

The hot water felt terrific, relaxing my muscles that I hadn't realized were stiff. I scrub at the dirt on my skin, the dried, caked mess finally leaving me. My hair was another matter, the thick waves refused to cooperate. I ended up having to wash it twice, doubling down on conditioning as well. When I finally felt clean, I stepped out, wrapping myself in a towel. I stepped back into our room quietly, trying not to disturb Felix.

"Hey gorgeous," his voice still husky from sleep. He was propped up on his side, a hungry look in his eyes. My body heated instantly in response to him, I would never get enough of this man.

"You, my mate, are trouble." I pointed towards him, turning to the closet to put clothes on. I needed some type of barrier here, or I would not make it out of this room. He chuckled behind me, more than likely smelling my arousal.

His arms slid around my waist from behind as he kissed my neck softly. I bit my lip, trying to conceal the moan I wanted to let escape. I wasn't trying to encourage him, even if I wanted him to take me right then and there. We slept most of the day, leaving no time for extra fun. We had the Super Moon Ball to get ready for.

A knock on the door interrupted my mate's sneaky assault. Valentina's voice rang out on the other side of the door. She was coming in whether we liked it or not. I couldn't help but smile, she had perfect timing. Felix growled as she entered the room, then turned, muttering to himself, heading towards the bathroom.

"Aw, I'm sorry. Did I interrupt your sexy time?" she fake pouted at him. I held back the laugh, trying to escape me. My poor mate did not find her antics funny.

"How was your night?" I asked Valentina, wagging my eyebrows at her. The smile on her face said it all, I had hoped she would have secured her mate bond with Evander.

"You were right. Having a fated mate is a feeling that can't be explained. It was magical, but don't you dare tell him. I like to keep him guessing." She winked at me.

"You have my word," I giggled, holding my hands up.

I was excited to find out who else had met their mate last night. I could feel the excitement in the pack as we made our way down to the kitchen. Breakfast was already made, so we grabbed a plate and ate quickly. We needed to meet Mindy in an hour for final dress adjustments. Gina skipped into the kitchen, a happiness radiating off her I hadn't seen before. I smiled a knowing smile, excited to hear it from her.

"Guys, I have something to tell you." She fidgeted as we waited for her to speak. "I found my mate, he is from the Thundercrest pack. He is Alpha Ezra's brother." Her eyes lit up as she spoke of him. I was personally excited because I had met Ezra and Briana. They were both good people, and this bond could bring our packs closer together.

"Well, where is the lucky guy?" I asked, wanting to congratulate them both.

"I told him I would introduce you all tonight, we girls have to get ready for the ball." She was right. We did have to get moving. I was so proud of her for becoming her true self. Giving her the choice to be my Delta was the best thing I had ever done. Felix chose that moment to enter the kitchen, his gaze finding mine. I walked towards him, placing my hands on his shoulders.

"We are headed to meet Mindy and get ready. I love you and can't wait to see you later." I kissed him, trying to pull away quickly, but he had other plans. He snaked his hands around my waist, pulling me flush against him. He deepened the kiss, sliding his tongue along my lips. My lips parted in response, a soft moan escaping me.

"Until later, my love," He abruptly pulled away, a wicked grin on his face.

I stood stunned momentarily, how could he make me want to jump him and punch him in the same breath. I pushed his shoulder, walking past him.

"You will pay for that later," I whispered, knowing he would hear me. He winked at me as I walked out hot, bothered, and aching for my mate's touch.

Mindy was waiting for us at the Elder packhouse. I hadn't had time to take it in before, but it was practically classified as a castle. It held the conference room, and the Elders each had their own living quarters. There were multiple rooms for the packs to dress in before the ball. I was excited to see the ballroom. I had heard it was breathtaking. I would have to ask for a tour one day from Elder Mason.

Mindy's eyes lit up as we entered the room, her excitement buzzing in the air.

"Queen Jasira, I have everything ready for you to try on. I hope you love it as much as I think you will." Her excitement was contagious. I trusted Mindy's work, but now I could hardly wait to see what she came up with. I had secretly asked Mindy to pick out dresses for V and Gina. She had eagerly accepted.

"Are the others ready as well?" I asked, hopeful.

"Yes, I brought them, I was hoping to do a fitting on those two as well." I turned to both ladies, a smile on my face.

"I had Mindy make both of you something special as well." We all three squealed, ready to try them on.

"Wait, Mindy, how did your night go?" I had really prayed that she would find her mate. She deserved it after everything she had been through. Mindy tucked her hair behind her ear, a shy smile on her lips. I rushed forward, taking her hands into mine,

"Well?" I pressed.

"I met my mate," she whispered.

"That is amazing. Is he everything you hoped for? Will he be at the ball tonight?" she nodded happily.

"Well then, let's get these dresses on so you can go with us for hair and makeup," I announced. Mindy was shocked, her jaw opened and closed as if she was trying to say something making me laugh. "

You want me to go with you guys to get ready?" she stuttered. She was so sweet, I hoped her mate knew how lucky he was.

"Yes, I do," I claimed.

Mindy finally pulled herself together, gesturing to us to each take a changing room. She brought us each a garment bag.

"I expect to see your dress on you as well," I hollered through the closed door. I unzipped the garment bag slowly, excited to see what lay inside. I gasped at its beauty. Mindy had undoubtedly done it again. I couldn't wait to put on this dress. I gently removed it from the bag, ready to step into it. Mindy knocked softly at the door, asking if I needed any assistance. I opened the door, ushered her in, and embraced her. "Thank you. I can already tell this dress is perfect." She took the dress from my hands, smiling.

"Well, let's get it on you then." She helped me step in, pulling the gown up and adjusting me.

She zipped the back and stood off to the side, admiring her work. I stood there staring at myself, the gown was violet bringing out my eyes. Its contoured v-neckline with spaghetti straps, a plunging back, and a high front slit showed off just enough skin. Sparkling crystal stones intricately covered the gown along with the cascading overskirt. Every curve of my body was held just right.

I exited the dressing room, ready to show V and Gina. They were both in their gowns as well. They both looked incredible, V wore an emerald green dress with a fitted bodice. It had a plunging sweetheart neckline and spaghetti straps. The back was laced up in a crisscross style. Sparkling curved patterns covered the top down to the trumpet silhouette of the skirt, which was covered with feathers and flowed down to the floor with a sweeping train.

Gina's gown was silver with a straight across-neckline and off the shoulder sleeves. The fitted top was adorned in glistening sequins flowing into a layered tier of tulle. Creating a beautiful A-line shape.

We took time to admire each other as Mindy made sure no adjustments had to be made. She had nailed our sizes, each one fitting us perfectly. After she was done, we insisted on seeing her before we all went to get our hair done. We unzipped each other, slipping out of our gowns and redressing into our comfy clothing. Mindy stepped out moments later, stunning as all.

"Wow, Mindy, you look amazing," Gina exclaimed. Gina was right, our shy little Mindy looked anything but that in her navy-blue gown. Its sleek mermaid silhouette was covered in a glitter print with an asymmetrical neckline. Sheer layered ruffles trailed along the bodice, with a sheer overskirt cascading to the floor. There was a high slit that screamed sexy that flowed into a sweeping train.

"Girl, you're going to have your mate begging for you by the night's end." V beamed. I nodded excitedly in agreement. I couldn't wait for all our mates to drool. Mindy returned to the dressing room to change back into her regular clothes. Excitement buzzed in the air as we all chatted on our way to get our hair and makeup done.

Entering the suite, we were quickly ushered to put on white robes. We did as we were told, not daring to argue with our sassy stylists. It felt nice to let go for a while, to simply think about having a fun night. I needed this break from the reality that we would return to.

Elder Jasmin entered the suite, pulling me from my thoughts.

"Elder Jasmin, are you joining us to prepare for this evening?" I asked. She smiled warmly at me.

"No, my Queen, I am simply here to request your presence for Elder Mason. He is in his study and would like an audience with you." Anxiety made my stomach turn. Was there something new he had learned about the darkness? I swallowed the bile that threatened its escape.

"You wanted to talk to him about your parents anyways," my wolf chimed in. She was right, my curiosity won out.

I looked at my stylist, her face clearly agitated with her work being interrupted. She sighed.

"Let me just finish putting some rollers in for your hair to set. Then you can go, but don't take too long. You still need your hair finished and makeup done." I looked back to Elder Jasmin. She seemed pleased with the stylist's answer. She gracefully sat down in a chair to wait for me. I could feel her aura rippling off her in soft waves. She may only look in her sixties, but the power spoke for itself. Werewolves lived to see generations past what humans did. Unless, of course, their life was stolen from them.

My mind drifted back to Elder Mason's story. Could the power that killed the elders before be the same one now? I was filled with questions and had no one to give me answers. Except, maybe my mother knew what this force was. I hadn't thought of that before. I knew the Gods were not supposed to interfere with fate to a certain point. But Selene might be the only one who can give me guidance. I have to make it a priority after the Supermoon Festival, I would pay her a visit.

Elder Jasmin guided me to the study, I was grateful because I would have gotten lost. We were both quiet for the walk, I wasn't sure who I could trust which meant I was not open to sharing. Elder Jasmin opened the door to the study gesturing for me to enter, she then shut the door gently behind me. The room held a specific power, I felt it caress my skin as if it was checking to see whether I was a friend or foe.

I stepped further in, taking in the room. Books lined one side, and a fireplace dominated the other. A desk sat at the far end of the room, several old books stacked upon it. A window dominated the wall behind the desk, allowing the Full moon in all its glory to light the room. That, of course, and the roaring fire, where Elder Mason sat in an oversized leather chair.

"Thank you dear for joining me, please come sit" He chimed warmly. I sat in the matching chair across from him, the fire warming my skin and creating a homey sensation.

"You wished to speak with me, Elder Mason?" I started impatient to hear what he had to say. He chuckled.

"Please call me Mason, there is no need for formalities here." I nodded my acceptance.

"Good, yes, I wanted to chat more about the darkness you saw. But mainly what you didn't want to say in front of your mate."

I froze, fear coursing through my veins. How did he know? I suppose you don't get to be his age without being perceptive.

"I am not quite sure what you are talking about." I stuttered out.

Mason crossed his legs, looking at me with expectation.

"I can smell your fear. This tells me that it involves harm to your mate. I suspected as much this is why I only invited you, you clearly need help. My loyalty lies with you, I will not share what you say with anyone."

I smelt no lie, his body language spoke of the truth and his aura showed pure intent. I was out of options, but I had one question before I could tell him.

"You say you are loyal to me? What if I tell you the choice of suffering or death is between Felix or me? Will you still promise your secrecy?" Mason seemed to not be surprised by my line of questioning.

"I am no fool Jasira, I knew that was the choice. I only mean to help you. You have my word." I felt a slight weight lift off my chest, the fear not so constricting. This could be what I needed to figure everything out to change the outcome of my vision. I began telling him every detail, not that there was much to go on. The room had been so dark, my senses not as sharp because it was simply a vision.

"It appears that you don't have much to go on location wise. However, I may be able to help with that part if you are willing to have another vision." He stood walking towards the shelves of books, running his fingers along them.

"I don't have control of having the vision. It just kinda happens when I'm asleep." I shrugged. He paused at one of the books pulling it out, it was worn and clearly old.

"That is why we are going to give you a vision, and I will go in with you. We will also be able to protect ourselves from the effects you were feeling before." My mouth gaped open. Hope blossomed in my chest, but I quickly shoved it aside. I needed to focus, I was far from out of the woods.

"Do we have time before the ball to do this?" I looked towards the clock, there was still three hours until I would be expected.

"Yes, time is different when in a vision. We won't need much because we are on this land. It will protect us." Mason quickly set to work, he gathered some stones to represent the elements laying them around us. He lit a white candle between us.

"This will help guide us back. This will be very similar to before, except we are searching for you." He began burning several herbs in the white candle, laying them in front of us in a bowl, their scents wafting around us.

He reached for my hands, and I allowed him to take them. I took several deep breaths, the smell of the herbs calming me, allowing me to focus. I pictured myself in the cell like Mason instructed. My mind darkened, pulling me under.

I opened my eyes and stood in blackness, mason by my side. A door was ahead, and something pulled me towards it. I turned the handle, and the door opened to the cell. Mason stepped in right behind me, reminding me that this time was different. I realized that I wasn't choking on my fear, my wolf growled in my head. She was not happy about being here. Mason moved around the room,

"We must be quick. We don't want to draw too much attention." His voice soft. I took a deep breath, calming my nerves. This was just a vision I needed to pull myself together.

I looked over at the cot where future me was sleeping. That was different. Future Jasira was always awake when I had come before. Maybe it was because I came this time willingly. I touched my shoulder softly, future me stirring. She sat up suddenly, backing in the corner, fear evident in her eyes. I held my hands out showing her I meant no harm, she blinked staring at me with shock.

"I must be seeing things. How are you here?" THE QUESTION IN HER *voice had me pausing.*

Something had changed, she treated me as if this was the first time for my visit. Mason came over to us,

"This is another version of the future, that is all. She doesn't recognize you because you have not come before. There are many paths and planes the future lives on." He explained in a whisper. Curiosity overtook me. What happened in this future?

"Can you tell me anything to help me?" My voice gentle, not wanting to frighten her any further.

"I saved them all, but then I wouldn't give master what he wanted. Now... Now," she sobbed, her body shaking with the force. "Now they're all dead, Felix, my mate, my heart."

"What did the master want?" I grabbed onto her. I had to know I wasn't coming this far to let it be worth nothing. Mason gently touched my shoulder.

"We have to go, someone is becoming aware of our presence." Mason grabbed me, pulling me with him. I couldn't leave, not without knowing.

"Tell me," I shrieked, tears running down my face. Right before the door shut, her eyes met mine. She was broken.

"You," she whispered. It echoed through the blackness as I fell back into the study.

I felt like I couldn't breathe, panic making my heart race. The room was spinning. I tried to stand but fell back down. Mason was by my side, holding onto my elbow. I heard shouting from the hall, then the door swung open. A snarl left my mate's mouth as he rushed towards me. His chest was heaving, fur had already sprouted along his arms and chest. He pulled me into his arms, the panic instantly lifting. Mason had stepped back, not wanting to get in the way of my protective mate.

"What have you done to her?" He roared out at Mason. I placed my hand on his chest, his anger easing.

"He did nothing to me, Felix. I am fine." Felix's eyes met mine, a fury burning in them. They softened slightly.

"Do not lie to me. I felt your fear, your sadness." I knew I had to lie, I couldn't tell him about the vision. I also knew I was a horrible liar, so this would not be easy.

"I came here to get answers about my parents, Felix. It turned to us talking about the incident the other day. Mason was kind enough to show me how to enter the vision world again." It wasn't a lie exactly, just not the complete truth. Felix studied my face for a second. He knew how scared I had been the other day.

"Why didn't you tell me I would have been here to support you." He accepted my answer, but concern was still evident in his voice.

"I knew you were trying to get ready for the ball just the same, plus this wasn't planned. I am glad that you came though, I feel much better."

He pulled me in closer, wrapping his arms tightly around me. I breathed him in, his scent speaking to my soul.

"Next time call me" he demanded grabbing my chin, I leaned in kissing him. Letting him know I would through our bond. The kiss ended too quickly for my liking, but we both had to finish preparing for the evening. "Let me walk you back," Felix said, taking my hand in his.

"That would be great," I agreed. We both headed for the door, saying our goodbyes to Mason. I knew Mason and I needed to discuss everything that had just happened, but that certainly wasn't happening right now. My mate was to wound up. He wouldn't leave me alone to speak with him. He could not know anything, now more than ever. I was going to cherish tonight and every moment by his side. I would ensure he knew my love for him and that our bond was unbreakable. So that when the time came, he would have no doubts. He was my heart, and I would fight for him.

27

JASIRA

Felix had walked me back to the stylist's suite. To say he was not happy he couldn't stay by my side was an understatement. I promised to see him soon, sending my love and comfort through our bond. He eventually gave in, especially when I told him he did not want to ruin my dress reveal. Walking in, my stylist shot daggers my way, complaining about how long I was gone. I repeatedly apologized until she finally sighed, telling me she would work her magic.

My head felt like it was spinning, I should have been enjoying getting ready for the ball. Instead, the silence reminded me how alone I was in this. The girls had finished their hair before I returned, moving on to the next segment of the pre-ball meet-up. All the females from each pack met up with their Luna for words of praise. I was on time but wanted to be among the first to arrive. Valentina reassured me that I was fine, but I was anything but.

As they finished with my hair and makeup, I took myself in. I couldn't help but smile at myself, they had done my makeup perfectly. I felt beautiful and confident, unlike what I had felt moments before. This was the face of someone bold and powerful who commanded a room. They had given me a natural look, making my porcelain skin glow. The smokey eyeshadow made my purple eyes somehow brighter than usual. My cheeks were rosy, bringing some color to my face, with a pop of pink lipstick on my pouty lips, bringing the whole look together.

I admired my hair next, soft waves framed my face with several crown-like braids wrapping around my head. The rest of my thick black hair fell down my back in curls, stopping around my hips. The stylists that had gathered to speed up the process and help chattered about how beautiful I looked. I was beyond grateful for them, thanking each one before running out the door to meet my girls.

I raced down the halls, letting Valentina know I was headed her way. When I reached the room, she had directed me to, I felt some of my earlier tension ease. I could do this, the room would be full of she wolves from my pack that cared about me. Whether they knew me or not, they respected their Queen. I stopped before the door and took one more deep breath before entering.

The moment I entered the room fell silent, Valentina and Gina were quickly by my side.

"Our Queen has arrived. Let the party begin," V rejoiced. Gina snagged a champagne off a tray, handing it to me.

"Here Jaz, relax and enjoy yourself. You deserve it," Gina whispered in my ear. My pack moved in, surrounding me. They sang their praise about my hair and makeup. Happy chatter filled the air, making a warm feeling settle in my chest. I laughed with my people and learned about who they were and their lives. Many of the she wolves expressed their gratitude for bringing them here, having found their mate from another pack.

This was precisely what I needed. My mind cleared of the doubt that had plagued me earlier. I finally belonged, the feeling of hope blossomed inside me, and I accepted it. No matter what came my way, I would protect my pack, mate, and family. Valentina nudged my side, drawing my attention. Happiness shone in her eyes as her face lit up with a smile.

"Seeing you like this is truly the most beautiful thing. Your happiness is radiating off you in waves." She mind linked. She knew of the pain I had experienced, not just the physical aspect but the never-ending pit of loneliness that buried who I was inside. I raised my glass, beaming with pride at my pack.

"Thank you all for making me feel at home. I am beyond happy that so many of you found your mates. Now it is time for the most important part, let's all go get on our dresses and make our mates drool." Cheers rang through the pack, all of us ready for the Super Moon Ball to begin.

As the room cleared, I spotted Nadia, she briefly looked my way a darkness in her eyes. Before I could really make out what I had seen, she turned away, leaving the room with the rest of the pack.

"She still frightens me," Mindy quietly admitted. I placed my hand on Mindy's shoulder, offering my comfort.

"You are safe with us Mindy, I won't let anything happen to you." I felt Mindy slightly relax but could see how much Nadia's presence had affected her.

"Mindy, Valentina will walk with you to the dressing rooms. Gina and I will be right behind you." I instructed. Valentina raised an eyebrow at me, clearly curious about why we weren't going together. She looked as if she wanted to say something but turned, grabbing Mindy's arm, and dragging her from the room.

"Come on, Mindy, we can help each other get back dressed."

I sighed in relief, grateful she hadn't tried to push the issue. Gina studied me, trying to read what was happening in my head. "I have something important for you to do. You will not like it and may want to ask questions, but you cannot. I need to know that I can trust you with this." I declared.

She was silent for a moment, "I already don't like this, but you, of course, can trust me," she acquiesced. I pulled the letter I had written out of my robe and handed it over to her. She paused before taking it, her gaze meeting mine.

"Do not open this, if something happens to me then you are to give this to Felix."

Gina placed the letter within her robe.

"Understood" She gritted out almost painfully. I blew out my breath, relieved she had made this easier than expected. We walked in silence back to the dressing room. Valentina was zipping Mindy's dress up as we entered, they were both breathtaking. I eagerly grabbed my dress, ready to slide it on once again. I couldn't wait to show Felix and see him again dressed in a suit. Valentina helped me, while Mindy assisted Gina. Soon, we were all four standing, looking at ourselves in the wall's mirrors. These women had become such a big part of my life, and I was so grateful for them.

"Let's go, ladies. We have a Super Moon Ball to attend," I announced, making the girls all squeal. We exited the room ready to dance the night away, excitement and eagerness hummed around us.

Elder Jasmin waited for us in the hallway as we neared the ballroom.

"Queen Jasira, you look stunning," she complimented. I blushed, thanking her for her kind words. "Elder Mason has requested you and King Felix to hang behind. He would like you to have a grand entrance," she added.

The girls pushed me forward eagerly, not giving me a moment to respond clearly. They were all for Elder Mason's idea. I tried to explain that it was unnecessary, but no one was listening. I followed her since there was no sense in trying to fight it. We walked up a flight of stairs that I suspected led to the upper floor of the ballroom. My mate stood with Elder Mason, his back turned to me. I could see the tension in his shoulders, his stance unyielding. Damn, he was sexy even if he was not happy this moment.

As if sensing my eyes on him, he turned to me, our gazes locked with one another. I rushed toward him, needing to be in his strong arms. I hadn't realized how badly I ached for him all day until now. He embraced me, breathing me in the earlier tension, leaving his body. He pulled back, holding me at arm's length, taking me in. A soft purr escaped him, letting me know of his approval. My wolf basically rolled over on her back, begging for her mate's touch. I totally got it.

I took the chance to admire him as well. His suit fit him perfectly. It accentuated his powerful body with its perfectly tailored fit. The grey complimented his eyes, making me feel like I could get lost in the ocean and never search for shore. The best part was that he was mine. Elder Mason cleared his throat, pulling our attention from one another.

"Are you both ready?" he asked happily. I took a deep breath, slightly nervous.

"You have nothing to be nervous about, you look breathtaking Jaz," Felix cooed. He knew just what to say when I needed it most. We turned to Elder Mason giving him the go ahead. He opened the two grand doors, stepping out onto the landing.

"Welcome everyone to our Annual Super Moon Ball," Elder Mason bellowed. Everyone responded with cheering and clapping. He waited for the crowd to quiet before continuing, "It is my greatest pleasure to announce the arrival of our Queen and her King. Queen Jasira and King Felix." We moved onto the landing, and the crowd kneeled as we entered. I was surprised to see so many quickly submitting, especially of their own accord. "Let the ball begin," Elder Felix announced, and the music was back in full swing.

Felix held my arm tightly as we descended the stairs to join the fun.

"I can't wait to get you out of that dress later, my queen," he whispered, causing me to stumble a bit. He chuckled at me, and I glared at him even if my insides were screaming about how much they liked his idea. Lucky for him, I couldn't stay mad at him, not with the incredible energy that buzzed within the room. There was too much to feel joyful about tonight. The moon goddess had blessed so many with their fated mates.

A crowd of my favorite people formed at the bottom of the stairs, their mates by their sides. I smiled, eager to be introduced to both Gina and Mindy's mate.

"Who do we have here?" I gestured to the men.

"My Queen and King, my name is Killian. I am from the Thundercrest Pack." Killian bowed his head.

"I am Matthais of the Redbridge Falls Pack." Matthias bowed his head as well. Gina and Mindy were both beaming at their mates.

"It is wonderful to meet you both. Please call me Jasira, as you are mated to my closest friends." I saw them visibly relax with my words. We began chatting, I wanted to get to know Killian and Matthais. I assumed they would be joining my pack, and getting to know everyone who remained that close to me was important.

I excused myself after a while, needing to find a restroom. Felix offered to come with me, but I waved him away. It was amazing seeing him amongst his people. I don't know how, but he seemed to have a special bond with each one. I was inspired to be like him in that way, everyone deserved to feel important like they had a place. I wandered off to the side of the ballroom, hoping this would allow me to find the bathroom with the fewest stops from others wanting to speak with me.

The ballroom was huge, and of course, the bathrooms were on the furthest wall. I sighed in relief, my bladder grateful that I had finally reached my destination. I was careful not to ruin my dress through all of it, eager to return to my mate. I stepped out the door, running directly into someone. My body froze, and panic threatened to creep in as his hands grabbed my arms, steadying me. I would know his scent anywhere, it instantly turned my stomach, and bile rose in my throat. Liam stared down at me, his eyes blazing.

"Well, look who it is. I was hoping I would see you here." My chest tightened, my throat closed, taking away my ability to speak. "Have you missed me, Jasira?" He reached up, running his finger slowly down my face. I was trapped in that night again. I was nothing, too weak to fight. He pushed me up against the wall, his body pressing against mine. I tried to shrink away, "Now that you are Queen, maybe I could teach you a thing or two." His grip tightened on my arms painfully, and I shook, lost in a black hole of memories.

I closed my eyes, waiting for my punishment to come. Who was I kidding? I would always be the girl in the shed. Everything else had been a dream, a perfect dream. I felt his hot breath on me as I built my walls up, closing the world out. But then the weight of him disappeared, and I heard muffled voices. I opened my eyes to the world whooshing in at a dizzying speed. Hudson swung, nailing Liam in his face, before turning to me. The warmth of his touch breaking through shock slightly.

"Jaz, look at me." I did as he commanded.

"Hudson," I choked out, and he pulled me into his arms.

"It's ok I'm here. No one is going to hurt you," Hudson assured.

That is when Felix came around the corner, a snarl leaving him as he saw Hudson embracing me. His eyes softened as he met my gaze. He raced over to me, pulling me from Hudson into his arms. I breathed him in, my walls falling instantly with his touch. My wolf was pissed. I had shut her out and closed off my connection with my mate. I didn't even know that was possible, but rage tore through me now that she was back. How could I let him have that much control again?

"What the fuck did you do?" Felix growled at Hudson. I placed my hand on his chest, stepping back to look at him.

"He did nothing, he saved me again," I explained. I looked at Hudson briefly, then turned back to Felix. "Liam is here, he said some things," I muttered the last part. Felix would lose his shit if he knew the extent of what had just happened. Rightfully so, except we were on scared ground here, and no fighting was allowed.

"Jaz, are you serious right now?" Hudson said through gritted teeth. He looked at Felix. "He had his hands on her pinned against the wall, his mouth inches from her." I felt Felix's anger roll off him in waves, his aura ripping through the air. Hudson stumbled slightly but held his ground. I could feel him losing control. This was precisely what I was trying to avoid.

"Felix, calm down," I commanded, using my alpha aura. He fought it at first, his wolf was stronger than any other I had felt before. I pressed harder, wrapping my body around him and comforting him with my touch. He glared at me, but his wolf rescinded. "I know you need to do something right now, but I need you to be calm and with me. We cannot fight him now even if we wanted to. Remember where we are." I caressed his face, holding his gaze until he finally let out a huge sigh.

"I will kill him when this is over, but you are right. This is not the place." He looked to Hudson, "Thank you for protecting my mate." He grumbled, his arms wrapping tighter around me, anchoring me to his body. I nestled in, enjoying his touch, allowing it to soothe my soul.

"I would do anything for Jasira," Hudson stated simply, but his words rang with so much truth. I felt the same. He may not be my mate, but we had a connection beyond what I could explain.

I knew we needed to return to the ball, but my anxiety was at an all-time high. How had I forgotten that other pack members who had met their mates in previous years could attend today in celebration? More importantly, why did my mind and body betray me? I was supposed to show my strength. Not that I was the same weak girl that let him push himself on me before. Another wave of nausea hit me as my body shook slightly.

"Talk to me, Jaz, don't shut me out." Felix pleaded.

"I just cowered, weak, and wolf-less like I did in the past. I became nothing in an instant." I looked down, unable to look at him, but his hand wrapped gently around my chin, pulling my face to his.

"You have never been nothing, you are everything. You survived unimaginable things that shaped you into the strong woman you are today. Jasira, the reason you cowered isn't because you're weak or mean nothing. It's because you still don't fully believe in yourself like we all believe in you." Felix attested.

I tried to push back the tears that fought to escape, but there was no use. This man had just spoken directly to my heart, knowing me better than I knew myself. He was right this whole time. I still had let that nasty voice inside me have its control. That ended tonight, that bitch was getting an eviction notice.

Hudson stayed this whole time, watching over us quietly, ensuring we were not interrupted. I stepped back from Felix, pulling Hudson into a quick hug.

"Thank you for always being there," I whispered. Hudson searched my face, reassuring himself that I was okay. I held my chin high, looking at both of them. "The night is not over yet, so let's enjoy it. Before rejoining the party, can I have a minute with Hudson?"

Felix's eyes darkened slightly, his jaw ticking slightly. I knew this was hard for him, being away from me after what just happened was a big ask. Yet I had no choice, I needed to steal this moment with Hudson.

"I will be waiting for you," he said gruffly. He gave Hudson a warning glance and then turned, leaving us alone in the hall. Hudson turned to me, concern laced with curiosity all over his face. I called the wind to me, creating a bubble around us, sealing out noise and listeners. I knew how good wolf hearing was. This was the only way to ensure that no one would eavesdrop.

"What the hell was that?" Hudson reeled, his jaw dropped. I had not used any of my elements around him yet. He grew up in a pack where magic and elemental wolves were never discussed.

"It is one of my elements. I created a bubble so we could have a private conversation." I chuckled at him. He blinked a few times before giving his head a shake.

"That's wild, Jaz." I smiled at the wonder in his face, it really was wild.

"We don't have much time before Felix barges back in, but I need something from you. I need you to take this envelope, do not open it. I need you to promise me that you won't say anything to anyone, and you will not read it." I began. His face was already shifting into doubt, so I pressed on.

"I need to know I can trust you with this, that you will only give this to Valentina if something happens to me." I saw the fight in his face.

"Why would you even say that, Jasira. Nothing is going to happen to you. I won't let it. If you know something, you need to tell me." his voice rising slightly with anger.

"Please, Hudson, I know this is hard, but I need you to do this. It is important," I pleaded. His anger wavered, and so did his resolve.

"I am yours, Jasira. If this is what you need, I will do it."

I released the letter, watching him take it like it was a death sentence. A war waged inside of me. I had used our bond against him, and that wasn't fair. I hoped he would understand that I used it to save everyone's life, including mine. I dropped the bubble around us, feeling better that this part of my plan had been taken care of. Hudson didn't look at me as he walked out into the crowd. My heart broke a bit, hoping that he would forgive me when this was all over.

28

FELIX

I hated every part of stepping away from her after what had happened. Anger swirled inside me, threatening to explode, but I pushed it down. Putting it away for another day, adding it to the anger already there beneath the surface towards Liam. I would take great pleasure in killing him. There would be no mercy, it would be a slow death for that piece of shit. I took deep breaths, calming my nerves, trying to ignore the fact that my mate was not beside me. I couldn't help but think back to the fear I had felt from her before I reached her. It stole my breath as if it had been my own, a pain unimaginable lived inside of Jasira.

One she clearly has been locking away, forcing herself not to deal with. We would need to talk about it, she needed to be free of that pain. It clearly was close enough to the surface to take control like it had tonight. I never knew someone could block out their mate and wolf. Jasira had done it somehow though, I am not sure she even understood what she was doing at the time. That scared me more than anything.

I hadn't been able to reach or find her once I finally caught my breath. The possibility of her death crept in, causing my soul to break. I lost it completely. The only reason I was able to pull myself out of that dark hole was because of Valentina. Valentina had assured me she was not dead. Their bond was different, powered by a type of magic that was more witch than wolf. I never wanted to feel that anguish again. My wolf was still whimpering from it.

I took more calming breaths, watching as everyone danced, when I saw him. Liam was speaking with his father, Stella by his side, fussing over his bruised face. My wolf snarled loudly within me. This is not the place to fight, I thought, trying to soothe my beast. I clenched my fists, willing myself not to move. Before I knew what I was doing, I stalked over there, my aura rippling off me in waves. Others cowered away clearing a path for me, well looks like I failed to let it go.

Liam's eyes bulged as he saw me approaching, making his father turn to me. Trenton stepped in front of his son, arms crossed, a wicked grin on his face. He knew I could not touch either of them here. I stopped an arm's length away, not wanting to tempt myself by getting in either of their faces.

"I came to tell you that I may not be able to take your life tonight, but you will be meeting death soon." I threatened. Stella looked at her mate, anger flashing in her gaze before returning to me.

"Whatever that waste of space said is absolutely false. My mate would never touch her." Something inside me snapped, and I reached out, grabbing Stella by the throat.

"Do not ever disrespect my mate or your Queen like that again." She clawed at my hands. Liam tried to step forward, but his father held him back. I released the wench, letting her fall to the floor, coughing.

"How dare you touch her?" Liam growled, still trying to break free of his father.

I sensed Hudson approaching from behind, his anger was palpable. Hudson stopped at my side.

"How dare he touch her? You are both lucky to be alive. This place is the only reason why you are still breathing," Hudson growled. Shock, then betrayal, passed through Trenton's gaze.

"Be careful who you speak to in such a way. This is your future, Alpha," he gritted out.

"Not anymore," Jasira proclaimed loudly, the crowd again parting for her.

Her Aether power swirled around her making her look like the demigod she was. I was so damn proud, yes, we needed to work through her fears, but she was using her powers to provide her with strength.

"Hudson belongs to my pack," she stated as if this was a known fact. Trenton's eyes lit with rage.

"You can't just do that. Hudson is my son," Trenton snarled. Hudson laughed, but it was filled with hatred.

"I stopped being your son the moment I knew what and who you really are." Liam looked as though he was going to say something, but Elder Mason stepped out from the crowd before he could.

"I believe it is up to Hudson what he would like to do, but this is not the place." His words had a finality to them that had Trenton begrudgingly stepping back. I went to Jasira, wrapping my arms around her, her scent a soothing balm to my wolf. She leaned into me, her love rushing through our bond.

I took her hand, pulling her towards the dance floor. She deserved to enjoy this day. So much had already been taken from her, and I refused to let this ball be another thing. Elder Mason cued the music, as I whisked her to the center of the room.

She smiled up at me, causing my heart to race and my chest to fill with warmth.

"I'm sorry that tonight has not gone as expected. I wanted it to be a night of celebration that you would be able to put on the good memory list." I whispered, my face pressed against her hair.

Our friends moved onto the dance floor, their mates joining them. More of our pack members joined in creating a circle around us. They were protecting their Queen, forming a bubble of loyalty around us. Jasira beamed, making any tension I held from earlier melt from my body. I spun her around, her laughter filling the room. I loved hearing that sound and promised myself I would do anything to keep hearing it.

The song ended, becoming more club like music, and the crowd cheered. Valentina, Gina, and Mindy rushed forward with their mates behind them. All the women wanted to dance with each other. I pressed myself against Jasira's backside, my hands on her hips as she swayed to the music.

She knowingly moved her ass against me, a slight growl slipping from my lips. She giggled as she turned her head to look up at me. I couldn't help but smile, her face looked carefree in that moment. A look I hadn't seen often, I nuzzled her slightly.

"You are in trouble when I get you home." Heat filled her face, her eyes screaming with need.

"Promises, promises," she sassed back, making the hunger inside me grow. My wolf surged to the surface with anticipation, ready to devour his mate. I ran my hands along her body with the music teasing both of us. I enjoyed how curvy she was. The room's energy changed. There was a new heat in the air, one of lust and need. The moon shone down on us through the glass ceiling, power filling us and driving our base animal.

Our bodies clung together, Jasira's arousal was heavy in the air. It was time to go before I claimed her right here on the dance floor. I grabbed her hand, weaving us through the crowded floor. Everyone was captured in the moment, feeling the same heat we had just experienced. Once we reached the hall, I scooped Jasira into my arms, my wolf needing his mate near him. She giggled, nuzzling into my chest, her hands moving into my hair. I groaned, just the feeling of her hand caressing had me reeling.

I held her tightly, running back to our room so I could finish this night with my name being screamed from her lips.

29

JASIRA

When sleep finally found us, the sun's light began creeping into the morning sky. I looked at the clock, seeing that it was noon. Felix had turned the night around, making it one I would never forget. I bit my lip at the slight ache between my legs from how many times he had taken me. I looked over at my mate, his breathing still deep with sleep.

Being sure not to wake him, I silently slipped from the bed. I desperately needed a shower and coffee. I turned the water as hot as I could stand, enjoying the slight burn as I stepped in. I showered quickly today, even though I wanted to just stand beneath the water, letting it wash away the anxiety of leaving this place. I knew that once we left this protected land, there was no stopping what would come next. I wish I had no idea in some ways, because thinking about it was driving me insane.

I stepped out quickly, dressed, and then snuck out of our room the best I could. Felix was still sleeping peacefully, and he needed the rest. Once in the kitchen, I brewed a cup of coffee at the coffee bar. I heard someone enter, my hearing better than ever now that I had my wolf.

"I hope you're not trying to startle me. you will have to do better than that." I teased. Hudson's deep, throaty chuckle filled the room, making some of my anxiety back off.

"Not today, Sunshine, I sensed it was you in here and knew that meant coffee." It was my turn to laugh, I poured another cup and made my way to the island sitting next to him. I placed the coffee down in front of him as I took a sip of mine.

"I guess I never asked you this, but did you not find your mate this weekend." Some wolves didn't find their mates immediately, so it wasn't abnormal.

"Jaz, I don't think there is a mate out there for me. I am happy with what I have right now anyway." He muttered, sipping his coffee, but I didn't miss the longing in his eyes as he stared at me. I felt like shit for hurting him, maybe it wasn't right to ask him to stay with me. Perhaps I was selfish, yet something inside me told me I couldn't let him go. I might have an idea of who I could ask to get down to the bottom of this.

I finished my coffee quickly, "I have to go do something. If Felix or the others get up, will you tell them I will be back shortly?"

Hudson huffed. "Are you serious, Jaz? You are leaving me to tell your broody mate that you left by yourself? Are you trying to get him to kill us both?" I smiled at him, kissing his cheek.

"Thanks, you the best," I hollered, racing out the door before he could stop me. I heard him mutter about my stubbornness, which made me chuckle as I ran through the forest back to the waterfall.

The air was hot and sticky. The sun blazed down on my skin, beads of sweat already forming. I stood at the water's edge, the cool water tempting me to climb in. I had other matters to attend to before I indulged in cooling off. I called to the Moon Goddess, allowing my body to move through the planes. Even though I stood by the water, this place was dark, the moon high in the sky. I could sense the shift of the air around me, things felt lighter here, almost ethereal. There was an unnatural silence. I realized I had never noticed it before. My mother appeared with a vision of grace, as always.

"My daughter, I have missed you. How have you been?" she reached out, gliding towards me. She hugged me briefly, then stood back, waiting in expectation.

"I have missed you too, Mom. This whole you being a goddess thing really does make it harder to have a relationship." I laughed, and she joined in.

"I know Jasira. I would show you my world more, but it is unsafe. The gods and goddess are not all kind, power controls their actions. There are those who would seek to harm you because it would hurt me. It is against our laws to interfere to a certain extent within your world, which provides you with some safety." I heard her words, but a gnawing feeling grew in my stomach.

She said it was against the laws, but what if she was right? What if it was another god or goddess that was the powerful darkness?

"Mom, what would happen if one of them did attack our world." she paused, her face tilting slightly in thought.

"Well, it would depend on their actions and how they affected the natural order. They would be punished more than likely, and you do not want a punishment from an immortal." She studied my face momentarily, and I could see the question behind her eyes. I could not afford for her to ask because I refused to put the people I loved at risk. The way she was looking at me, I had to change the subject and fast.

"Enough about all that," I shrugged, trying to play it cool, "how about we talk about why I really came to see you." She nodded, allowing the change in conversation, which I was beyond grateful for. "I have a friend that has a connection to another wolf that is not their mate. They can't explain the bond, and it's deeper than a sibling or pack bond. Any idea on what's going on with that?" I spoke so fast that I was slightly out of breath. So much for playing it cool, Jasira, I thought to myself. My mother raised an eyebrow, a smirk on her face. She didn't believe me for a second.

"Your friend," she drawled out. "It's an interesting case. I have not heard of such a bond before." That is not to say there isn't a reason for it. Perhaps if I met the two, I could feel the bond and decipher more for you."

"Would you look at that," I stumbled slightly over my words. "I know we are short on time, but I am happy we could chat, Mom. I need to go. Tonight, we have dinner to celebrate the beauty of our Moon Goddess." I winked at her, making her smile.

"Very well, but if there is anything else you need, Jasira, I am here." She pulled me in, giving me another hug, and then I spiraled back.

I steadied my breathing, I knew this meant I would have to come clean and introduce Hudson to the Moon Goddess. But today was not the day to worry about doing that. I just hoped that I would be able to do it before what was coming. There was something positive that came from that visit, though. My mom telling me what she did about the gods and goddesses may have been what I needed.

I stepped into the water, walking waist deep before I went under. I didn't care that I still had my shorts and tank top on still. I needed the water to surround me, to wrap me in its security. I felt the water shift, alerting me that someone else was here. I rose slowly from the depths, knowing without seeing who it was.

My mate stood water glistening off his muscular body, a smile playing on his strong face. His blue eyes shimmered as they stared at me playfully.

"I thought I would find you here." He walked in deeper, approaching me. He had a mischievous look on his face, and that's when he splashed me. It was not your standard splash, either. He used his powers to send a good size wave of water that landed in my face. I stood shocked for only a moment before retaliating. Two could play that game, I summoned my water element as well, sending giant splashes his way. Until he dived at me, wrapping me up in his arms. We were both breathless with laughter as he held me flush against his hard body.

"I love it when you laugh," he purred, making my insides heat up. I kissed him, lingering only for a moment before pulling away.

"I really love this place, it's beautiful, not to mention I feel more in control of my powers," I explained as I stayed in his arms, my legs wrapped around his waist. He began walking towards the shore,

"It makes sense. Yes, this land is filled with magic and power. That is not what soothes you, though. This land is directly connected to the gods and goddesses. Especially your mother, I am not surprised that your power reacts that way or you.

It did make sense when he put it that way. He set me down gently, my toes curling in the sand. I shivered slightly from my soaked clothing, but the hot air would warm me quickly. Felix came prepared, wrapping an extra-large towel around my shoulders. I should have known my mate would think ahead. I stared at him as he dried off, taking another minute to admire the strong, beautiful man who stood before me. He caught me, his gaze locking with mine, a knowing smile on his lips.

"We should be getting back to the house to pack our bag so we can head out after dinner." I blushed.

"Yes, you're right. Considering what happened last night with Trenton, I am unsure how the ride home will be," he confessed. We both knew that once we were out of the protection this land offered, the Cross River Pack would try to come for us. The only comfort I held on to was that they had brought fewer members this year, and just like our pack, many were younger members. They are not warriors ready to fight a war. I held on to the hope that we had more time as we walked towards the house.

The house was filled with chatter as everyone readied for the journey back home. Several pack members stopped us along the way to pack our own bags. They wanted to speak with us regarding their mates, which many of our pack members had found. Each one asked for our blessing that their fated mate join our pack. My heart threatened to overflow with happiness for our people. They wanted to stay with us, to grow the pack.

Many had marked their mates already, bringing out elemental powers in the other wolf. They would need to be trained, and their abilities would need to be nurtured. I pranced around excitedly once we reached the privacy of our room. Felix's deep, hearty laugh filled the air as he watched me.

"Can you believe it? Our pack is growing, our people have found their mates." I knew how incredible it was to have a mate. The feeling of your soul being whole was unexplainable.

"It's all because of you, Jaz. I will forever be in your debt for what you have done for our people." His look of admiration had tears forming in my eyes. No one had ever made me feel so proud to be me like I was worth something. Yet, here he stood, giving me all the feels. Making me feel as if I was worthy to be Queen.

"Thank you," my voice gentle. Felix crossed the room, taking me in his arms and kissing my head.

"Of course," he cooed. He released me, then turned me towards my bags, giving me a slap on the ass, "Now get packed. We have dinner in an hour." Felix commanded playfully. I giggled as I quickly collected my things. I hadn't brought a lot, so it wouldn't take me long, but I wanted to have our things placed in the SUV and help load the rest of the pack's bags.

We finished with twenty minutes to spare before dinner. Felix and I joined Valentina, Evander, Gina, Killian, and Hudson to load the vehicles. Moments later, Mindy, Mathias, and Gage joined us, their bags in tow. We quickly loaded the two SUVs before heading to help the rest of the pack load the bus. I spotted Rebecca, the pack doctor. I had only had a moment to speak with her at the ball and was thrilled that they had been one of the couples to approach us in the house. Felix and I were thrilled for her and that she would be bringing her mate to the pack.

We walked in her direction, "Doctor Rebecca, how is everyone doing?" Felix asked. She was trusted by everyone in the pack, so she always stepped up when it came to rallying the pack members.

"It looks like we have just about everyone loaded up. I have a few stragglers that should be here any second." She bubbled, and happiness radiated off her in waves. Having a mate after all this time would do that.

"You're the best," I chimed, her mood infectious. She smiled happily at us, the few pack members she spoke of rushing out the door, pulling her attention away.

"I guess this means we can head to dinner. It looks like a lot of the pack has already headed in that direction," Felix hummed. My stomach growled its approval of the idea, making Felix chuckle. We walked hand in hand, our friends or, should I say, family by our side. We sat amongst the pack members, enjoying the conversation that floated through the air.

Luna Briana entered the dining area, her gaze finding me immediately. She had joined us last night at the ball when we were all gathered socializing. It was great hearing stories of her pack and learning more about their lives. I had just wished we had gotten more individual time. I stood walking towards her as she approached me.

"Queen Jasira, can I steal a moment of your time." Her voice was light but came with an urgency I could not ignore.

"Of course, Luna Briana, let's step into one of the side rooms off the hall." She turned, leading the way, "Felix, I will be right back. Briana just needs a word," I mind linked.

"Alright, hurry back, you need to eat." He demanded. I rolled my eyes. Alpha's always being so demanding, I thought to myself, even though I loved it.

I followed her until we were alone with the door shut. She turned to me with a serious look on her face. My stomach twisted, if she knew too much, would she tell Felix. I had to find out what she knew and convince her it had to stay between us. I calmed myself, maybe I was just jumping to conclusions. The fact that she sees things doesn't mean it has to do with the darkness coming for me. That gnawing feeling in my stomach was back, though, telling me I was kidding myself.

She began to pace slightly, making my nerves worse. My palms were sweaty at this point. The room felt as if someone turned the heat on.

"Bri, you're killing me here. What is going on? I burst out. I couldn't wait any longer, I had to know. She stopped pacing.

"I had a vision, it was not very clear. There was so much darkness that it made what I was seeing unclear. I could feel its power," Bri shivered, rubbing her arms before continuing. "Its power was cold, cruel, but then there was your power. I felt it even though it was hidden in all of the shadows." She reached out, grabbing my hands, "You can fight through the shadows, you are stronger than it, and they fear you."

I stared at her, absorbing everything she had just said. She seemed so sure of me that my power would be strong enough to beat this. I held on to that even if I was rattled.

"Brianna please keep this between us, no one must know" I pleaded. She searched my face, understanding washing over her.

"You know about the darkness coming for you already, don't you?" she questioned. I bit my lip, unable to lie. Even if I had, she would know.

"Yes, but no one else can know. I have had several visions of myself in a cell, the darkness surrounding me. I am unsure in the visions where I am." She released my hands, her face twisting in thought.

"I understand I will not speak of this to anyone. We should return to dinner before our mate's search for us." She moved past me, reaching for the door handle and ending the conversation. I breathed a sigh of relief, knowing she would keep her word.

We made our way to the dining room and returned to our mates. The weight of the conversation had my stomach turning, but I forced myself to eat anyway. I didn't want Felix to suspect anything was off. I listened as everyone bantered back and forth, allowing myself to get submersed in the nonsense. By the time dinner was finished, I had tucked the earlier conversation away and joined in what was in front of me.

Elder Mason stood making a small speech filled with thanks and prayers to the Moon Goddess. A sadness filled me as he concluded the Super Moon Festival with his departing words. Things were going to change. I was leaving the safety of this place. There was no more hiding from the darkness, I couldn't run from it. Too many would get hurt, or worse, die. I reached for Felix's hand, gripping it tightly as we piled into our vehicles. It was time to begin my long journey home.

30

JASIRA

Leaving was harder than I had expected. We were two hours out crossing the land border. The land called to me, begging me to come back. It wrapped its powerful embrace around me, holding me like a small child. I sat silently as the last trickles of energy that caressed my skin drifted away, leaving me cold. I rubbed my arms as I leaned into Felix for comfort. He wrapped his arms around me knowingly. I relaxed against him, at least my body did. Unfortunately, nothing could ease the thoughts plaguing my mind.

I continuously reviewed the steps I had taken, and it comforted me to know I had done something. I had written the letters after what happened with Elder Mason and then gave them to Gina and Hudson. I knew I could trust them both to follow through with my instructions. Gina held on to Felix's letter. I could tell Gina wanted to ask questions, but she restrained herself. Promising me that she would not speak a word to anyone. Hudson was a bit harder to convince not to ask anything. In the end, he had promised me the same.

My eyes became heavy, sleep calling me, but I fought it. I took in the people I love that surrounded me, memorizing them. Felix held me closer as his eyes grew heavy as well.

"You should sleep, my love. It is going to be a long ride," he whispered. His scent swirled around me, his warmth relaxing my body. I tried to fight, but exhaustion won in the end.

The brakes squealed as we came to an abrupt stop. Strong arms wrapped around me, holding me in place so I didn't go flying.

"What is going on?" I asked, still groggy from sleep. Then I felt it, the surge of dark energy ahead of us. I reached for the door handle, quickly climbing out before anyone could stop me. Felix then Hudson climbed out growls on both of their lips. I shushed them as I reached out with my Aether. I could feel the darkness pouring off the creature, its red eyes piercing the night as it stood in the street. I would swear it was a wolf, yet something wasn't right about it. The creature was unnaturally thin, and it stood on two legs. Its mouth dripped saliva as if it were rabid. This creature had no humanity left in it, and it was not alone. I could feel that there were more waiting for us beyond the trees.

"I can feel them," Felix whispered. Everyone was out of the vehicle now.

"Gage, take the buses and get our people to safety," I commanded. Gage looked at Felix, hesitation in his eyes. I was asking him to leave his friend and King.

"She is right. There are too many that cannot fight." Felix agreed. Gage nodded his understanding as he took off towards the others. Dr. Rebecca appeared with her mate on her tail.

"How can we help?" She exclaimed.

"Keep yourself safe. We may need you after this fight. Gina put two guards on Dr. Rebecca. Then let's prepare to fight our way out."

"I don't like this," Felix growled, "you should be staying back with Rebecca. "

"I actually agree with Felix on this one," Hudson huffed. I rolled my eyes at both of them.

"It's not going to happen, guys, so get over it."

The creature sniffed the air in search of something or someone. Its gaze landed on me, snarling. The others that had been deeper in the forest moved out of the darkness. We were out of time. They were coming for us. Our soldiers shifted, charging forward, Gina leading them. Felix gave Hudson a look, then pressed on as well. Evander followed Felix, which I was grateful for. I knew he would watch his back. I shifted, heading towards the buses. I could feel the creatures using some sort of shadow power to conceal themselves.

They were trying to go after my people, and I was not about to let that happen on my watch. I pushed myself harder as I ran toward the moving buses. I could feel Hudson and Valentina by my side, ready to fight. I leaped in the air, lighting the darkness up with my fire breaking through the shadow barrier they used to cloak themselves. There were eight of them hidden.

Hudson jumped on one's back, going straight for their neck, blood spraying from the creature as he ripped his throat out. I brought my fire forward again, engulfing myself in flames. I pounced, my claws catching its shoulders, and burning flesh filled the air as we tumbled. It screeched in pain, struggling to get away, but I wasn't done yet. I sunk my teeth deep into its neck, ripping the flesh from its neck. Blood poured into my mouth a rancid taste from the foul beast. I moved to the next one, doing the same to it.

We made quick work of the eight, not showing any mercy. We rushed back to the larger fight, our bus was now able to continue on a route to safety. It was clear everyone was struggling as we approached. It wasn't that the creatures were good fighters or overpowered us. There were just so many of them. I tried to fight through them to get closer to Felix, but they had formed a wall between us. I could tell through our bond he was fine, so I focused on the fight in front of me.

The wind shifted, bringing a familiar scent in my direction. I snarled, recognizing it as Trenton. I looked around knowing no one else would be able to track him in time, they were too consumed in the fight. I turned, running toward the woods, letting my wolf guide me.

It couldn't be a coincidence that he was here when those messed up wolves attacked us. I was done with his games.

I found him in a small clearing, waiting as if he expected me. He had a smug look on his face.

"Well, well, if it isn't the bitch herself," he sneered. "My friends giving you trouble," he cackled. He was behind this, I knew it. I shifted back, ready to end this.

"What is this about Trenton?" I asked, watching his body movements closely.

"For starters, you took my son from me. Did you think I would let you get away with that? That is not the main reason, but it will do for now he shrugged. Anger swelled in my chest, this man had done nothing but cause me pain my whole life. I took a step closer, ready to attack. He laughed again. "You stupid girl, did you think I would come alone?" His Beta stepped out from the tree line with a cruel smile. A shiver of fear ran down my spine. Five more wolves followed, with a couple of twisted creatures in tow.

I was outnumbered and surrounded now. I wasn't just a wolf, I was a Demi God and it was time to show them what that meant. They weren't going to take me down that easily. I called upon the earth, feeling it shake beneath me. Roots reached out, grabbing several pack members, and holding them in place. They struggled against them but were stuck for now. I used my chance to rush forward, shifting into my wolf's form again. I quickly took down the beasts, ripping out their throats.

This allowed Trenton and Stephan to attack me from behind. Stephan bit down on my shoulder and then tossed me. I twisted mid-air, landing on my paws, but lost balance due to my shoulder injury. The pain jolted through me, and a scream threatened to rip out of me. I dug my nails into my palms, focusing on the pain instead. I would show them no weakness.

I stumbled slightly, allowing Stephan to pounce on my back. I fought to get him off as he dug into my fur covered back with his claws. I called fire to my body, allowing my back to heat up, burning him. The smell of burnt hair was heavy in the air.

Blood dripped from my shoulder and back now, but I ignored it for the time being. Stephan rolled on the ground before me, trying to put the fire out. Trenton charged forward, now still in human form, a hunting knife in hand. I dodged several strikes, snapping at him. My body was exhausted from all the fighting, making my movement slower. He lunged again, this time hitting my side. I pivoted at the last moment, the knife grazing my flesh instead of stabbing into me. He stumbled forward too much, allowing my teeth to sink into his leg. He hollered, trying to shake me off his leg. I tightened my hold, trying to gain my footing.

Stephan charged, attacking my already hurt side. I cried out, releasing Trenton as my body flew through the air. I got back on my feet quickly, but Stephan was already charging again.

A flash of fur flew past me, intercepting Stephan. The shock was apparent on the Beta's face. Hudson clawed into his chest, sinking his teeth into Stephan's shoulder, barely missing his throat.

Thats when time seemed to slow, I never expected what happened next. Trenton had been down. I should have been paying attention. He had managed to crawl his way towards Hudson. He stood, raising the knife, stabbing down quickly into Hudson's back.

I couldn't move. I was frozen in place. Hudson yelped, falling off Stephan. He lay on his back as his wolf shifted back to human form. Stephan quickly shifted back, grabbing his Alpha as they rushed away. I ran to Hudson, no longer caring about Trenton. I shifted, kneeling in front of him, not caring that I was naked. Blood poured from under him, coating me. I tried to reach under him and apply pressure from where the blood was leaving his body.

"Please, Hudson, please don't leave me. I need you," I begged. I could feel his aura leaving his body. His heart was slowing, he was fading fast. There was too much blood, and he wasn't healing. Footsteps came from behind me, my pack and Felix approaching. My element air poured out without me even asking, it formed a bubble around us. Not allowing anyone to come close.

Hudson lay lifeless in my arms, his warmth that used to comfort me gone. This man was not my mate, but our connection was soul deep. My wolf howled inside as my heart shattered. He was here because of me, of my selfishness. How could I have let this happen? My grief was all consuming, an emptiness settling in my chest. I could feel Felix trying to get to me, pressing on the mate bond. I shut him out, I didn't want to be comforted right now. This pain was not one that he could fix.

"Moon Goddess, please," I cried out, "Mother, if you hear me, please help," I pleaded. "I need you!" I screamed desperately. I laid my head on his chest, begging him to heal, to come back to me.

I felt the air shift. I looked up to see my mother before me. Hudson still in my arms, she moved towards me.

"My child, I heard your calls, so I came to you." She said softly. I sobbed, the pain in my chest growing by the minute.

"Can you save him?" I had to ask. I couldn't see this world without him. Selene shook her head, my worst fear coming true.

"No, I cannot, but you were right about the connection between you two. I see it so clearly now," a sad smile on her face. "Alpha Maeve, your other mother requested that when she died, a piece of her soul be put inside you. I fulfilled her wish, even though I would be messing with fate. I had no idea what the outcome would be. I see now." Anger rose inside of me. How could she be talking about this right now?

"I don't understand how that matters right now," I snapped. What was the point of any of this if she couldn't save him?

"Jasira, you feel connected because you have your mother's soul inside of you, and Hudson has your father's soul inside of him. They were fated mates, and fate made sure they stayed together." She explained, her voice soft. I choked on another sob racking my body. How could she tell me this when she couldn't save him?

"Why are you telling me this if you can't save him?" I yelled, the grief tearing me apart inside.

"You can save him, my child. It will strengthen your bond further. I am not sure how much." I paused, trying to process what she had just said.

"Will it affect my bond with my mate?" I asked. "Nothing can change your fated bond with Felix, but the bond between Hudson and you is a fated one as well. Technically you have two mates," she explained.

"As long as my bond is safe with Felix, I don't care. Now tell me how?" I managed out my voice raspy.

"You must give him your blood. This will solidify the connection, finalizing the bond. You will also have to give him one of your elements." Her face was serious with the last part. I knew that was a small price to pay to bring him back.

"Send us back". She nodded her understanding, doing just that.

"You must hurry," her words a whisper in the wind.

I tumbled back to my body, still holding Hudson. I bit into my wrist, pouring my blood into his mouth, and repeating the words my mother had told me.

"My blood is your blood. With this, you are mine." After I was sure I had enough in his mouth, I pressed my hands onto him. My elements flowed through me, responding to my needs. They wrapped around his body, "I give you a piece of me to seal our bond." The elements continued to glow around him, exactly like my mother had said. I waited for one to choose him. I suspected I knew which one.

They began to mesh, forming one element. Air. I wept knowing that it worked. The rest of my elements returned to me, a wave of exhaustion hitting me. Hudson took a shuddering breath, opening his eyes. I cried out, wrapping my arms around his neck.

"Nice to see you too, Jaz." I couldn't help the sobs that racked my body. I helped him sit up, looking at him.

"You're alive, and okay? " I asked.

"I think so, but I feel different and a bit foggy." I nodded as we stood.

The bubble that air had formed around us dropped, it was no longer my element. My father's element had chosen Hudson, it was only fitting. I felt another wave of exhaustion hit me, pain lancing through my body. I tried to hold on. I had just gotten him back, and I needed to make sure he was okay. My body had other plans, I pushed away not wanting to put my weight on him. My legs betrayed me, giving away, but arms wrapped me, catching me. The last thing I saw was my mate before darkness consumed me.

***

Beeps filled the room as I began to wake up. What happened flooded back to me. I heard voices I recognized speaking softly around me. I tried to focus on what they were saying.

"You two need to stop fighting. Jasira doesn't need to hear that when she wakes up," Valentina huffed. I cleared my throat, trying to sit up.

"Jasira already hears it," my voice a raspy whisper.

"Thank goddess, you're okay," Felix touched my cheeks, resting his head against mine. I placed my hands on his, letting his love fill me. Our bond was still there, strong as ever. My mother had been right, nothing had changed with Felix. He pulled back, holding my gaze. "I am going to lock you in a room and never let you out," He chided. I chuckled at him, holding his hand. He stepped back, allowing me to see the rest of the room, my gaze locked with Hudson's. Tears threatened, but I pushed them away. He was alive and in front of me.

"Hudson, I wasn't dreaming. You're okay?" He cocked a smile. I could feel our bond, so I gave it a tug.

"What the fuck is that, Jasira?" A shocked expression filled his face.

"I have a lot to tell you, may I have a moment with Felix and Hudson" The room cleared quickly, silence clinging in the air. I knew Felix would hate what I was about to say, but he deserved to know.

"I can feel it, Jasira, I know," Felix stated, hiding his emotions.

"I figured as much, but I want you to know why. The connection I had with Hudson isn't just because of our past. When my mother died, Selene gave me a piece of her soul as my mother's last wish. Fate decided to put a piece of my father's soul in Hudson." Understanding dawned on Felix.

"What does that mean for us?" Fear made his voice shake, breaking my heart.

"Nothing has changed between us, Felix. Our bond is as strong as it has ever been." He relaxed slightly. "I love you, I always have." He moved forward, claiming my lips softly at first. I parted my lips in response, deepening our kiss. I pulled him closer, weaving my fingers through his hair. I needed him to know that it would always be us.

He pulled away first, knowing there was more. I held his hand as I looked at Hudson.

"I couldn't live without you, I'm sorry." I whispered a tear falling down my cheek. He stepped forward taking my other hand.

"You have nothing to be sorry for, Jaz. I would have done the same." He assured me. I looked at both men standing beside me. I knew it was against every alpha's instinct to share a mate. How was I going to make this work without someone getting hurt?

"Stop whatever you are thinking right now Jasira. It doesn't matter that you have two mates. It just makes us stronger" Felix promised.

"He is right Jasira. We will make this work, you are the only thing that matters." Hudson agreed.

"You both are okay with this? How is that even possible?" I stuttered.

"You make it possible. Loving you is what I was born to do and if that means I have to share you then I will," Felix confessed. They both leaned in wrapping their arms around me.

Dr. Rebecca cleared her throat as she came in, and we pulled away reluctantly.

"I see the patient is doing much better." Dr. Rebecca smiled warmly at me.

"Yes, I am, thank you," I said, blushing slightly.

"I just want to check some blood work to ensure everything bounces back normally." I nodded as she approached to draw blood.

"We are under attack," Gina announced as she busted in the door out of breath. I could see the war waging on Felix and Hudson's face. Our people needed them. Plus, I had no idea where we were, so who knows how many fighters were available.

"Both of you go. I am staying right here unless I am needed." I knew I wasn't up for fighting unless I had to. I was drained.

"I will run these to the lab and stay with her." Dr Rebecca assured.

"Please be careful, I can't lose either of you." I said through the mind link.

"We are together. We will be okay." Felix assured. He was right. They would be okay, the three of us together would only make us stronger.

Dr. Rebecca had been gone for ten minutes, and worry crept in. She said it would only be a minute. I pulled my IV out and the monitors off me, getting out of bed. I grabbed a few napkins holding them to my arm, the bleeding would stop quickly. I walked out to the hall, pausing to listen. Silence filled the air, emptiness. Something was wrong, I held on to the wall making my way down the hall looking for her.

"Rebecca," I called out as I went, but no one responded.

Fear coursed through my body, freezing me in place, the same fear from my dream. I realized too late that I was surrounded by darkness. My hair stood on end, and shivers ran down my spine. Nadia and Trenton Stepped out from the shadows, cruel smiles on their faces. I tried to move, to fight, but I couldn't. I reached for my mates, but the connection was blocked.

"Remember, this was supposed to happen. Both of our mates are fine. We need to let them take us. That way no one else gets hurt," My wolf reminded me.

I calmed myself, this was it. I needed to leave my trail. I closed my eyes, reaching for my Aether. It was sluggish but still there, answering my call. I pictured it as a rope tying one end to me, like Madeira had instructed. I then searched for Valentina's magic, I found it easily. I tied the other end to her. Even if I could not connect to my magic, she would be able to tug on mine. Now I just had to hope it worked. I brought my attention back to the moment.

"You're lucky he wants you alive, you know, because if it were up to me, I would kill you." Trenton snarled. Nadia came forward looping her arm in Trenton's.

"Don't worry my love, we will kill her when he is done with her." She purred at Trenton. These two were together. How was that possible? I thought to myself. Plus, didn't he hate elemental wolves?

"I am going to enjoy this," she cackled. Pulling me from my thoughts. She shoved a syringe into my neck. I dropped to the ground, aware of my surroundings but paralyzed. I screamed at my body, but it did not respond. A breathtaking man stepped out from the shadows, his hair black as night. The shadows danced around his god like body, following his every command. He wore a crown with a wolf insignia on it. He crouched before me, running a cold finger down my cheekbone. My stomach turned, bile coursing up my throat.

"I have been waiting for you, for so long" his hot breath on my neck. He traced the mark with his finger before, licking up my neck. "Time to come play with me," He whispered, then stood up and held his arms out. Shadows snaked down his arms and wrapped around my body. They tightened ensuring I would not escape. He picked me up off the ground, walking back towards the dark portal he had come from. As we stepped into the darkness, I built up walls around my heart. The Shadow Wolf King wanted me, I was his prisoner. I had to protect my heart from his darkness, until my mates came for me.

Find Out What Happens Next In

Darkness In My Heart

Available 2024

About The Author

I am a proud wife, devoted mother, and passionate writer. From a young age, the desire to put my thoughts on paper has burned deep within me. However, life's inevitable obstacles seemed to conspire against my dreams, constantly pulling them further and further out of reach. But now, as my three beautiful children fill my days with love and joy, I have realized that it is never too late to pursue my true passion. With unwavering determination, I am ready to break free from the constraints that held me back for so long and embrace my calling as a writer.

Check out my website to find out what is happening next!!
https://alduncanauthor.com/Untitled

Made in United States
North Haven, CT
03 February 2024